not let go

not let go

a novel

Paul Bruno

Swirling Mist Press

Special thanks to: J. deBeer & Son No. F. 12 Official Clincher Softballs, Budweiser, Jäegermeister, Guinness, New York Mets, New York Yankees, Dante Alighieri, Mario Puzo, William Golding, Robert Heinlein, Joseph Conrad, J.R.R. Tolkien, Dave Arneson, Gary Gygax, Stephen Covey, Starsky & Hutch, Friendly's, Gateway 2000, America OnLine, Nalgene, Star Trek, James Gosling, Larry Wall, Ogilvy & Mather Direct, Gartner Group, Metro North, Star Wars, An Officer and a Gentleman, Metropolitan Museum of Art, High Staff (ALPOE, Doc Oc, JVC3, The Dessert Fox, Squidman), Buddy Holly, Humphrey Bogart, Willie Mays, Spider Man, The Bronx Zoo, Dani Chance, Gino Colangelo, Mia Kim, Laura Kuhn, and Larry O'Connor.

ISBN (paperback): 979-8-9879025-2-3

ISBN (ebook): 979-8-9879025-3-0

Swirling Mist Press

swirlingmistpress.com

Published in the United States of America

For Karen

a perfect day

My day starts suddenly, with a pillow fight.

"What are you doing today, Michael?" Ellen asks. She's kneeling on the bed, still holding the pillow she woke me with.

"Me? Um. The gym?" I pull the sheet over my head and hope she lets me go back to sleep.

"You always go to the gym. It's a perfect day, Em. I'm taking the day off. Let's do something fun."

"Do what?" I don't want to open my eyes yet. It's Monday. I was expecting Ellen to go to work. My day was planned around that, that she wouldn't be around. I could wake up whenever, go to the gym whenever, play some video games, maybe watch an old movie, and be here when she got home.

"C'mon, Em." She hits my head with her pillow again. I block the next blow with my forearm. She hits me a couple more times, then stands on the bed and jumps up and down, trying to get me to pillow fight her or just to be so annoying I have to get out of bed. I grab her ankle and pull her down. But she doesn't stay in my arms long. She gets off the bed and drops her pillow on me.

"I'm calling in sick," she says. But when she calls, I hear her say she's going to take a personal day. That raises the stakes. She only has a handful of those. In three years living together, she's only used a personal day once, and that was for her grandmother's funeral. She makes a second call; Ellen is responsible for several important accounts.

I sit up. "What do you want to do?"

"I don't know. Something. Something outside."

That spares me from a museum. "Central Park?"

"No, silly, it's a day for us. I don't want to run into any of your softball cronies."

"They're all working. It's a weekday."

"Let's go outside the city. The Zoo."

Ellen means the Bronx Zoo. Connecticut girls think the city is just Manhattan.

The Bronx Zoo is one of my favorite places to go. It's been that way ever since I was a little boy. I get out of bed and stretch. "Take the train?"

She comes up behind me and wraps her arms around my waist. "Let's take the car. It's a day off. No train."

I turn around, slow so she doesn't let go of me, and loop my arms around her too. "It's a date." She smiles and her eyes laugh. She kisses me and then pushes me away.

I put on jeans, sneakers, a Mets t-shirt. Ellen wears her hair loose and dresses like me except for a white baseball jersey with blue three-quarter length sleeves. It barely reaches her belt loops. It's not one of mine; it fits her too well. For breakfast I have a bowl of Lucky Charms. Ellen has yogurt and granola.

We get the car and take the West Side Highway up into the Bronx and drive through Riverdale toward Belmont and Fordham University and the Botanical Gardens and the Zoo. The parking lot is not even half full. It's a beautiful day but people—the unlucky ones—have to work. There are several yellow school buses, which would usually put me in a bad mood, but I'm indestructible today.

We walk from the parking lot over a small stone bridge and along a shaded asphalt path to the gate, holding hands. The gate is like the ones in the subways: three ladders of horizontal bars forming a revolving door. I grab a map. I don't really need it. It gets folded and put in my back pocket.

The first exhibit is the wolves. Children climb and play on the wooden fence. There's another, almost invisible fence behind that one, with rectangles of dark wire. A couple of wolves are lazing all the way in the back; I find them and point for Ellen. "They're hiding way back there. They don't want to come close to these noisy kids."

Then another wolf appears, right in front of us. It must've been standing there the whole time. It just stands there on its four legs and stares at us. Its eyes are blue. Not like Ellen's, though. This blue is cold and dangerous. You can tell there's intelligence but it's alien, not something you could ever understand. *Maybe* a little like Ellen's.

"You would be dead meat in there," Ellen laughs. "You wouldn't have seen that coming."

"I wasn't looking that way."

"That's what little red riding hood said."

I laugh. I love making Ellen laugh, but this is even better. I take the map out of my pocket and study it.

"Are you afraid of getting lost?"

"You know what I'm looking for."

"And you'll find it. Without the map." She tries to take it from me but I'm too fast, I fold it up quick and shove it back in my pocket.

Another class is coming up to the exhibit. Two ragged rows of school children, falling apart no matter how hard their teachers try to keep them in check. We move away. We'll be running into these groups all day. At least it's not a weekend.

It's not crowded. You could almost pretend you're walking alone with your girl. Not dodging kids.

Maybe the wolves will get them.

It's a short walk from there to the old center of the Zoo. We pass bison, but they're motionless in the distance. The sea lions are calling.

We're still holding hands. It's like our first date all over again. Not our first date, but real early on. One of the first public—outdoor?—places we went together.

Not much has changed around the sea lions, and that's part of the fun of the Zoo. Rediscovering things exactly as you left them. Seals swim clockwise around the sides of the pool. Sometimes when they come by, they surface and breathe, and sometimes they don't.

"I want to see!" Ellen pleads like she's a little girl. Just like the first time here. I put my hands on her waist and lift her until she can get her sneakers on the bottom rail of the fence. It's not like she couldn't do this herself; she's five foot ten. We make up silly little things to do, then we do them again the next time, then we call it a tradition.

The first time we came here, in '94, I had never seen Ellen outside of work, restaurants, and, well, her place. It took me by surprise. How loose, how open, how playful she could be. I was fascinated by her. I already couldn't get enough of her. But I fell in love with her that first time at the Zoo. I'm not ashamed to admit it. Sure, it was early in the relationship. But I could suddenly see myself telling her that I was in love with her.

Of course, I held back. She was way out of my league, and I worried she'd realize that. I didn't want to scare her away. Which is funny, because later she told me she was afraid of scaring *me* away. So we didn't say it for a while.

Then something catches my eye on the other side of the pool. She's pretty, and she's with a friend. Maybe they're college students; maybe they go to Fordham and are here between classes. The pretty girl sees me looking and says something to her friend, and now they're both looking at me, smiling.

"Michael, please," Ellen says, and I look quickly back at her.

"What?"

"Can you *not* do that, today?"

"I don't know what you're talking about." I pull Ellen toward the Monkey House.

It's dark in there, and it takes a little while to get used to it. All the monkeys are behind glass, but there's a strong zoo smell. There are exhibits on both sides of the building. I try to figure out how the monkeys are organized. "Are all these monkeys in size order? Like the lines of school kids?"

"Maybe it's done by geography," Ellen says. "The South American monkeys are at one end, and the ones from Madagascar are at the other."

A troop of those kids are making noises at the monkeys and each other and we wait for them to leave. Then it gets quieter for a few moments.

I take the opportunity to hold Ellen. She leans back against me and I move her hair out of the way and kiss her throat while a Capuchin makes faces at us.

"Mmm," Ellen whispers. "He's watching us."

The door opens and another group of kids comes in. It gets noisy. We don't stay long; it's too dark and noisy and smelly and we want to be outside, in the sun and fresh air.

Outside it's bright, so bright, and we shade our eyes until we get adjusted to the sunshine. For just an instant I worry that we're going to see those two coeds again. Now we walk past the big cats. Ellen tugs on my arm, but I try to walk fast here. I don't want to stop to look. I love the big cats. Both of us love the big cats. There are tigers, Siberian tigers, and snow leopards.

"Please, Em," Ellen says.

I let her pull me toward the cages. They're part of one of the older brick buildings that made up the original zoo. Not a lot of sunlight gets in there. Most of the tigers are lying around like they're bored or sedated. The cages have metal bars and thick metal screens in the front, and concrete floors.

"They're suffering," I tell her. "I don't like this."

"How else are we going to see these kitties up close?"

"They belong in the wild. They're solitary, they have home ranges. Putting them all together in one cage has to mess with their heads."

"Their habitat is disappearing. They'd be hunted and killed."

"This isn't living," I say, but she insists, and we watch them lying there for a while. A tiger slouches back and forth in front of us, back and forth, throwing a glance at us occasionally, pacing like it has a nervous condition.

"I wonder if it blames us for this situation it's stuck in."

"Oh, Michael. Lighten up. It's probably wondering if it'll get a chance to eat you."

I wish I felt better about stopping to admire the tigers. There are signs saying the Zoo is planning a total rebuild of the exhibit; it'll look more natural. That's at least a year away. Ellen and I will come back then, and maybe I won't mind so much.

As soon as we get out of the shadow of the big cats I cheer up. Ellen squeezes my hand. "You know what's next, Em."

The brown bears are in a big, open exhibit that has a deep concrete trench between the bears and the humans. The trench is hidden by strategically placed bushes up near the rails. The bears never fall into the trench. One walks on top of a stone cliff, and makes a little spin at the end and heads back in the other direction. Over and over. One of them scratches his back on this huge tree trunk in the center of the exhibit. There's nothing that could hide them from visitors, like the trees hid the wolves.

Ellen decides she doesn't need my help this time. She puts her feet on the bottom rail and tries to look over the top of the bushes. "Nope." She sounds disappointed. "Nobody has fallen in."

We let the sun warm our backs and watch the bears. It's a much nicer exhibit than the last one, except for the bear pacing like that tiger. None of these cages will ever come close to their natural environment. I must be frowning. Ellen pulls on my sleeve and tells me to stop.

"I love the Zoo," I tell her. "I love coming here, I love bringing you here, but sometimes I don't like being here."

"I know, Michael."

"It's not fair. All these animals were meant to be free. Now they're trapped. They live in cages."

"They're taken care of."

"If you can call it that." I want to say something else. I want to brighten things up. I want to beat back this mood. I don't want to ruin Ellen's perfect day.

While I'm thinking how I can do that, the coeds from the sea lions come up to the rail a few feet away. Every so often one of them looks at us and I stop worrying about the animals. Ellen sees the girls. "Let's go look at the polar bears," she says.

We walk over, and along the way we pass this boarded-up area that I remember from my childhood visits. There used to be a tunnel there, a short one, that had a window into the polar bear den. We always thought we would see a cub in there, but if there was a bear it would have its butt pressed up against the glass, and that's all you could see. Still, it was always an adventure when I was young. We would take turns hiding in there, jumping out and surprising each other.

As we circle around and down some steps, we can't keep our hold on the metal rail that wraps around so many of the exhibits. There are people in our way, also holding the rail.

This is the best spot in the Zoo, my favorite. Ellen and I stand in the back. We're both tall enough that we can stand on some rocks and see over the children's heads. The exhibit is like a stage and there's a waterfall and a big red steel beach ball and the concrete is painted glacier white and Arctic Ocean blue. The ball is dented in places and there are a couple of rusty patches where the paint wore off.

The day's getting warmer, but the bears hardly seem to mind. They're not fooled by the white and blue paint. That's what I think they're thinking. I have no clue what goes on in their heads. Or in anyone's head. Even my own.

One of the bears is pretending to do an Olympic backstroke. Really, just the start: it holds on to the edge of the pool, its feet against the side of it under water, and it pushes back. It doesn't go very far; it comes right back and does it again. Like most of the animals in the zoo, it keeps doing the same thing, over and over and over. It doesn't know what to do with itself.

Both of the polar bears have fur that's dirty in spots; it's yellowish and matted. I'm surprised they're not sleeping.

I nod at them. "These were always my favorite."

"I know."

"Did I ever tell you that I visited the Zoo every Thanksgiving Day?"

"No. Why would you come to the Zoo on Thanksgiving?"

"My dad used to bring me here. He would take me and a couple of cousins. All boys. It was to get us out of the way while our moms were cooking the turkey."

"The Zoo was open?"

"Yes, but empty. I don't know if they still do that. It was like we were the only ones here. My dad had a heck of a time trying to keep us all together. Until we got to the polar bears.

Then we'd all be lined up on the rail, just like those kids over there."

"Why didn't you ever tell me this before?"

"I don't know, El. That stopped when I was twelve. As I've gotten older, it's lost some of its magic. Not the part now, that I have with you. But you know how when you're a kid, anything is possible?"

"I believe anything is always possible."

"You optimists."

"Go on, Em."

"When I was a kid, those were real glaciers and real icebergs. Sure, I knew they were stone and concrete, but they were also real."

"I know what you mean."

"I know you know what I mean. Things are worse than they look."

"No, they're not. What's wrong?"

I wipe my eyes with my palm. "Yeah. Something must've blown in there." I can't help thinking about my father. Dad always smiled; he was never angry with me. I'd listen to him and do whatever he said. He didn't have to yell. He didn't have to ask me twice to do something. Well, maybe twice.

Ellen stares into my eyes, worried, and I have to stare back. It's usually pleasant, but now it's discomforting.

When Ellen looks at me sometimes I freeze like a deer in headlights. I have to catch my breath. I forget what I'm saying. Her eyes are Arctic Ocean blue. Like the blue under an iceberg. Translucent, turquoise. Cool, clear blue. That's almost it. But they're not cold. I'll figure it out some day.

I don't want Ellen to think I'm crying. I blink and look away. My nose feels like it wants to run. Not in front of Ellen. This is not supposed to happen to me. I try wiping my face with my hand, then wiping my hand on my jeans. Ellen pulls out a tissue like she's a magician; I don't know where she was carrying it.

She waits until I clean my face properly with the tissue, then says, "Come on, Michael. Let's go look at something else."

We see the Safari Shop and I pull Ellen into the store. I go over to a glass case at the end and crouch down. There are rows of tiny figurines here, of all the animals in the Zoo and then some. I look for the polar bears. There are two figures there. Both polar bears are on all fours.

"What are we looking for?" Ellen asks.

"It's a polar bear cub. On its hind legs, holding its two front paws in the air over its head. My Dad bought it for me when I was a kid."

"Sorry. I don't see it."

I scan the rows four times, hoping maybe it's hiding behind something, hoping the crying won't come back. I'm safe for now, but the cub is not there.

"I'll be outside," Ellen says.

I give it one more try, another look, and still come up empty. Every time I'm here, I check. Just in case. But I've never found another one and I wish I never lost the original.

Ellen is leaning against a stone wall across from the shop. She's got her right foot on the wall next to her left knee and her hands are in her back pockets. Her jersey is cropped short, and you can see a little skin there. If I were a teenager I'd have her poster on my wall. I glance around to see if any guys are checking her out. There's one guy, he's pushing a stroller and looking at Ellen over his wife's shoulder. And there's another guy, trying to sweep litter without looking down at it. I don't feel threatened; I feel proud.

Ellen sees me and lifts her hand and gives me a beckoning finger and a flirty look. Just then the Zoo train drives by, and I smile at her through the passing cars. After it's gone I cross over and she meets me halfway with a kiss and says, "I'm hungry."

We split fries and a cup of soda on a wooden bench by the concession stand. Between fries Ellen says, "I want to go visit my folks this weekend."

"It's a perfect day," I remind her.

She feeds me a fry. "Still, I do. But we don't have to talk about it now."

There are things we don't want to talk about today: her parents; me getting a job; why we don't drop in on my folks in New Rochelle. Things that would ruin the perfect day. For a while, we're quiet together. Then Ellen gets up and gets a cup of ice cream, half chocolate and half vanilla, and she pulls off the cardboard top and starts stabbing the ice cream with her flat wooden spoon. She keeps stabbing it until it gets mushy and drippy and then she drags her fries through it.

Between fries, she says, "What was bothering you before?"

"Nothing. Allergies."

"Allergies. Huh. Why don't you talk more about your parents?"

"There's nothing to say."

"Why don't you ever bring me to visit them? Are you ashamed of them, or of me?"

"It's not that."

"Then what?"

She's not supposed to talk about this stuff. Not today. I look up at the sky through the leaves of the trees. It's safer than looking around and accidentally discovering a pretty girl.

My folks are not a part of my life. It's my fault. I can't tell Ellen that, though. She wouldn't understand.

We get quiet again.

Ellen nods toward a couple struggling by on the path to the gorillas. "Look over there." The woman is pushing a stroller and the man is trying to contain two young children. Ellen says, "that's never going to be us."

"Three is out." I'm okay with that. Ellen's sister Caroline has three, and the couple of times I met them it was chaos. I wait for her to say something else.

She offers me an ice cream fry, but when I open my mouth she deliberately misses.

"That's not nice," I laugh, and wipe my cheek with a napkin. "I'm going to get even."

"No you won't," she says, but it's cute what she did, and doesn't bother me a bit.

"There are things I want to do first," she says.

I thought she was going to drop the subject. "There's no rush."

"Maybe, after. One day. But only one."

We're negotiating the tricky neutral ground here with extreme caution. I want two; at least I think I do when I bother to think about it at all. I know what it's like being an only child. I say the safest thing possible. "Mets lost again yesterday."

Ellen scoops the last drops of ice cream out of her cup with the last two fries. Her hair has gotten a little windblown. There are straw-colored tendrils in her face. She pushes them back. "I want to go to the petting zoo."

"They're still not going to let you on the camel ride, El."

"It's not fair," she pouts.

"Let the children have the ride, we'll feed the goats."

I like the Children's Zoo. It's one of the oldest things in the zoo, and it's not far from where we're sitting. It doesn't have the best animals, but you can touch them, and you can put dimes into a machine and get pellets to feed the goats. The goats have scary eyes that come out of nightmares. Odd looking things. But they won't eat us and they're not afraid of us and they're not suffering like the other animals.

There's children everywhere. There are parents, too. One father is ignoring his son, who is pulling on his pants leg while the man is staring at his cell phone. It seems wrong, like he's not really there. But I'm there, and so is Ellen, and the man notices her and looks up and puts his phone away.

Ellen gets some pellets and gives them to a little girl who seems to be too afraid to approach the goats. Ellen says something to her and the little girl holds out her hand and a goat licks the pellets off the little girl's hand. She squeals and laughs.

I want to tell her she's a natural but maybe it's not a good idea to bring that up again. Ellen has said all she wants to say about children for today.

We go look at the elephants and the giraffes and then walk over to the lions. We don't see the college girls again. Ellen hooks her arm through mine and leans her head on my shoulder. We pass under the sky cars. I imagine looking down on us from up there. It feels like we're just another exhibit.

The lions are in an open-air environment that doesn't look like it can contain them. I look around for moats or concrete trenches but can't see anything. It's very well done. "This is nice," Ellen says. "Maybe they can do this for the tigers."

"Maybe lions don't jump as far as tigers. Or there's some other reason why they get different treatment."

Ellen and I lean over the rail, trying to see what the lions are doing. They seem very close. Three females and a male, just flopped on their sides under a big tree, panting. The smell of other animals must be confusing. The sides of the male shake every so often to get rid of flies. He swishes his tail. We sit on a rock and just watch them for a while. I remember playing with my little toy polar bear cub while sitting on this rock a long time ago.

I brush a fly off my forearm. "That fly was just on that lion, El. Where do you think it was happier?"

Ellen doesn't answer.

"Was it happier in there, on that lion, or out here on me?"

Ellen tries to push me off the rock. I try to tickle her, and we both end up giggling.

"I would have dumped you by now, but you're too handsome," she says.

In the distance, behind the lion exhibit, some zebras are standing around. Whatever the Zoo did with these exhibits makes it look like the zebras, like us, are in danger of being eaten by the lions. If only the lions would wake up.

I nudge Ellen again. "See that? I bet if one of these lions goes over to those zebras there, he's going to come back and say the grass is greener on the other side."

She cuffs the side of my head. Not hard.

"What was that for?"

"Nothing. I—sorry. Nothing. I didn't mean it."

I should just take her word for it. But I can't. "Did I say something wrong?"

Ellen gives me a big dramatic sigh. "Yes. No. You didn't. Can't you enjoy anything?"

I pull on her sleeve. "I didn't mean it."

"You don't even know what you said."

"Tell me."

"Michael. That expression—the grass is greener—that doesn't mean it really *is*. It just *looks* that way." She stands up. "Let's go home. This has been a nice day. I love coming here with you."

As we walk back to the car, I try to figure out what got her upset, what made her want to end her perfect day now. It wasn't the joke about the zebras, it couldn't be. Maybe it's been building since the girls by the sea lions. She caught me looking. But there's nothing wrong with wanting to be sure that you're not missing something. We all do it.

unidentified flirting objects

Tuesday I get home from the gym around four o'clock. The phone is ringing.

"You don't know who I am," someone says. She's right; I don't. Maybe it's for Ellen. "I mean, you do, or you will." She's talking fast, nervous. "You pushed my friends' car off the Turnpike when we ran out of gas. It was raining. We ran out of gas right at the exit. You and a couple other guys came running over and pushed us up the ramp to the pumps. I wanted to thank you."

"No problem. I remember now. This happened... about a month ago?"

"Five weeks ago. But you just pushed us up the ramp and to the pump and ran back to your car. Why?"

"It was raining. Were you pushing or steering?"

"Pushing."

"We were all pushing. There was no room. Tell the truth, I was trying to make sure I didn't slip and fall on my face. I should've told you to get in the car."

"You did. I wanted to help too. God, it was pouring. Anyway," she says, and she picks up speed again, "I wanted to thank you but I turned around and you were gone but then I saw you get in your car by the other pump and before you left I have photogenic memory and Cindy's brother—she was driving—is a state trooper and he owed me a favor so I gave him your license plate and now I feel so… thank you." And she hangs up.

Photogenic memory. I wish I had that.

The next day I'm writing a computer program that will calculate the members of the Fibonacci sequence when she calls again. "Sorry I hung up," she says. "I feel really stupid. I mean how I tracked you down like that and called. Maybe you don't want to be bothered. Maybe now you'll never help anyone again. Maybe you have a girlfriend."

"Maybe I'm married."

"You're not."

"Maybe, but what if my girlfriend answers the phone? You'll start right in, and she'll find out all about us and that'll be it, she'll kill me."

She hangs up.

A little later I'm watching *Dark Passage* on the classic movie channel when she calls back.

"You don't have a girlfriend. I didn't spy on you or anything, I just know it."

"I thought I got rid of you."

"Not that easy. You sounded mad. Then I figured you were only teasing. There's nothing to find out all about us." She chuckles. "Yet."

"What does that mean, 'yet'?"

"Just, yet."

I try to picture her. I had forgotten all about it, even if I did play the hero that night. Me and two other guys. She came up to the pumps and asked for help.

It was a hot, humid night and the sudden downpour was a relief. It had been hot for a week before the rain. I'm trying to remember her, but I may only be imagining her out of fragments. She had dark curly hair. Her nails were painted. I know because her hands were next to mine on the back of the car. No, they weren't painted.

"'Yet,' what?" I repeat. But she's hung up again.

Maybe I should go to a hypnotist. They can help you get back all the memories you can't recall. I saw them do that on a detective show on TV. When I looked down to check my footing, I looked at her legs, of course, a natural reaction. She was wearing sneakers, ankle socks, her legs were smooth and tan. She was an athletic girl, or at least the girl I'm creating in my imagination was. Mid-twenties? Younger. Coming back from the Jersey shore like the rest of us? I don't know. We all were, all of us on the northbound Turnpike on a Sunday night. She was shorter than me. Was she was pretty? Why don't I remember?

The next time the phone rings I pick it up and say, "Before you start just tell me who you are."

"It's Phil, Mike. What's going on?"

I tell him about the phone girl and my trouble remembering her. "She's preemptive. Doesn't bother with opening pleasantries. That's why I answered the phone like I did just now."

"Did you star-69 her?"

"You mean call her back? No. I'm not sure I should be talking to her. But I'm curious."

"Don't you know anything about UFOs, Mike? Only people who don't want to see them, see them. People *want* to see a UFO, go looking for one, they never do. Same thing with this girl. Sounds like she came from another planet anyway. You tell Ellen?"

"No way. She'd flip."

Of course I haven't told Ellen yet. Why should I? What would I tell her? It's a prank call. Some crazy girl keeps calling me. Ellen was in the car waiting at the pump when I ran out to push that car. I told her what happened, but she didn't see it. What would be the point of trying to explain this to her now? Ellen might want to get an unlisted number. That's a real pain. You get to decide who to tell about the new number. I'd have to reach out and say hey, remember me, the guy who never returns your calls? Here's my new number, in case you need it.

Ellen would've used star-69. I check the call record on the phone and delete all recent callers. There's no sense making trouble when there should be none.

Phone girl doesn't think I have a girlfriend. And I didn't tell her the truth, didn't correct her. She won't call if she knows I have a girlfriend. But that would start to make this into something it's not. These are just anonymous prank phone calls. I'm not guilty and have nothing to be guilty about and I refuse to do anything to hurt Ellen. Alright, I am guilty but it's a rather petty offense. I still *will not* do anything to hurt El. I'm just answering the phone when it rings; phone girl is someone I helped one rainy night, that's all.

Besides, the only reason I didn't tell phone girl about Ellen is because it's something she *doesn't* know about me. It's no equalizer compared to how little I know about her—like her name—but it's something.

I think about Phil's theory, and I decide not to expect her to call again and I realize that's because I want her to call so she won't and that's why I've never seen a UFO.

Next day I'm coming home from the dentist. As I get close to our apartment I walk faster. Ellen said she'd be home before me, and the phone calls usually come around now. So far there have been no messages left on the machine. I buy some flowers from the grocery store on the corner. I can't help feeling like I'm apologizing for something.

Ellen's not home. A note tells me she went for a run in Central Park. I set the flowers on her pillow and put on a t-shirt and shorts and grab my sports bag. I can't wait around; I've got a softball game. Maybe I'll see her. The game is in the park, too, but it's a big park. Before I leave I turn off the answering machine.

In our half of the seventh we're down by a run. Phil gets on base. But they get the next two outs and it's up to Sully.

Our second baseman, Andre, asks, "Why is this guy still playing for us? Doesn't he work for Williamson now?"

"Sully changed agencies this spring and Williamson already had a full team," I tell him. "So he still plays for Kraven Morrisey."

I quit KM a year ago, so I shouldn't be playing for them either.

We don't trust Sully to come through. He's a very good hitter, but he's not been clutch for us all season. He surprises everyone and skies the ball over the right fielder's head and we win. It's the longest and highest home run I've ever seen. It's almost like a Darryl Strawberry moon shot from back in the '80s.

After the game we go to our usual bar. Most of the team leaves after a couple of beers. Sully says, "I have an idea."

Scott's been staring at our pitcher, Melissa, so he's not really paying attention as he says, "You won the game. What-ever you want."

He doesn't know Tom Sullivan as well as I do—I grew up with the guy. We end up in a strip club in Queens. At the club Sully insists that one of the dancers looks like someone we know. We end up arguing about it and it starts getting loud and we get ourselves thrown out of the place.

I get home very late and I take a shower before I crawl into bed. Ellen doesn't wake, or pretends she doesn't. I figure she's mad at me for being late and drunk. In the morning I reach for her. It's early but I want to make sure we're okay. She's got her arms over her head, and light brown hair covers her eyes. I kiss her belly. It surprises her and she rolls over, away from me. I kiss her back, right between her shoulder blades, then a little lower. She lifts her head, tries to blow hair out of her face.

"Good morning," I say.

She kicks me off her and sits up. "Where were you last night, Michael?" She pushes her hair back. I can't tell for sure if she's been crying but her eyes look waterlogged.

"We won the game yesterday. It was a big win. We went out after."

"Who?"

"The team. Well—Scott and Phil, after everyone else left. We got hammered. Sorry I got in so late."

"Were you out with the boys?"

When Ellen says 'the boys' it makes me think of a different group of guys. Guys she has never met, except for Sully. I haven't spent time with the rest of them in years. I'm not planning on it.

"Yeah. Not the boys, only Scott and Phil, and Sully. It was a big win. Really." I should have left Sully out of it; Ellen knows his preferences. I put my arms around her. "I had two RBIs. Sully won the game. We came from behind. I love you, El."

"So you say, Em." She's still stiff. The flowers are in a vase on her dresser. She sees me looking at them. "Someone left me flowers," she says.

"That would be me."

"Someone left them drying out on our bed."

"Me again."

"How would I know? There wasn't a card or a note. Just the flowers."

I shrug. I don't know what to say. "Did I do something wrong? I thought you would like them."

"You only give me flowers for a reason. Valentine's Day, my birthday, our anniversary. When you do something I don't like. I'm wondering why you're giving me flowers now."

"I thought it would be nice."

"But you didn't think to put them in a vase. You just left them there on the bed. And no note. Were you in a hurry? It makes me wonder why you bothered."

"This isn't a big deal."

"No. Apparently, it's not."

"So I shouldn't have gotten them for you?"

"I'm sorry, Michael. I just—you don't follow through on anything. They're nice. I love them. Thank you."

After that, Ellen doesn't say much. She showers and gets ready for work. I dress to go to the gym. Sometimes I like to go early, and tag along on her commute to work. I try to make small talk but she only answers in monosyllables.

We take the same train; she has to transfer at 59th Street. We get on the train and find a place to stand in the middle of the car, holding the straps hanging from the overhead bar. Ellen is on my left. The woman on my right has straight auburn hair that wasn't combed and wasn't sprayed into place. It looks natural, but not messy; just not fussed over. I'm using 'woman' instead of 'girl' because she looks older than me. She's maybe in her early thirties, and has this aura that says *mind your own business.*

"Michael," Ellen says, quiet enough that with the train noise only I can hear. "It's not polite to stare."

Ellen hates walking through the city with me. Whenever we pass a pretty girl, or maybe there's one across the street, I feel Ellen's head turn. She seems to pick them out before me, and as soon as she sees one, she's watching me to see if I'm looking. I've become conditioned so that whenever I see a pretty girl—or anything remotely associated with one, like a flash of long hair or legs—I try to focus my eyes straight ahead and concentrate on walking. I've started doing that even if Ellen's not there. I hate walking through the city with her.

This one took me by surprise. I try to turn my whole body toward Ellen. "Hey," I say, not knowing what else to say. "We just have to win one more out of the next two games and we're in the playoffs."

"When's your next game?"

"Wednesday. Next week."

"Can I come? I want to watch you play."

Ellen has never cared about softball. Or baseball. She's come to a couple of Mets games with me. She had something to say about everything at the stadium: how far away we were sitting, how slow the game was, how the dirty water dogs tasted. I could tell she was completely bored. I stopped asking her long ago to come watch me play. She'd always have a big presentation to work on, or something. But I'm glad she wants to come now.

The train comes to a screeching halt in the tunnel, and the lights go out. I look toward the front of the train, not that I could see anything, but this makes me look to my right again. As soon as I realize that, I snap my head around to face Ellen.

"I hope this doesn't make you late," I say. There's not enough room in the subway car for me to move my gym bag from my right hand to my left, and I don't want to push my bag into the sitting passengers or the newspapers they're hiding behind. I feel like I'm tied up into a knot.

The train starts moving again. Every now and then the lights go out. I can see that woman reflected in the window. It makes me doubly uncomfortable: she sees me looking at her in our reflection, and smiles; I can see Ellen glaring at me.

Ellen gets off the train at 59th Street. She says she'll call me later but I follow her.

She notices I'm there. "What are you doing? What about your gym?"

"I can catch another train. Or walk. Better than having to wait for a treadmill."

"But what are you doing?"

"Following you. Walking you to work."

"That's sweet."

"It's nothing."

"It's not nothing. It means a lot to me."

We walk to the next train platform.

"Why do you have to do that, Michael? Can't you stop? At least when you're with me?"

My policy has been to deny everything, whenever she confronts me. This time, I say, "It's just that I like to look at everyone."

"You don't look at *everyone*."

"I do. You just don't notice it when it's not, you know."

"It bothers me. Please stop."

"I just like to make up stories about them, try to figure out what they're doing, where they're going, who they are."

"You're practically drooling sometimes."

"That's an exaggeration. If I see a pretty girl, I like to imagine she's making some guy's life a living hell. That she's a real bitch. If I saw *you* across the street, I'd probably think that."

"You would think I'm a bitch."

"I would think you're very pretty. I would not be able to stop staring."

A train comes and we get on. The car we're in only has a dozen people in it.

"I'm late," Ellen says. "This train is usually packed."

We find a couple of seats next to each other and sit down even though this is going to be a quick ride.

"Look over there," I say.

Ellen pretends not to look. "That scruffy guy?"

"Yes. He's not looking up from his shoes. He's depressed,

because here he is starting to bald, and he still lives at home with his mother."

"Does he have a job?"

"He's a police hostage negotiator. That's part of why he's dressed so bad."

"What's the other part?"

I lean close to Ellen's ear like I'm passing on a secret. "His mother stopped doing his laundry."

Ellen laughs. "What about that one you were staring at before?"

"I wasn't staring, I swear. I didn't even get enough of a look to make anything up about her."

The train stops and we get off.

"You're a liar," Ellen says, but she's smiling. Then she stops smiling. "And I'd still like it if you stopped doing it around me. I don't like the way they look back at you. As if I'm not there."

This isn't the reason I'm walking her to work. "I'm sorry I was out so late."

"Oh, don't worry about that. I get that you want to spend time with the team."

"Then why were you upset this morning? Was it really just the flowers?"

She doesn't answer.

When we get to the KM building we kiss goodbye. "I'll call you later," Ellen says.

I'm going to stop playing this game, I tell myself. Then I turn and bump into a girl who says "Excuse me" and quickly slips past. Once she's behind me I don't stop and turn around for a better look. There. This is easier than I thought it would be.

When I get home after the gym the phone rings. "I miss having lunch together," Ellen says.

"So do I." We never really had much of a chance to have

lunch together. When I worked at KM we managed it less than half a dozen times in two years. Schedules were always the problem. That, and we didn't want to draw attention to our relationship.

"You wanted to know why I was acting like that this morning," Ellen says.

"Yes. Why were you upset?"

"There was a phone call yesterday. After I got home from my run." Ellen sighs. "Maybe it was just a wrong number."

"Who was it? What did they say?"

"I don't know. All she said was, 'I meant about us.' Then I asked who it was and she hung up."

"It must've been a wrong number."

"What do you think she meant by that? You're not seeing someone, are you?" I can't tell if she's kidding. She has never asked me anything like that before.

"No, El. No, I'm not. I really was out with the team last night."

"Please forget I asked that question. I feel pitiful even thinking it."

"I'm not seeing anyone else. We're together, right? I'd never do that to you."

"But what do you think she meant?"

"I have no idea. It was a wrong number, she misdialed the phone. That's all."

I don't know why Ellen wanted to talk about that call over the phone. We could've talked about it while she was getting ready for work. Or on the way there. I'm just glad it worked out this way. I don't know how I would've acted if she asked me in person.

Friday afternoon Ellen comes home early. She still wants to

visit her parents for the weekend. While she calls her mom, I start packing.

Behind my suitcase in the closet I find an old shoebox full of photographs. I flip it open out of curiosity. Some of these pictures go back to college, high school, even earlier. The people in them, including me, feel like strangers, like memories from someone else's life. There are some older pictures of my little polar bear cub, with interesting backdrops. Shea Stadium. The World Trade Center. The hood of my father's car. I used to take that little toy everywhere.

I find a photo of Anne and Alison by the popcorn machine.

That's Anne alright, that's her nose, her face. As if I'd forget. They're both in uniform, white shirts and black vests, but Anne's shirt is open at the neck and she's not wearing her red bowtie, she's wearing a black velvet collar with a little silver pendant. Nice neck. Allie's wearing her bowtie, very pretty. They were—well, Alison was seventeen, Anne eighteen. There's a light in Anne's eyes that's not the flash. Her bangs are out of control and she's wearing too much makeup. Anne was always pretending to be older than she was. In this picture they both look so young. I was dating Allie when I took this picture, but nobody knew, we kept it to ourselves. Almost nobody knew about it. Anne knew, told me she hated me for it. Called Allie a tramp. Her best friend.

It's something I want to show Sully. He was convinced that one of the girls in the strip club the other night looked just like Anne. I slip the photo into my copy of *The Seven Habits of Highly Effective People* and throw the book into my suitcase. It's not a book I want to read, but Ellen asked me to, so I'm giving it a try.

I wonder what Anne is doing.

stranger in a strange land

The drive down to Cape May is tedious. We're stuck in stop and go traffic with everyone else heading down the Jersey shore. Ellen isn't talking; she's either napping or staring out the windshield. The Mets are losing again. FM radio seems to have gone to an almost all-commercial format; they keep promising forty minutes of uninterrupted music and fewer ads and after every song they remind you of it. All the ads sound the same: lazy, as if the writers scanned the creative brief, stuck the customer benefit in the mouth of a character, and ended the spot with a pointless joke. Life could be worse. Instead of listening to these spots, I could be writing them.

"What lane are you in?" Ellen asks.

"Wanna drive?"

No answer for a couple more minutes because neither one of us wants to drive. Especially in this traffic. Then I get too close to the Pathfinder in front of us. Ellen says, "Slow down. Okay. I'll drive."

At the first opportunity I pull over and get out. While I run around the car Ellen climbs over into the driver's seat. The door's locked. I have to get her attention so she lets me in. I buckle up, adjust the seat, recline it, and shut my eyes. I could be asleep in minutes. But Ellen's driving now, and she wants to talk.

"What did you do today?"

Maybe I could ignore this, pretend I'm already sleeping.

"It's just that when you were still at KM I always knew where you were. Now I don't know what you do with your days. I'm not suspicious or anything." But it's like she's been thinking about that phone call all this time.

"You've got nothing to worry about, El. There's no reason why I'd want to look at anyone else."

"But you do."

"That's nothing, El. I can't help it if someone walks into my field of view. I'm really not looking. Not intentionally."

"Oh, I know it. Maybe I'm just jealous of all the free time you have. It's like you're not really looking for another job."

"I'll try harder. Starting next week. I promise."

"Oh. Gretchen MacArthur called to ask about you. She remembered the great work you did for Rampart."

Gretchen MacArthur... I know where this is going.

Ellen continues. "She called you 'brilliant.' She said, 'That boy of yours is brilliant!' I had to agree. I said, 'You won't regret...' well, I agreed with her. It wouldn't take much to get back into it, Michael."

I don't say anything. The conversation is over. I'm not participating in this, and Ellen knows it.

Gretchen MacArthur, MBA Brown '87, and Ellen Stanford, MBA Brown '93 treat creatives as if they were food for clients. Fed clients are good for the agency, but hungry ones are better because hungry clients mean more work. Ms. MacArthur and Ms. Stanford insist that their clients are fed on time. They also encourage their clients to develop insatiable appetites. The hungrier the client gets, the better for the agency, for the account executives, for fine restaurants throughout the city where these appetites are stoked over expensive lunches and dinners. But the people getting squeezed to feed these clients, the creatives, get discarded when they can no longer satisfy the hunger.

Ms. MacArthur and Ms. Stanford have their own styles. Ms. MacArthur, when she was at KM, didn't like it when I wasn't working through dinner, never took me seriously, and would have put me out on the street if I hadn't left first. From what Sully tells me, she's doing the same thing to him at Williamson now.

Ms. Stanford was different. She rewarded my work on her accounts by smiling at me during and between meetings. She listened to my stories, laughed at the right parts. Next thing I know, I'm moving in with her. It started, as things in ad agencies do, at a brainstorming session that went past six o'clock. Ellen asked me out for a drink when we were done. After, the only thing I missed was flirting in the office. That had to be hidden, once we were a real couple.

Before I go on, I should apologize to all those in the advertising industry who are made for this work, who were born for it or have come to love it. Anything bad I have to say comes from my own experience and is my fault, starting with how I wasn't suited for being a copywriter. It didn't make me happy, and it showed. It showed in my attitude. It showed in my work, which was pulled from me when it wasn't ready, tampered with, mishandled, brutalized. I didn't like seeing that happen, I couldn't separate the things I wrote from myself, I couldn't just let them go, and it's true I started to create less. I'd come in late, miss deadlines. They couldn't destroy what I wouldn't give them. I knew I was wearing out everyone at the agency, and even Ellen would not be able to stop them from giving me the boot. Before they could fire me, I quit.

Turns out changing careers isn't so easy.

Ellen hates that I quit without having a plan or better job lined up. She hasn't kicked me out, she's been giving me some time. But all I've done with that time is watch old movies, play video games, break copy protections, write game cheats, and teach myself programming languages. Things I've done all my life. For fun.

Mr. And Mrs. Stanford don't live in Cape May but in a community of luxury homes nearby. We call it Cape May because that gives it an identity that seems to mean something more than *Whispering Pines* or *Roaring Brook* or whatever part of nature was removed to make room for it. This is their northern base of operations, where they spend a few months in the summer to escape the heat of Florida.

They're retired, or he is. She's still going strong with tai chi, pottery classes, and tennis filling her mornings and various community service activities taking up the rest of her day. Mr. Stanford plays golf competitively: not well but with anger. He's improving and is determined to be club champion. He'll probably succeed. He gets what he wants. He used to be a powerful executive at a Fortune 100 company. I don't remember the details. I believe his title in retirement is Chief Executive of Everything My Daughter Decided Wasn't Important When She Let That Bum Move In With Her.

Visiting her parents gives Ellen the chance to try once again to win their respect. Like all long-running family sitcoms, nothing really changes episode after episode.

I wonder what would happen if one day Ellen's mother would look up from carefully rearranging a floral centerpiece and say something like 'You look beautiful in that' or maybe her father could say 'I'm proud of my little girl.' I wonder if Ellen would be able to function. I wonder if this serious, professional woman, who has accomplished so much—who has attained physical perfection, who is never out of fashion, who manages million-dollar accounts, who handles people effortlessly, who can demand and get a refund for our tickets because the sound in the theater isn't up to her standards, who is propositioned by nearly every man she meets, who can learn foreign languages on her own, and who has mastered every tip or trick a modern woman should know in or out of bed—I wonder if a few magic words of approval would shatter her, vaporize her into a cloud of millions of tiny, sparkling shards, and there'd be a little girl standing there, smiling, weeping.

I'm glad I don't have this kind of potential time bomb lurking with my folks. Not seeing them helps.

After cocktails we sit down for dinner.

"Why in hell didn't you tell us you were coming down earlier in the week?" Mr. Stanford wants to know. Three years into this and he's still Mr. Stanford, or maybe Sir. "You have a snowball's chance of playing tomorrow."

"I didn't bring my clubs. I'm taking it easy this weekend. Had a rough week."

"Suit yourself." Then he tells his forkful of lettuce, "Must've sprained your wrist on your keyboard."

Mrs. Stanford steps to the plate and swings for the fences. "How was your week, dear? You look exhausted."

Ellen, who has cursed out bike messengers and cabbies, and who has experienced this many times and should know what's coming, can only say, "Why? I feel fine."

"Sweetheart, your eyes. They're packed for a long trip."

Defense mechanisms finally kick in. Ellen stares at her mother. She casually raises her glass of wine, takes a sip. Her eyes are suddenly even more Arctic Ocean blue than usual.

"It's Michael's fault. He kept me up nearly all night. He's insatiable when he's stoned."

Now it's her mom's turn to stare. Oh, and her father: I feel his glare but I'm not looking up from my plate.

I'm trying to keep my mind blank so I don't start laughing. I focus on one thing: I really do love my woman.

After what seems like an hour of shocked silence, Mrs. S chooses to ignore the remark altogether. "I'm going into town tomorrow. You can come with me, and maybe we can find something nice for you to wear tomorrow night."

"Sure, Mom."

"Tomorrow night?" I have to ask.

"Dinner at the Clubhouse. Reservations at eight." Mr. Stanford points his fork at me. "You brought shoes, no jeans, at least a golf shirt, something with a collar."

"Yes."

Not exactly, but I'm not telling him that. I was hoping that he'd be out on the course and mother and daughter would be torturing each other in town and I could kick back for a few hours at the pool, and now that's not going to happen. I'll have to hit the mall tomorrow. All I wanted to do was sleep late, and spend as little time around them as possible.

He's pointing the fork at me again. "My daughter thinks she's funny. You will not get 'stoned' in this house, or around her."

"Your daughter is funny. I wasn't 'stoned' last night. More wine?" I hold the bottle out for him.

"Your sister is coming with our grandchildren in a couple of weeks," Mrs. S says.

Ellen puts down her fork. "Caroline? I know. I talked to her yesterday."

"Keith has to work, but he'll join us a couple of days into the visit. I don't know how she manages those children on an airplane by herself."

"She told me she wants to go back to work."

"That's nonsense. She's too busy."

"That's what she told me, Mom."

"She can't leave her children with strangers all day," Mrs. S says.

"Maybe Keith can help."

"Keith has a very important job," Mr. Stanford says. He doesn't look at me when he says it, but we all know what he means.

"Well, it will be good to see our grandchildren." Mrs. S gets up from the table. "I think it's time for coffee," she says.

After coffee, Ellen excuses herself and goes to bed.

We're adults, we've been living together for a few years, Ellen has just brought up the Unmentionable, but we still don't both of us head for the guest bedroom at the same time.

I end up watching a recap of today's games on the sports channel silently with Mr. Stanford. Not silently, because the TV is too loud. But not talking to each other about any of it. Because the TV is too loud. And that's how Mr. Stanford likes it.

Ellen's in bed by the time I get away.

The sheets are cool. There's a breeze coming in from the window. The bed squeaks. At the slightest movement. There's an unspoken agreement that Ellen and I will never have sex in her parent's house, mostly because of this bed.

Ellen's awake. She doesn't fall asleep easily, and I'm sure the stress of the week, the drive down, and dinner are not helping. She won't drink more than two glasses of wine in front of her parents. And she shouldn't have had that coffee.

My settling-in noises go on for a while. Then crickets chirp.

Ellen says, "Did you hear what Mom said? 'Our grandchildren'?"

"Caroline's got you there, El. That's why she's their favorite."

"That's not the only reason. She's the older daughter, and she's married, and I'll always be compared to her."

"And, Keith has an 'important job'. I'm sorry I disappoint your parents so much."

"Don't let them bother you. *I'm* the disappointment."

"I noticed they didn't ask when *we* would be giving them any grandchildren. They don't want me around. They're still hoping you'll come to your senses and dump me."

"It's not that. I talked to Mom. About children. She knows what I want. She's not happy about it, but she knows. That's why she brought up Caroline's kids."

"El, I don't want you to come to your senses."

Ellen shakes her head. "I don't get why everyone thinks I've lost my mind."

"Everyone?"

"Well, my parents. You. You're always saying if I woke up I wouldn't want to be with you."

"It's true."

"That's what I mean. I'm awake, I'm aware, I'm fully sensible, and I want *you*."

"Now?"

"That too, but not right now. I want to be with you, Em. You're my guy. Please don't question that."

"I'll try not to." It feels so good to hear her say that. It feels great.

Ellen returns to the conversation we weren't having in the car. "Williamson's a good agency, Michael. You won't be able to do much better than that."

"They're all the same. Sully hates it there."

"They're not, and you know it."

"All right, Williamson's a good agency."

She turns, squeaking the bed. We're facing each other now. "So why are you trying to blow it? Gretchen likes your work.

The client likes your work. She's giving you another shot, to come back. To a real job, a real company."

"Williamson's good, but not better than KM. In case you forgot, I quit KM. Besides, Gretchen hated my attitude. It wouldn't last."

"Attitude? You're the one who makes that a problem."

"You've complained about it many times."

"No. No I do not. I mean at work. But if I didn't like the way you approached us, our relationship—do you think we'd be together?"

"Of course. There are certain things that only I can do." I playfully reach for her under the sheet, the bed squealing in alarm.

"Stop it. Oh, forget it." She rolls over so now I'm talking to her back.

"I hated that job, El."

"It's a job, not a game, Michael. You don't make a living playing games. Time to grow up."

"Have you found what you're looking for?"

The girl in Eddie Bauer is not as tall as Ellen and has short, very curly blonde hair and impossibly green eyes. She's wearing a golf shirt and khakis like a good Bauerite. Sounds like she has an Australian accent. I'm not sure; it could be anything from the British Empire.

"No, I haven't, but really, have any of us?"

She gives me a half-smile. "I can't help you with that. What about something that's in the store?"

That was quick. Nice comeback. But if I ask her for help she's going to be in on the secret I've been trying to hide for a while, that my waistline is now a bigger number than my inseam. On the other hand, I don't want her to go away.

"I'm looking for a pair of these, 33 x 32."

"Let's see. No wrinkle, pleated front, relaxed fit." She says it in such a nice way, whatever that accent is, but why did she have to say it out loud? "Sand. Here we are."

"I swear I just checked that shelf. It's more like wet sand."

"I suppose you're right. Would you care for something in a lighter shade?"

"No. That's a fine color." In my head I hear *would you care for something blonde?*

"Would you like to try them on? Our dressing rooms are across from the register."

I go into one of the stalls and shut the slatted door and try these pants on without incident. They fit like I expected them to, and she doesn't 'accidentally' open my door while I'm undressed and then ask if she can help me privately. A boy can dream, can't he? I come out of the dressing room with the pants. She's standing near the cash register.

"They fit just right," I tell her.

"My name's Jenny."

"Hi, Jenny. I'm Michael." Maybe this is going too far.

"Is there anything else I can help you with today?" She is so polite. It must be the accent.

"Yes, but for now I'll just take a golf shirt."

This gets me a bigger smile and a little laugh. That's all I wanted, really. I feign incompetence and let her pick out the color. She picks one that looks like orange sherbet.

On my way out of the store, she says, "I hope you find what you're looking for, Michael."

I smile and thank her and in my head I'm thinking *I just did.*

The shoe store isn't nearly this much fun. I try to find something I can wear to the clubhouse and maybe even some-place else. I end up with everything I need to avoid reproach by the staff or Mr. Stanford. We always eat at the clubhouse. I should remember to bring this kind of stuff, or just leave it here.

When I get back to the house I head straight for the guest room. I take the tags off my new pants and shirt and see that Jenny has written her phone number on the sales receipt. Keeping it would be wrong, so I tear it into small pieces and crumple them into a tight ball and go out to the kitchen and put it in the garbage carefully, below some other trash, where it won't be found.

The house is cool and quiet and empty. The bed still squeaks but not as loud as it does at night. I reach for that self-help book I'm reading, which is sitting on the nightstand next to the clock. The picture I'm saving for Sully falls out. I look at it, Anne and Alison looking so young, then I put it in the back of the book and find my place so I can read a little.

But I can't concentrate on it. There's something about self-help books that drives me crazy. I would much rather be reading a programming book. I have *Data Structures and Algorithms in C* in my suitcase, but Ellen gave me this book, and she will be happier if she catches me reading it.

I get through the first two pages and fall asleep.

Mr. Stanford is jabbing his fork at me again. This time it's got a hunk of New York strip steak impaled on it. Well-done, gray, dead. "You missed a terrific day for golf."

I put my own fork down. "When I saw the sun this morning, I knew I made a mistake. Next time I'll remember the clubs," I lie.

"Why don't you leave them down here?" Mrs. S asks. "You wouldn't have to lug them back and forth. And they're probably only in the way in that little apartment."

I don't think storing my clubs at Ellen's parent's house is a great idea. If they were here I'd have to come here to use them.

That would mean every round of golf in my future would be sandwiched by three hours in the car with my girlfriend, not good for our relationship. I'd be playing with a foursome that included an obnoxious, competitive braggart. I play golf for fun, and I try to enjoy myself. For me, golf is serenity and reflection, satisfaction with your personal level of play, calm acceptance of double and triple bogeys. Mulligans.

I look to Ellen for help. Her hair is in a ponytail tonight. I prefer it loose, but this way I can see more of her neck, which is just fine with me. She's staring at me, through me is more like it, waiting for me to say how great that would be. But then she focuses on her father and says, "I don't think Michael can leave his clubs here. One of his clients is a big golfer. He just doesn't want to say no to you, Daddy."

"Which client?"

"Rampart," Ellen says for me. "Their EVP of marketing, Frank Hendershot, really likes Michael's work. He plays a lot."

Mr. Stanford is curious. "The lock company?"

"They do home security, cameras, sensors. It's not just locks."

Mr. Stanford waves his fork dismissively. "Crime's way down."

Ellen's on her home field now. "Daddy, Rampart's target market is suburban, upper middle class, the white flight crowd. They're security conscious, which is why they move to small towns away from the city, but they're not ready to give up their old habits and leave their doors open at night."

She tosses me a glance as she makes this stuff up. That's my cue, just like it's a pitch meeting.

"And you'd be surprised how many small-time burglaries happen in these places," I chime in. "It's local kids, they've got nothing better to do in these towns, they get drunk in the high school parking lot and go do something stupid."

"Maybe we need a camera system for this place. For when

we're not here." The fork isn't pointed at me anymore; Mr. Stanford starts eating again. "Not worried about Florida," he says around a mouthful of New York strip. "Our geezer neighbors keep an eye on everything, nothing gets by 'em."

Ellen and I share a smile across the table over our little charade, and I add, "That's a pretty dress. Did you get that today?"

"It's batik. Mom showed me this cozy little place. You really like it?"

"I like the pattern. I've never seen you wear something so... patterny."

Ellen's smile fades a little.

"I mean, I like it! Green looks good on you." To Mrs. S I add, "But then everything does, doesn't it?"

"I thought the blue was nicer. Went with her eyes. But this is nice, and it's not black," Mrs. S says to Ellen, probably continuing something from this afternoon. Still, it's been a good dinner.

Then Mr. Stanford starts to choke. He drops his fork, clutches his throat, turns all sorts of colors, and falls out of his chair.

He must've tucked the tablecloth into his belt, maybe thinking it was his napkin, so he takes most of our table settings with him. The noise of all this hitting the floor makes me jump almost as much as seeing the look on his face.

Someone screams "Doctor!" which, in the clubhouse, is like crying "fire!" in an Irish bar. At least three men step toward us; maybe another two hesitate, thinking of lawsuits. I always wondered what I would do in a situation like this and what I do surprises me. Before anyone gets close I pick him up, get my arms under his and make a fist and do the best imitation Heinlein maneuver I can, and I know I said Heinlein but that's the name that pops into my head, no time to remember the real name, and I'm thinking of those big pieces of steak and his habit of talking with his mouth full and the poster I have that shows how to perform this maneuver on a choking Red Sox fan, and it sounds like he says "grok!" The offending morsel is flung quite a distance, landing at the feet of one of the doctors. Mr. Stanford suddenly fights to break the hold I have on him. He grabs my arms and pushes me away.

"I'm alright, I'm alright," he says.

Waiters and managers surround us, bus boys cleaning everything up, people returning to their tables. Strangers shake my hand, compliment me on my quick thinking, pat my shoulder. Then Ellen's next to me.

"How did you know what to do?"

"I didn't. It just happened."

She squeezes my hand.

Mrs. S is looking into her husband's face, asking him questions, concerned. "How are you feeling, Edward? Do you want to go to the emergency room?"

It takes me a while to realize who Edward is. Suddenly I get this wicked grin and tell Ellen, "I'm going to call your dad 'Teddy' next time we're playing golf."

This makes her stifle a giggle against my shoulder.

Mrs. S takes charge. "We're going to go home," she tells the manager, and he tells her not to worry about the bill. Mr. Stanford—Teddy—looks a little shaky and he's probably annoyed his wife has to do this for him. He keeps trying to focus on a spot on his shirt, rubbing it off with his jacket cuff.

On the way out the manager shakes my hand again and calls me a good man. The valet brings the car around and I'm given the keys. I never drive when Teddy is in the car. Even though it's less than a mile to the house I feel weird, driving his car with him sitting next to me.

When we get back to the house Mom—where did that come from? Mrs. S goes into the kitchen. We sit down in the living room. I sit in a big armchair near the window and Ellen sits on the big arm of the chair, her fingers playing with my hair. Teddy flops on the sofa, grabs the remote, turns the TV on. He starts flipping through stations but leaves the volume all the way down. Mrs. S comes in with espresso, four cups and saucers on a tray, puts it on the table in front of the sofa. Ellen gets up, gets hers and mine, comes back.

"You saved my father's life," she says.

"I'm here to help." All those years wanting to be a super-hero, and that's my catch phrase?

"You should thank Michael," Mrs. S says to her husband.

We wait for Teddy to figure out a way to do that. "Well, I'm glad Michael was thinking quick," Ellen says. "And so's Dad. We all are. How are you feeling, Daddy?" She gets up, goes over and gives him a hug, gives him a big kiss on the cheek, and sits down next to him. The dress really does look good on her. He grunts something and continues to watch TV.

"Daddy?"

"I'm fine," he says.

"I'm so glad Michael was there."

"Uh-huh."

"Are you sure you're okay?"

He pats her arm. "I'll be okay without all this fuss, little girl."

Ellen stands up and looks at me. "My hero," she mouths, and smiles. Out loud she says, "I'm going to bed. Good night... Michael? You coming?"

I launch myself from the chair at the invitation to retire to the guest room together. "Uh, me too. Nite!"

"Get some rest," Mrs. S rationalizes. "You do need to drive back tomorrow." Teddy grunts something else that I don't catch.

Ellen's waiting for me just inside the guest room, and when she shuts the door she presses the lock at the same time so there's only one click. Then she turns and we share a long kiss and start to undress each other.

"Neat color," she says, as she pulls my golf shirt over my head. "Makes me think of baby aspirin."

"Picked it out all by myself," I answer, turning her around to find a zipper. "You too. Green's good on you." I give her a kiss where the opening zipper exposes her back. "But I bet the blue was better."

Ellen turns, shimmies, and the dress falls to the floor. "Don't get smart," she says, and pulls on my belt. "Don't ruin a nice evening."

"Teddy gagging on a slab of meat is a nice evening?"

This makes her giggle again.

"Your problem is," she starts

"you think when you shouldn't," trying to make a point,

"but when you just react," and I keep

"you are so much" kissing her

"smarter."

We fall on the bed, which rips out an agonizing scream. It sounds like there are roomfuls of rusted hinges and old wooden floors in there. Ellen pushes me away, gets up quickly, and looks down at me and the still screaming bed.

I shrug. "What do you think they think we're doing?"

"Get up."

I get up and she shows me where she wants to do it. I put a pillow on the floor next to my side of the bed, as far as possible from the bedroom door, and she stands there, waiting for me to lay down on the floor, which I do, my head on the pillow right at the bottom of the nightstand. She straddles me, then moves up a little, so she's over my chest, her hands on the nightstand. She undoes her ponytail and shakes her head. I look up at her through a cloud of golden light, illuminated at the edges by the bedside lamp like an angel's halo. She puts the scrunchie down on the nightstand next to my book. She picks up the book, looks at the cover, and I hold my breath. I know what could fall out, and I know it's going to need an explanation, and I know it's going to interrupt and probably end what we're doing. She bites her lip a little, like she's thinking. "Stephen Covey," she says. "I approve." Then she puts it down, turns off the light, and lowers herself to kiss me.

We eventually get enough courage to get into the bed. It's not heroic courage, because we're only doing it so we don't have to sleep on the floor. A summer thunderstorm rolls by; we get heat lightning and distant rumbles. I'm not sleepy so I count when I do see a flash to see how far the storm is.

"A nice evening?" I whisper. "Your father almost died."

"Yes, but he didn't. You saved him."

"So all's good?"

"Better than good."

We practice cuddling deliberately, without rattling the bed. There's muffled shouting coming from somewhere in the house outside our bedroom. Ellen's parents are in a heated argument. It's mostly her mom yelling; he sounds more defensive than anything else, but I can't make out the words.

"I wish they wouldn't do that," Ellen says.

"What are they arguing about?"

"She's telling him he should've ordered the fish. I don't know. Maybe it's about you."

"Me?"

"Mom likes you. She told me while we were out shopping. She said you're a hunk. Now she probably likes you more."

"She likes me?"

"I told her how happy you make me. Michael... who are those girls?"

"Girls?"

"I didn't mean to poke into your things. I just wanted to see where you were in the book."

"The picture."

"Yes."

"It's a couple of girls from the candy counter. When I worked in the movie theater. Years ago. Back in college."

"Why?"

"It's something I need to show Sully. He thinks he saw one of them recently, and this will show him he's wrong."

I hope that's enough detail. Ellen's breathing slows and she falls asleep. Too bad. I want to ask her why Teddy thinks I'm still a copywriter.

brand new clincher

Phil, Sully, and I jog into the outfield, bringing a ball to toss around.

Glove, cleats, cap, that's all my equipment besides the ball. Uniform? Shorts, a t-shirt with the KM logo on the front and a number on the back. I'm number twenty-two. I've always worn that number. Sometimes there's an Ace bandage on my right knee. The ball? It's a gray softball, a Clincher, soft fuzzy leather, worn.

Hit an old Clincher hard enough, really hard, and you can alter the shape of the ball, turn it into an egg. The more the ball is used, especially if it gets wet, the heavier it feels, and it loses its 'juice'—it doesn't travel as far. We only use the new balls for the game. The new balls soar. It's like they have an anti-gravity field. Hitting a new Clincher is a joy.

Starting close to each other, we throw the ball high in the air to simulate fly balls. There's a steady rhythm to this. We gradually increase our spacing until we're roughly in our positions, Phil standing in left field well behind the shortstop, me in center field, Sully in right.

Today we're playing on Randall's Island under the Triborough Bridge. On a field like this where there's no fence, balls getting past the outfielders turn into home runs. We've got a deep left field that ends in underbrush and then trees. Phil would like to avoid going near that place. There are used needles in there. There's no fence, nothing but the outfields of the other diamonds laid out under the bridge behind me and Sully.

We've loosened up our arms so we can make throws from out here to the infield. Sully rolls the ball in toward the dugout, just a bench behind a chain link fence on the first base side of the field. The infielders are done taking practice grounders. Melissa, our pitcher, tosses the last of her warmup pitches. We're ready.

First batter steps to the plate. A righty. Phil moves a little deeper and closer to the left field line. I shade a little toward him. Sully moves in a step and a few feet closer to me.

Our infielders also eye the batter and go through their own calculus. The third baseman, Bobby Campbell, guards the line against sharp grounders and line drives. Scott, our shortstop, plays deep in the hole between second and third. Andre slides a little closer to second base. Laura, our first baseman, stays near the bag; she's ready to take throws from the infield on ground balls. Our short fielder plays close to the infield to stop line drives.

The umpire throws the new Clincher out to Melissa. She holds it up and turns around to show us, as if we need reminding. It's bright white and I can feel its lightness even here in the outfield. The catcher settles in, the batter takes a couple of practice cuts. Melissa goes through a whole routine, pulling on the brim of her cap, tugging at her tank top, kicking the dirt, before she pitches. It's kind of cute, the way she does it. She's an account executive, not as senior as Ellen, and she's always involved in extra-curricular corporate activities. Her energy level is motivational, even for someone like me.

The first pitch is high, a ball. From the way the batter shifted his weight and pulled his bat back as the pitch came in, it looks like he's going to try to slap the ball the other way, to take the pitch and hit it toward right field.

I wave Sully another step in and a couple away from me; he's got to watch the line, this guy might be trying to slice it. Scott moves a few steps back toward second base. I take one step in and lean toward right field.

I know what it looks like. I understand Ellen's complaints. Nothing happens. Players stand around waiting, doing what looks like nothing. Softball is almost like baseball, nearly the same rules, so it looks just as boring and motionless to the uninitiated.

The next pitch is a little outside and the batter swings.

As he starts to swing I'm stepping toward right field because he's swinging late at an outside pitch, keeping the head of the bat back in his swing, and that's going to go the other way if he makes contact, which he does. He smashes the ball, it's a drive into right field, the ball tailing away from Sully because of its spin.

Sully's sprinting, hoping to get to it before it rolls past him into the other field, and I'm running at a deeper angle so I can back him up. Andre comes out a few steps into the outfield to take the relay. Scott stands on second base in case the throw goes there.

Sully gets to the ball and turns, throws, a real strong throw. Andre catches the ball and runs it back toward the infield. The batter has gotten to second base. A clean double. Nice play by Sully to hold it to just that. Now we get ready to do it all again, except this time we've got to think about that runner on second. A line drive or bloop hit in front of us could score him.

You miss all this other movement if you're watching the game on TV because the camera's only tracking the ball and one player. Or, if you're at the game, you might be doing the same thing, just tracking the ball, or looking for the beer guy. You certainly miss what's going on in the fielder's heads. Most of it, they miss, too—it's reaction and instinct.

I can't blame Ellen for not showing up

It's her company team but she doesn't really know or spend any time with this crowd. We play together, drink together afterwards. We're clinging to a world where play is everything, not making the all-out commitment to our careers and our adulthood that maybe we should. This takes some effort and dedication to principles that directly contradict the ones vital to career success. Ellen has her priorities straight. She can be fun, but you can see where she would be uncomfortable around us.

I reminded her about the game this morning, but she was distracted. When she called me this afternoon she said she needed a ride but wasn't sure when she could get out. I told her to grab a ride with Henry if possible.

Henry pulled up five minutes before the game with Bobby, Andre, and two traffic coordinators, one of them a redhead. Half our infield and a couple of cheerleaders. I spend less than four seconds trying to figure out who is with who. I'll find out later at the bar. But no Ellen.

There have been no calls this week. Maybe that was it, maybe it was just that call making her a little jealous, but she's never been like that before. Maybe the thought of sitting through a softball game and then a couple of hours drinking in a crowded, loud bar was too much for her.

The next batter is a lefty. I know this guy. He's a line drive hitter. He doesn't like to show off, he won't try to hit a big fly. He just wants to get the runner home. I try to get short field's attention but Andre has told her something outrageously funny and she's laughing. Melissa's into her windup and even from way out in center field I can see the batter's eyes looking at the gap behind second base that nobody can get to. Sully's playing too deep against this guy. I start charging in toward that gap.

You really can't appreciate the game watching it on TV. The stride of the batter toward the pitch, the way he's swinging the bat, the path of the bat toward the ball, the contact, the *ping!* of ball against aluminum bat, the ball jumping off it, the first few feet of flight—within milliseconds the impression of all this on my eyes and my ears is fed into my brain. It factors in all of the softball I've ever played, projects the trajectory of the ball, takes wind into consideration, and propels my body in the right direction, even adjusting for the jump I've taken based on what I saw happening in the instant leading up to the hit.

The ball's going right where I knew he'd hit it. Andre raises his glove and jumps but it's half-hearted, the ball passes over his head. I love this part because everything slows down and I can flow with it, I'm already there, the ball is staying in the air long enough, I only have to reach out and down below my knees to catch it running full speed toward the infield. Even more fun, the runner on second watches the ball over his left shoulder, sees it going into the part of right field where no one should be, and starts running for home, and now there's nothing he can do. I pull up a little and throw the ball over to Scott standing on second base for a double play.

It looks like I'm a lot faster than I really am, like I flew to that spot, but it's only because of the good jump that I got, sort of like seeing what was going to happen before it happened.

It feels good getting there and making that play.

Melissa shouts *yes!* from the pitcher's mound. Scott, our best player, gives me a thumbs up.

"How the hell did you get to that so fast?" Sully asks as he hands me my cap.

That's why I play. When I play there's no second-guessing, no one looking over my shoulder, no back-seat driver, no struggle, no failure. There's only the game, just like there's always been. Simple and fun.

We get the next out and I lead off and they know me, they go four across and deep with the short fielder between the left and center fielders. I'm feeling good. I lay off the first pitch, but I get the next one and I pull it and I *know* it's going over the left fielder's head, I don't care how deep they were playing me, it's going to bounce into the trees. Did I mention the discarded needles in those bushes? They'll have to be careful looking for the ball. Rounding first I see their backs as the outfielders chase it and I don't hear or see anything after that but second base, third base, and Andre's outstretched hand which I slap after I touch home, running past him (he's up next), slapping a few more hands, not focused on anything else but how much I love this game.

I stand at the end of the bench and catch my breath. Henry's sitting on the grass there, with the girls he brought. "Nice one, Mike!"

I walk over, meaning to ask whether he talked to Ellen. "What's up, Henry?"

"Mike, this is Rebecca and Joan."

We wave at each other, smile. Rebecca's the redhead, so I probably won't forget her name. The other one I've already forgotten.

"This is Mike Santino," Henry tells them. "He's a ringer. Used to be a copywriter. Now he does something else, but he still plays with us."

Rebecca smiles at me and doesn't say anything. The other one, not as charming, says, "Does your company have a team?"

"Do they, Mike?" Henry echoes.

I shake my head. I've kept my unemployed status a secret from most people for almost a year. Anyway, these are my friends. I've known Sully since high school. And Phil, a few years anyway. And the rest of the team. This is who I want to play with.

We score two more runs and go back in the field.

In the top of the fourth I'm out there, thinking about playing softball for someone else, knowing I can't keep playing with KM forever, when a silver Jaguar coasts into the parking area. Pete Sera gets out, then Alison (Alison?) gets out on the passenger side. It *is* Alison. She holds the door open for someone in the back seat. It's Ellen.

I haven't seen Pete or Alison in a long time. Pete is one of 'the boys,' as Ellen would put it. He's someone from my past. I'm surprised, but not exactly thrilled.

The batter hits a single through the middle, which I have to field and play in.

Well, I'm glad she found a ride. And there's Pete. And Allie. I've known them forever, like Sully. But it's odd, because Ellen has never met either of them. And I'm not sure I like the idea of introducing her to them. But it's too late for that.

They go and stand near Henry and the two girls, Rebecca and the one who asks stupid questions. Alison waves and yells, "Michael!" and I wave my glove at her. I look over at Sully and he gives me a big, goofy grin. Melissa's waiting to pitch. Bobby is yelling to the catcher to get back behind the plate. Finally, we're ready to go. The batter's a lefty, strong looking. We shift toward right field now. Sully takes several steps back.

I check the game on the diamond behind us. The outfielders on that field are deep, too. They could get in our way. Have to watch where we're going. I inch backward, and a few steps toward right field, a little closer to Sully.

Melissa pitches, and the batter smashes the ball right between us. It looks like Sully should be able to get there, but I move over too. My eyes are on the ball but in my peripheral vision I can see Sully coming hard toward me, and the left fielder from the other game is moving toward where the ball is coming down. I angle my run so I'll be behind Sully just in case. He's yelling "I got it! I got it!" and the other left fielder keeps coming closer so I yell "Watch your back!" trying to clear him out of the way and warn Sully at the same time.

The ball floats down, heading right for Sully's glove. It's a beautiful run and catch but he doesn't make it, he slows down and closes his glove just a little too soon and the ball skips weakly off the top of the glove. Skips off and arcs right at me, about twelve feet behind the play, but I'm running past it and have to slam on the brakes and reach out with my right hand, the one without the glove, and catch it bare handed. My momentum is still taking me away from the infield so I have to turn, throw the ball off balance, and nobody's come out for the ball so Scott takes it on several bounces. The runner on first smartly tags and goes after the catch, and gets to third with no trouble.

I pick up my cap and start walking back toward center field. Sully says, "That was mine."

"It happens," I say.

He mutters, "Hot dog," and heads back into his position. We've got another batter coming up so I don't question it.

They only score the runner from third, and when the inning ends, I've forgotten about what Sully said.

Alison is the first person to greet me as I come off the field. "You're looking better than ever," she says, holding my arms but keeping me at arm's length as she leans up to kiss me. She's gone blonde, that's why I wasn't sure it was her at first. I'd give her a hug but I see Ellen over her shoulder, watching.

"Hey, El. Glad you could make it."

She's smiling. "Hi, Em." So everything appears to be okay.

"I haven't seen you since forever," I tell Alison.

"Whose fault is that, I wonder?" Alison says. "Ellen was telling us how you still love to play softball." She's got me by the arms, squeezing them. She's only about five feet four, and she's very pretty. Even more than I remember. She's grown up.

Sully comes over. "Oh, yeah. Absolutely. Mike *loves* to play softball."

Alison doesn't let go of me. "Hello, Thomas. How are you?"

"I'm fine. Or maybe you should ask Mike. Mike, am I fine?"

"What are you talking about?" I ask.

But Alison says, "Michael, how is Thomas?"

"Ask him if he'll let me catch a ball," Sully says.

Phil's been watching this develop. "Sully, that was yours. You dropped it. You're lucky Mike was there to back you up."

"He called me off it!"

"I didn't call you off, you yelled that you had it. I was just backing you up."

"Don't call it if you can't catch it," Phil says. He's not helping any.

"I had it! He called me off!"

"Drop it, Sully," I say. "You're on deck." For now, it gets forgotten. He grabs his bat and walks away. But I know it's not forgotten. It's Sully. I walk over to Pete.

"You can tell these guys have known each other forever," Pete tells Ellen, and Rebecca and what's her name. "It was the same way when we were back in high school."

We shake hands. "Been a while. Didn't know you were coming," I say.

"I had lunch with Ellen this afternoon, and she mentioned the game," Pete says, "and I thought I'd drop by. Made her keep it a surprise."

Ellen having lunch with Pete: that's the surprise. Not that they shouldn't, or couldn't; just that Pete has never *met* Ellen, as far as I know, and it feels wrong. I look at Alison to see what she thinks but she's talking with Ellen.

Anyway, Pete wouldn't do that to me. Or maybe he would. I never did trust him.

"What've you been up to?" I ask him.

"Traveling. Spent some time in Argentina."

"What's in Argentina?"

"Cowboys, Mike. 'Gauchos.' And some amazing sights. Patagonia. Hey. Remember my plan? I'm thinking of climbing Everest next year."

"Everest? That's great. How the heck are you going to do it? Don't you have to know what you're doing?"

"There are guides that will get you to the top. I've been doing a little preparation, training, that's partly why I was in Argentina. The training's going to get more intense. I'm going to do it, Mike. Just like we always dreamed."

"That's great, Pete. I gotta get ready, I'm up soon."

"Hey," he says. "You backed up Sully nice."

If one of us is going to do Everest, it'd be Pete. I wonder if Ellen is going to tell me about this lunch she had with him.

I get up with the bases loaded and drive the ball the other way, toward the right center gap where Sully and I had our trouble. The ball gets past their outfielders and rolls into the middle of the other diamond, disrupting that game. They're still chasing it as I round second and I don't look back, sailing all the way around the bases again.

We win the game easily and head for the bar.

atomic dive bar

I'm standing with Scott and Phil in the bar later, talking about the game. It's called Dive Bar, but there's always been a neon Atomic Buffalo Wings sign in the window, so we call it Atomic Dive Bar, or just Atomic. The inside walls and ceiling are covered in scuba-related stuff. Henry, Sully, and the two girls (I've forgotten both their names for the moment) are in the back of the bar, shooting pool. Bobby and Laura have already left together, but we knew about them.

"Who do we play next week?" I ask for the third time.

"Williamson," Phil says again.

"Think they'll let Sully play with us?"

"Could be a league violation. Not the only one we have on the team, but it might be a sore point for Williamson."

Scott's not saying anything; Scott, Sully, and I are ringers but most of the teams have at least one. I don't really consider Sully to be a ringer. Everyone in the league knows him; he works for an ad agency, just one that doesn't have any room on their team to take him. So he's playing for the last agency he was with. It's cool with most of the league. Also, ringers are supposed to be better than the rest of the team. That's me and Scott, not Sully.

Every now and then Scott looks at his watch. It's been a full twenty minutes now since Melissa made her perky good-byes with everybody, making sure we heard her tell Scott she would see him at next week's game. As she left, Phil gave me a nudge and nodded at Scott and then out the door after her. We're trying to delay Scott until he admits where he's going.

"We'd be better off if we could get them to take Sully," Phil says.

I head toward the back of the bar. "Let's see what's going on."

Alison and Ellen are sitting in a booth with Pete, talking.

"Michael! Come here and sit down with us," Alison calls. "Spend some time with your significant other."

This is something I was avoiding. Sitting down with past and present girlfriends. Worse, not sitting with them, and not knowing what they're talking about. I could watch Rebecca, who's bent over the pool table lining up a shot. Just to see if the girls are holding their own against the guys, of course. Scott's got his gear bag and is making his goodbyes.

Phil puts his hand on Scott's shoulder and points to the pool table. "Come on, this game is almost over. Where are you rushing off to?"

"Just remembered, early day tomorrow."

Phil wants me to say something, to keep Scott longer or get him to admit he's seeing Melissa, but I'm no longer in the mood. "Good game, man." I give him a high five. "See you next week."

Scott nods. "You pounded them today. That shot in the first inning."

"The new Clincher. Gotta love hitting the new ball."

"Yeah." He smiles. He gets it, he knows what I'm talking

about. He's a softball player. "Brand new Clincher. Love that feeling."

After Scott leaves, Phil shakes his head. "Why'd you let him go?"

"Why keep him?"

"Since when did you get soft?"

Alison comes up behind me, hooks my arm with hers. "Are you ignoring me?"

"Hey, Allie. You met Phil?"

"Hi, Phil. How are you?" Alison moves from my side to Phil's, wraps her arm around his waist.

Phil's somewhere between six and seven feet tall, and he looks like a giant next to her. "I'm good," he says. "How're you?" He's easy-going, but suddenly he's tight, with this little pixie he just met clinging to him.

"You didn't tell me you had such good-looking friends," Alison says.

"I don't."

"What do you do?" she says to Phil.

"I'm an art director."

"You probably have a girlfriend. Too bad."

"Allie, Phil's married. Two kids."

"And your wife lets you out drinking?"

"Only sometimes," Phil says. "And only for a little while." He looks at his watch. "And it's been a little while already. I better get going."

Phil does a quick round of goodbyes, ending with me.

He pulls me close. "Ever hear from that UFO again?"

"What? No. Guess I've been looking too hard."

That's not true. I haven't been expecting her to call me again. I had forgotten about her until Phil mentioned it just now.

As he leaves, Alison says, "Look at that. I scare guys. Even married ones."

"Phil's good. There's no bullshit. What were you talking to Ellen about?" This comes out far more suspicious than I intended.

"You, of course."

I don't know how to pursue it. We go over to the table with Ellen and Pete. She's drinking a screwdriver; he's got something that's clear. Sully comes by with a round of beers, so I'm armed for this.

"How was lunch?" I say to the space between Pete and Ellen.

Pete gets up, sits on the other side of the table giving me the seat next to Ellen. "I'm going to do a spot for the Super Bowl. I was looking for someone I could trust and bounce some ideas off of, and Ellen was a big help."

"Super Bowl? That's great. Ellen's the best."

Ellen finds my hand under the table and squeezes it.

"We're building something that can have a real effect on the way people shop. Give them time for living." Pete's holding back, which is just like him. He's being deliberately vague. "We need to get our message out, and I figure the Super Bowl is the event for it."

"Expensive."

"But still, maybe cost-effective. If done right."

"El, you tell Pete what Super Bowl spots run?"

"He says it's not an issue."

Pete does look serious. "Look," I say. "It was a good idea calling Ellen, now you have someone on your side who knows the business. But—"

Sully comes over. He takes off his Mets cap and runs his hand over his hair. He's got a bad case of hat head; his wiry reddish-brown hair is molded to his head on top, and frizzy all around the sides. He puts the cap back on. "Another round?" He's on a fast pace.

I show him I'm still half full. He nods and heads for the bar.

Pete says, "You sounded like you were going to say something else. Before Sully interrupted."

What was it. Oh, yeah. "How much can you do, El? I mean, can you help Pete pick an agency? Evaluate their work? Negotiate?"

She squeezes my hand again. "Pete is giving *me* the account. Kraven Morrisey is going to do it." Only because I know where to look, I can see how excited she is by this. To everyone else, she's making a matter-of-fact remark, as if she manages Super Bowl spots every day. But there's a smile hiding there, an excited, joyous smile, in the corners of her mouth and deep in her eyes. For an instant I am totally with her, totally happy for her.

In the next instant the nagging anxiety I felt about their sudden lunch today telescopes into naked, jagged, ugly, stupid fear over dozens of business lunches and dinners (and probably trips to exotic shoot locations) to come. And guilt. I have no right to feel this way. This is a guy I've known for years; sure, I've seen him do some sleazy things, but never to hurt me; and this is no way to treat the woman I love. Don't think I'm not also, in this instant, punishing myself for every transgression, every glance, every thought I ever had that was not completely faithful. Sprinkle in a tiny bit of envy, that I'm the only one who should be writing a spot for Pete. But I don't do that anymore. All this pretty much replaces my happy thoughts for Ellen.

I wonder if Ellen, knowing me as she does, can see any of this in *my* eyes.

I don't give her the opportunity. "That's great!" I say again. "Great! Look at that! Hey, Sull, hear this?" Sully's back, and he has a fresh beer for me anyway. What a guy.

"What's up?"

Pete's glaring at me.

"What's up?" Sully asks again.

"I'm thinking of doing a little advertising, maybe," Pete says.

Sully lights up. "Hey, give me a call in the morning, we can talk about it. You know, Williamson's a top-notch agency. It'll be awesome."

"That's the thing..."

Pete's too nice a guy; also, he's not one to talk plainly. But I can. "Pete already picked an agency, Sull. Not Williamson."

"Who?"

Pete and Ellen remain quiet, leaving it up to me. Pete is staring at me, serious. I stare back. Sure, I realize Sully will have a problem with it. How was I to know this was supposed to be a secret?

"Who?" Sully asks again.

Still staring at Pete, I tell Sully, "I had nothing to do with this."

"Pete?"

"Yes, Sully. It's not Williamson."

Pete's not going to do it, so I say, "Pete's going with Kraven Morrisey."

Sully stands there for a bit. "Whatever," he says finally. "I'm sure you have your reasons. I'm sure they're good ones, too." He glares at Ellen. "Whatever." He means to turn back to the pool table, to make a show of it that it doesn't really matter, but that's over, and Henry and Rebecca and whoever she is are all set to leave. Sully's stuck with us now. Or we're stuck with him. It's just the five of us.

We've got two dimensions of fifth wheel going at this table that seats four.

First there's Sully, who's out of sorts now. He's going to blow up any second. He won't be able to control himself.

Then there's Ellen, who's really the newcomer to the

group. The rest of us have known each other since high school, and Ellen only has the three years with me. I haven't seen Pete or Alison since before I met Ellen, and she only knows Sully through work, so she doesn't have any idea what we have between us.

My foul mood likes that. I'm prepared to stick to inside jokes and references to things she can only guess at. This feeds the dark thing inside me. It makes me angrier at myself for being like this. But it doesn't stop me. She does, by beating me to the punch.

"You didn't tell me you dated Alison."

"It never came up." I glare at Alison across the table.

"*I* didn't say anything!"

"I did," Pete says. "I thought everyone knew."

Sully, recovering a little, adds, "It was Mike's big secret. He didn't want anyone to know." He leans over toward me. "Mike, let me tell you something. *Everybody knew.*"

Ellen doesn't know what she started and doesn't know how to stop. She's amused by what Sully said. "Why didn't you want anyone to know?"

Alison's eyes are glistening. She's fighting it. She's always had a hard time letting stuff roll off her, to not get bothered by it. But this kind of act from Sully should be nothing.

"It wasn't anybody's business then," I say. "And it's not anyone's business now." She didn't want to keep it a secret, then, but we were working together, I was her boss. It had to be that way. And why doesn't Ellen remember that she and I had to do this secret dating thing ourselves at KM for almost two years?

Sully presses on. "We all have our little secrets. Gives us power over each other. Hides the weak spots." He drains his beer, uses the empty bottle to point. "Pete, he has lots of secrets. Important ones. Expensive ones. Ones he can't share with his friends. Maybe only his friends at MIT. Or that company he has. Ellen, she's got secrets. Sure. There's plenty of stuff we don't know about her. Don't expect to learn it from Mike. She's not really one of us, is she. She's an outsider. She's aloof. Like a cat."

"Shut up, Sully."

"You like it that way, Mike. You like keeping her to yourself. You like having girlfriends no one knows about. What's that all about? Ellen? You ever wonder? Are you the only one?"

What am I supposed to do? "Time for you to go, Sully." I don't want to have to stand up yet.

"I don't think so." He points the bottle at Alison. "Ms. Congeniality. How you doing?"

Alison mouths, "Thomas, please stop."

"I don't think so. How you doing?"

Sully's been an idiot before, so we shouldn't all be stunned by this display.

"You doing okay? You're pretty hooked up, now."

Pete says, "That's enough."

"Let your possessions speak for themselves," Sully hisses back.

"I mean it, Sully. That's enough." The problem is, Pete isn't physically capable of backing that up, of shutting Sully up. Sully's big. Pete's not going to do anything.

"I'm just asking a question. You happy now, Alison? Sweetie?"

"Stop it, Thomas," she says.

"Just answer me. Does Pete make up for your 'troubled' childhood? Hey—"

Before he's finished I'm up. I have his shirt in my fist and I push him across the back room of the bar and shove him against the wall next to the men's room door. I want to pound him, to break my fist against his teeth. "You are way out of line," I say.

Sully pushes back, we wrestle a bit and the pool players form a semi-circle but I shove him back against the wall. He has size, I have leverage. We have an intimate conversation.

"What are you doing?" I ask him.

He stops resisting. "She's using Pete. Can't you tell?"

"Pete's a big boy. Lay off her. Don't bring up her father again."

"I didn't—why not?"

That was a mistake. I can't tell him. Certainly not now, here. I'd never tell him. Hopefully he won't ask at some later time. "Go apologize. To *everybody*. Then go home."

"But I didn't mean it. Tell them I didn't mean it."

We go back to the table. Sully says, "Sorry 'bout that. Had a little too much to drink." He does this too easily; he's had lots of practice. He grabs his bag. "I'll call you tomorrow, Mike. About that thing."

I escort him to the front of the bar.

"Mike."

"Yeah, Sull?"

"You're not one of us anymore."

"What are you talking about now?"

"*Us.*"

I can't help a little laugh. "We haven't been 'us' in years."

"Why, Mike? We could always count on each other."

It wasn't really like that. It was four guys who were insepa-rable, true. But the only thing we could really count on was abusing each other. It's where I learned what friends are for. Manipulation, criticism, mockery. Trust was never an issue for us, at least those of us who already knew it was a waste of energy. It was all about competition. Who had the best computer, the biggest knife, the brightest future, the prettiest girl. I haven't thought about it for a very long time. Yet it still holds. Even tonight, when there are only three of us here. There's still plenty of foolishness.

"Go home, Sully."

"Think about it, Mike. Make Pete think about it."

Sully leaves, and I go back to the table.

"And so goes Thomas Sullivan, eternally damned to drunken buffoonery," Pete announces to the girls. It's irritating, given the way he sat there a few minutes ago.

"Shove it, Pete."

"As I was telling you earlier," he continues, directing this at Ellen, "We've known each other forever, and it's always been the same. We even had a name for ourselves. We called our little group 'The Syndicate.' Made us sound a bit criminal. But we were mostly harmless."

"The Syndicate?" Ellen asks, big smile, teasing me. "You never told me you were in a gang."

"It wasn't a gang," I try to explain. "It was just guys who spent all their time together. As we got older, in bars. Sometimes camping or other fun. Me, Pete, Sully."

"Zander," Pete corrects. "Don't forget Zander."

"I never met Zander."

"Ellen, as long as I have strength, you never will."

This is good for a laugh.

"So," I continue. "We all know Sully. Don't let him throw you with his talk tonight. He's just talk, mostly when he drinks. He didn't mean anything by anything." I stare at Alison when I say this, but she knows it already, because she's a long-time camp follower of the Syndicate.

"Allie. Pete. You two together?" That would be a relief, but my question gets ignored.

"So, what happened to Zander?" Ellen persists.

"Alexander Lombardi," Pete says. "He got married."

"Oh." Pause. Ellen is processing this information. "Who did he marry?"

Alison says, "My best friend. Anne. They got married, oh, five years ago."

"So that's when the Syndicate broke up?"

"You could say," Pete says. "We were the ushers at the wedding. Mike here was best man. It might've been our finest hour."

"That must've been some wedding."

Alison gives me a look that I hope Ellen doesn't see. "It was."

"Was my Michael the ringleader of this gang?"

"Oh no," Pete says. "It was Zander. Zander made all our decisions."

"Really? So when he got married, the Syndicate collapsed?"

"Actually. After Zander got married, we continued to get together, pretty regularly." Pete stops a moment to think. "Actually. The first one to leave was Mike. He just slowly disappeared, had other things to do, couldn't make it. Actually. It started before Zander's wedding. At first, we were worried. We thought he was ill, maybe hooking for dope. But he was just the first to outgrow it."

"*You* were," Alison corrects him. "But Michael was the first to leave."

"Michael, don't you want to get together with the boys? I mean, the Syndicate? It's been so long." Ellen has been causing trouble all night. This is what happens when the present meets the past. Disaster.

I shake my head. "No."

"You *should* have a boy's night out. You have my permission."

"Thanks."

"C'mon, Michael. What's the matter?"

"Nothing's the matter, El. Can we talk about something else?"

"I think El has a good idea," Pete says.

I glare at Pete. "*Ellen.*"

Pete looks at me and gets it right away. That's a private name. It's a small thing, but I'm already on edge.

"I think *Ellen* has a good idea," Pete says. "It would be something, to get the guys together again. Maybe we can go somewhere on a weekend. Camping. We used to do that. Ellen, would you mind if Mike went camping with some old friends one weekend?"

"Not at all. I think he should get in touch with his past. I think he really wants to." Then she reaches across the table, puts her hand on Alison's wrist. She smiles, but her eyes are serious. "He shouldn't get in touch with *all* of his past, of course."

Alison smiles back, a real 'I getcha' smile, and looks at me. "Of course."

I think about what Sully said. About us, the Syndicate.

"Go ahead, Pete. You try to put this thing together. Go work it out with Zander."

"Great. I'm sure Zander will be as excited as I am."

"You've got to be kidding me. When was the last time you talked with him?"

"I bet he hasn't changed a bit."

"That's the problem, don't you think?"

"Well, I'm sure he's mellowed some."

"He's not changed, but now he's mellow?" I laugh.

"You just want to disagree with me."

"I'm just warming you up for the big leagues. Did one of those Patagonian horses kick you in the head?"

"What's gotten into you?"

"Zander's going to feel the same way I do, only with more *oomph*," I tell him. "And Anne isn't going to push the issue, unlike *you*." I point my bottle at Ellen, the way Sully did earlier. "Who cares about getting together and acting like we're all in high school or college again? That time has gone."

"We could use another round," Pete says, looking at me as if I'm a waiter.

I think: Patagonia. Everest. Super Bowl. I would have been happy to get the round; there's something in the way he asked that sets me off. "Then let's go get one."

Misty is tending bar tonight. She recognizes me and comes over. "Hey, Mike," she says. "What's up?"

"Another one of these, a screwdriver, and whatever this guy wants."

"Make it two screwdrivers. And a club soda," Pete says.

While Misty is getting the drinks, Pete flicks his eyes toward her. "Nice one, Mike."

I shake my head. "That's not for you," I tell him. "When did Alison start drinking?"

"That's what she asked for."

"Okay. Forget about that camping trip for a minute. Everybody knew? About me and Alison?"

"Everyone," Pete laughs.

"If you don't mind me asking, what's going on with you two?"

"Alison? Oh, it's nothing. She called me out of the blue, I told her I was going to see you and Sully."

Nothing is not what I want to hear. What I want to hear is, 'Yeah, we're serious.' End this nagging feeling I've got. "Please, Pete. Be careful. Allie's practically family."

"I get it. No worries here. Not leading her on or anything."

"It's just that I'm very protective of her. Always have been. As you know."

"If I want to ask her out, I'll get your permission first."

"Just don't hurt her. Don't play games with her. She doesn't need that."

"You have my word."

"And how did this lunch with Ellen come up?"

"I was looking for an agency, and I remembered you were in the business, so I called you. She picked up."

And never mentioned it to me.

We get the round and go back to the booth.

"Help me out," Pete says, to everyone in general. "I've been thinking about happiness. People spend so much time trying to find new things. Always putting aside old things. What are they looking for?"

"To feel good. To find where they belong," Alison says.

He puts his arm around her shoulders, pulls her closer to him. "To feel good, to find where they belong. Maybe."

Oh, great. Pete's philosophizing. And he says he's not playing games with Alison.

"What else?"

"To find out what they want. Who they are," Ellen says, looking at me.

"Their identity. Mike?"

"I don't know, Pete. Why do you always ask these kinds of questions? I don't know. To escape."

"Escape?" Ellen turns in her seat, faces me. "Escape, Michael?"

"I don't know. To change. I don't know."

Pete says, "Maybe to hide. To forget."

"Yeah, okay." Even though I'm holding a full bottle I'm getting the urge for another beer, and another, and wish Sully was still here. We wouldn't be talking about this if Sully was here.

"Michael," Ellen says.

"What?"

"To escape?"

"Did I say something wrong? Save me here, Pete. What are you trying to get at that has me in so much trouble?"

"I'm just talking about happiness."

"Oh. Happiness. That's not what I'm feeling right now."

"Happiness is what we are all looking for."

"Some of us know where to find it," Ellen says.

"Some of us, but not all of us," Pete says. "Most of us turn our back on it."

"Pete, old friend, either you drank too much or I didn't drink enough."

"Mike, old friend, it's just club soda. Don't turn your back on happiness."

"It's getting late."

Alison says, "Why don't you listen to him?"

"Because he's full of shit." It's *my* turn to put *my* arm around *my* girl. "Look at me. I'm happy. See?"

Ellen pushes me away.

Pete tries again. "I didn't mean for you to take this personal, to start an argument. I've been thinking about this. All this looking, this finding new things. It doesn't lead to happiness. Everest is not going to make me happy. I know it. Maybe the trick is, not to look for new things, not to change, but to find your identity in who you are, how you became that way. Maybe instead of letting go of things, there are things we should not let go."

"And maybe, you're wrong," I say. "Maybe, it's a good idea if people forgot about what screwed them up so bad when they were younger, and got on with their lives. Sometimes it's better to let go of a problem, than to not let go."

"There's no anchor, Mike. You can't do that, without setting yourself adrift."

"Nothing good comes from dwelling on the past. Nothing."

"And I think you're exactly wrong."

"Nothing."

Pete puts his hands up in mock surrender. "Enough. We

agree to disagree. But I have to ask you one more thing. We were talking earlier about a certain Super Bowl spot."

"When you pissed Sully off."

"I gave the job to Ellen on the condition that *you* write the spot."

"Ellen, you can't let him—KM won't let him do that. I'm not at KM anymore. Did you tell him that?"

She doesn't answer me. Pete says, "Why don't you write it."

"No. Sorry. Thanks. No."

"Think about it."

"No, Pete. No."

"Michael, please," Ellen says. "Please think about it. Come in as a freelancer."

"There's plenty of talent at KM, Pete. It's a good agency. Ellen will take care of you. If you want a friend on the creative team, then go to Sully at Williamson."

Alison says, "Why, Michael? Why won't you do it?"

"It's not what I do, Allie."

"Michael, you're good, you're a good copywriter," Ellen tries. But none of this matters to me.

"No. I was a copywriter. *Was.* That's in the past. See? Was I happy, being a copywriter? No. So I changed. I don't do that anymore. That me, that was, is no more. This me is not a copywriter."

Maybe I did drink too much. I could probably use some serious editing here, or at least a pot of coffee to sober me up, but as it's coming out it sounds like a really impressive speech.

"Just like Pete says, I changed so I can find happiness. Not yet, but I will. I'm not a boy. I grew up. No more Syndicate. No more stupidity. That's it. You can call it hiding. You can call it whatever you want. You can say I'm escaping. I don't care. This is me. I don't go back."

The three of them stare at me, maybe like they were staring at Sully during his outburst earlier. Then Pete says, as quietly as you can in a bar, "That's nice, Mike. But are you happy?"

witness protection program

The phone is ringing as I come in the door with a full bladder. I haven't even put my gym bag down. I'm taking different trains now, avoiding certain lines, and it takes longer.

"What's her name?"

"What are you talking about?" I snap.

"The girl. Who answered the phone the other day. What's her name? Is she your girlfriend? Does she live with you?"

"That's not your business."

Eventually she says, "Why not?"

"Because it isn't. Who are you? What's *your* name?"

"Olivia. Liv, to my friends. You can call me that. Now, what's *her* name?"

"Olivia. Okay. Hello, Liv."

"Hello, Michael Santino," and she reels off my address, complete with zip code. "What's her name?"

"Liv, why are you calling me?"

She hangs up.

I could not care less. I have to go to the bathroom.

I'm standing there a minute later, visualizing subway and bus maps and planning new routes to and from the gym, to avoid certain… distractions, and the phone starts ringing again. That's it. This isn't funny. I remember to flush but don't wash my hands and it's only because I'm so pissed off.

"Now what?"

"Nice way to answer the phone, dick."

It's good to know that some things don't change.

"Zander, hey, how the hell are you?"

"A little more relaxed than you. Living large. Talked to some guy this morning. He claims to know us."

"Pete actually called you?"

"You knew about this? Wants us to meet him in the woods. I think he's some kind of pervert."

"I think he's nuts."

"That's right, I forgot about that, you're better than everyone."

"What do *you* think? You going?"

"I'm considering it. Yeah. I need to refresh my memory. Remember why I hate you fucking guys."

"I don't need to remember."

"Look, dick, if you want to join us be at my house by six Friday. We'll drive up and grab a hotel, be in the woods early Saturday morning, come back some time Sunday."

"Anne's going to let you go?"

"She's got no say what I do. Six o'clock. Don't be fucking late."

It's always such a pleasure to talk to Zander.

Pete moved fast, didn't waste any time with the idea. To get to Zander's by six tomorrow I'll have to go to the gym around noon, so I could take the usual way home and won't be in danger of running into this woman who always wears the nicest summer dresses. I get my backpack out of the closet but decide not to do any other preparation until I talk to Ellen. She sounded like she was encouraging it last night, but you never know.

The phone rings again.

"I wasn't calling to harass you," Olivia says. Her voice sounds different. Like she's not smiling. "I just wanted to thank you, at first. And then I thought it would be fun, the way we were flirting. I thought what if two people met, just met, like we did, how would they ever find out that maybe they're perfect for each other. But I guess we'll never know."

I don't interrupt her. She's on a roll and says what she says and hangs up. I hope that's it, that I just got rid of her. Which is fine. I woke up this morning thinking maybe I could eliminate these little games I play, maybe then I won't feel so miserable about Pete and Ellen spending time together. Maybe then Ellen won't give me guilt about looking to escape. Because I'm not. I'm not trying to get away from her.

It's just that I've been having this last ride of the night feeling, the one I always got when I went to Playland amusement park when I was a kid. The feeling that says maybe I should try to get on the Dragon Coaster one more time, maybe they haven't shut it down for the night yet—or maybe I should ride the bumper cars.

Maybe Ellen and I should do something this weekend, stay in bed, something. Going camping with my old friends isn't going to strengthen our relationship. Although knowing where Pete is going to be, that helps. I can't believe thoughts like that keep slipping in. I'm not jealous of Pete. He's decent. Most of the time.

I set the table and open a bottle of wine, light a candle. The spaghetti is in one pot, the sauce is in another. Ellen brings home Indian food.

"Oh, Michael, how sweet."

"It's okay. I'll save the sauce, maybe the spaghetti too."

"No, no, don't do that. We'll throw this stuff in the fridge. It'll keep. I'll have it tomorrow night."

"You sure? If you want Indian, that's fine."

"No, Michael. This is very sweet. But you didn't have to do it."

"Why not?" She doesn't answer me. What I want to say, what I was planning to say, what I don't say, is, 'I meant what I said last night, Ellen. I'm happy with you.' Maybe later.

She gets changed while I finish cooking. I throw some chickpeas and red kidney beans into the sauce. Gives it bulk. Everything's perfect.

"You are so sweet, Michael." Ellen kisses me. She's dressed for bed. She's wearing my Black Crowes t-shirt and a pair of boxer shorts; they're shorter, tighter, and pink, and they fit her just right, so they're not mine. Very sexy. She's always hot. "You really didn't have to do this, you know."

"I wanted to. And I was thinking, maybe we can have some fun this weekend. Whatever you want. You know me, I'll stay in bed all weekend. But if you don't want to, we can go somewhere, anywhere." Now to deliver the deal closer. "We can go to a museum."

"A museum?" She sounds a little surprised at this. Did I go too far? Is that too unbelievable? "I was thinking of going to see Mom and Dad."

"Again? Okay. We can do that."

"Michael, aren't you going to ask me if you can go camping with your old friends?"

"What are you talking about?"

"Didn't they call you? Pete said he talked to this Zander, and everyone was all set for this weekend."

"Pete did?"

"Yes. He called this afternoon to tell me. He wanted to make sure I'd say it was okay. He's very thorough."

"He is. Very. Like, somehow, he found *you* out of all the advertising people in Manhattan. Somehow he called *you*."

"What are you talking about? He called for you. He thought you could help."

"And it wasn't important enough to tell me. Why was that?"

"He called when I was on my way out. He said who he was and why he was calling. I thought I could help. Right away, I thought new client. I just... I forgot to tell you. It's not a big deal."

"Some stranger calls the house, someone you've never met, he says he's my friend, and you don't bother to check with me, you just go off and have lunch with him?"

"I'm sorry, Em. Don't make this something it's not. Anyway, it's not like I was wrong. He *is* your friend, and I have a new client."

"Try to look at it from where I'm standing."

"This is not some strange girl calling for you and hanging up when I answer. And besides, you keep telling me you're not interested in the advertising business."

"She wasn't calling for me. That was a wrong number."

"And Pete wasn't calling for me. But it all worked out. Can't you be happy for me? And you don't have to cook me dinner. You don't have to ask for my permission to see your friends."

"This is different," I say, but I don't want to push this any further. Maybe I am making a big deal about nothing. And Ellen still has that phone call on her mind. "I don't want to go, El." I put the backpack in the closet, shut the door. "I don't want to go."

"Go. It'll be good for you. See your old friends. Do something you used to do." She comes over to me, puts her fingers in my belt loops, puts one hand on each of my hips. I do the same. "Sometimes you act like you're in the witness protection program. These guys are just called 'the Syndicate,' right? What are you hiding from?"

I take her hand and lead her to the sofa. I have nothing to say.

"Well?"

"Let me get your wine."

She humors me, which buys me the time it takes to get up, go get our glasses, and bring them back to the sofa. Enough time to admire her legs and feel lucky that I'm with her. But not enough time to come up with a good argument.

"Well?"

"There's nothing to say. I just don't want to go."

"Michael, they're your friends. You grew up together. It can't be that bad."

"You saw Sully last night."

"Sully's... Sully."

"You don't mind how he acted last night?"

"What about Pete? He seems normal."

I'm surprised she has nothing to say about Sully's performance last night. She's always had something to say about him. And now, she thinks Pete is normal. But I can't bring myself to tell her a few stories about him. I can't enlighten her about Pete. He's become competition, and it would be dishonorable to use this opportunity to stab him in the back. It would not be playing fair. Syndicate rules.

All I can say is, "Pete is not normal. He's..." Some words I can use: shifty, a snake, untrustworthy; he's full of empty promises. He'll say anything to get what he wants. I don't know why I feel the weight of Syndicate rules. I thought I was done with that.

Fortunately, Ellen moves on to the next subject. "And what's so bad about this Zander?"

Zander is not competition. I can say what I want. "He's a megalomaniac, an egomaniac, a pyromaniac, a kleptomaniac.

Those are the nice things I can say about him. Picture every villain in every James Bond movie, every bad guy in the comic books. That's Zander."

"You're exaggerating."

"Yes, I am. He doesn't have eight mechanical arms, no eyepatch, no secret base or army, and as far as I know he's never stolen any nuclear weapons."

"Huh. I want to meet him."

"Ellen, please don't say that."

"You ought to have a party. Or take me to a reunion. Something."

"Please, El. I wish you would understand this about me. I didn't enjoy growing up with these guys. I wish I did. But I didn't. I didn't care for the pain of it. I didn't care for the backstabbing, the manipulating, the arguments. There *are* some things I remember fondly. But putting us four together, it's going to be a replay of all the stupidity we put ourselves through. The teasing, the plotting and scheming, the power trips, the peer pressure, the jealousies... that's enough. No."

"Michael."

She says it like she's not my girlfriend, wearing my t-shirt and those shorts and in arm's reach. She says it like she's my boss, and we're in her office and there's a big desk between us.

"I can't believe you're afraid to spend some time with the friends you grew up with."

I have no answer.

"I think you're not afraid of them, you're afraid of yourself."

"Afraid *for my self.*"

"I have never tried to change you, to make you something you're not. You know that."

She's right. I mean, a year unemployed.

"There are three things I never understood about you, though. And I've been afraid to talk to you about them, afraid that I might be going somewhere you didn't want me to go. But I think they're all the same thing."

I would love for somebody to explain me, to understand me, to fix me. I'll let her go on.

"The first thing is what you did to your career. That's the most obvious one. You were—are—a very talented copywriter, Michael. And you gave it up. You just decided one day that you were tired of it, and you walked away from a career. Not a job, a career."

"No. I don't want to go through this again. I was miserable. I *hated* that job. Except for the part you were in."

"And you're not miserable now."

"That's not the point. I'm miserable by choice. I'm miserable because in order to get a programming job, you need experience, and in order to get experience, you need a job. Are we going to talk about jobs? I don't want to."

"No, you're right. It's not what job you have. It's that you quit. That you walked away from one life and started another. Tried, anyway."

"Not many people can do that. It's a good thing."

Ellen nods. "It is. If it's done positively."

"What's that supposed to mean?"

"If you're going forward, if you're going toward something, not running away from something."

"El, I taught myself how to program computers in high school. I'm working on those skills now, so I can get a job in a field I find joy in. You can't get more positive than that."

"Em, you could do anything you want to do. You're brilliant."

"I wish you wouldn't say that. I'm not." Ellen's still talking about jobs, and it annoys me. "I don't drive a silver Jag."

"No, you don't." She was supposed to say, 'I don't care what car you drive.' But she didn't.

"Then there's your family. I don't get it. How you've cut them out of your life. Like you outgrew them. You don't outgrow family."

"My family?" She changed lanes on me. I want to keep talking about how much she likes Pete's car. Where they went. What they did.

"Yes. Your mom and dad. You never call them. Your mother calls here every Sunday at 10 am, and you talk to her as if she's trying to sell you a subscription."

"You hate that she has to check in on me."

"She shouldn't have to. And when you're talking to her all I hear is 'yes,' 'okay,' meaningless answers from you. As if you can't waste your energy on it. What do you think your mom hears? What about your dad? Do you ever ask how he's doing? Do you ever talk to him? It sounds like you just talk to your mom. And you just answer her questions. You never ask her how she's feeling, or how he's feeling, or if they need anything from you."

Then it comes out without thinking. "My stepfather is fine."

"Stepfather? You never said anything about that."

"You never asked."

"Why would you never just tell me that?"

"It never came up."

"What happened to your father?"

"He's dead."

Ellen takes a moment to process that piece of information.

"I can understand why you wouldn't want to tell me something like that when we just met. But you could have mentioned it between then and now."

"It never came up," I repeat.

"How can you withhold something like that, from me?"

"It's part of my messy past. It doesn't matter anymore. I moved on."

"Is that why we never visited them? Were we ever going to?"

I don't know why Ellen's trying to irritate me, but it's working.

"Look, we don't talk a lot. What's the big deal? At least we don't pretend…"

Some things are better left unsaid. It's hard to think of a way to get out of it. It's like I just stepped on a land mine, heard the click, and now can't move on without blowing up. I can't just tell her what I think of her relationship with her parents.

Ellen is waiting for me to finish the sentence. "Pretend what?"

On the other hand, this would get her attention away from whatever agenda she was pursuing with me. And get my own away from my stepfather.

"What were you going to say, Michael?"

"At least we don't have to pretend that I'm still their little boy."

Her eyes narrow. I should stop.

"Face it, El. You're playing out this thing with your folks where you're still their little girl, and can do no right. I know you hate it, too."

"You're kidding, right?"

"Not at all. And somehow you think I should have the same kind of relationship with my parents. No, thank you. I left. They let me go. I'm gone. All grown up."

"You're all grown up." Ellen is not normally sarcastic.

I've forgotten what this was about, but so has she, and that must mean I've won. I better start playing nice. She's kind of cute when I beat her in an argument. Although I can't remember the last time that happened. I reach out, to put my hand on her leg. Politely, just above her knee. To show her that I support her.

"It hurts to see you go through it with them, every time."

My palm somehow doesn't make contact with her thigh.

"You haven't grown up at all."

I smile. "Don't tell anybody." I just want to hug her when I win like this. But she stands up and steps back from me.

"What are you doing?" she asks.

"Trying to give you a hug?"

"I don't think so."

"Why? Because I said your parents treat you like a little girl? It's true."

"Maybe you're right."

"You know I am." I start to rise, but I can read in her body language that I better not go near her. So I sit down again.

"You think it's not a mature relationship. Between me and my parents."

"I'm not saying it's your fault. And it's not a unique situation. Probably lots of people go through it."

"You think I could talk to them? Sit down, air it out, work out whatever it is that's behind it?"

"Hey, maybe it's worth a try. You look great, by the way. Those shorts are something else."

She relaxes. The tension and the defensiveness go away. I stand now, and it's okay to go over and give her a hug.

"That's what I like about us," she says into my shoulder. "We can always talk something out."

If I'm Peter Parker, my spidey-sense would be tingling right now. But I'm not.

She keeps talking into my shoulder. "It's good to talk things out."

"Sure is." I start to rub her back. Who knows what this might turn into.

"You really think that just by getting together and talking, you could be able to work out years of a dysfunctional relationship?"

"You never know until you try." I notice her fingers have again worked their way into my belt loops.

She pushes away, steps back, we've still got our arms on each other but she's looking directly into my eyes. Her eyes are sparkling, the way she gets after laughing, the way that makes me unable to think. She says, "You never know until you try?"

That spidey-sense must have saved Peter Parker from many of Mary Jane's tricks. Who cares about the webs and swinging from building to building? Spidey-sense, that's what I need. But I don't have it. I just nod dumbly. In my head, I'm thinking I'm a genius, a master manipulator. I'm already in bed with her. I'm already staying in, the whole weekend—forget the museum, forget the trip to the parents'—forget whatever she said about my family and my job and the other thing. The other thing. She said there were three things. What's the third thing? Who cares. She's smiling at me, and it's only good when Ellen smiles at me, and she comes back in close and we hug again.

Then she pushes away and says, "Let's eat."

"Good idea. Forgot all about it."

Ellen needs a spoon to twirl her spaghetti onto her fork. I've tried to show her how to do it without training wheels, but she has never mastered it. She's in the middle of a twirl when she says, "How are you going to get there? I need the car."

"Get where?"

"Zander's house. Pete said you're all supposed to meet there."

"I must've missed something. I thought we already had this talk. I'm not going."

"This is good. I like the beans. Yes you are. You said so."

I put my fork down. I'm trying to replay the last half hour in my head.

"You said growing up with your friends was tough."

"Yes."

Ellen looks up at me. "You might characterize your friendships as dysfunctional."

"Very."

"You said just sitting down and working it out could resolve years of dysfunctional relationships."

It hits me suddenly, the feeling I had before, winning the argument. That was an old gray ball. Waterlogged and ovoid. Ellen has the brand new Clincher.

"Like you said, Michael. Maybe it's worth a try."

Lying in bed later, I'm replaying our discussion looking for where it went wrong. Maybe I can find a loophole that I know isn't there. I remember the third thing.

"El? What's the third thing?"

"Third thing?"

"You said there were three things you didn't understand about me."

"Oh. Yes."

It's been raining. Every now and then, there's a wet zipper sound of car tires in the street.

"Well?"

"Not if you're going to get upset."

"I'm going to get upset if I don't know what the third one is."

"You can't guess?"

"No."

She lifts her head from my chest. "If you know the first two, you'll get the third." Then she puts her head back down.

"You're going to make me say them?"

"Yes."

"You're tough." I play with her hair for a while, spread it around on my chest. "Okay. One, job. I left my job. Two, family. You don't like that I left them behind. Three, friends. I don't want to waste time with my old friends."

Ellen lifts her head so she can look at me.

"No. There's four."

"What's the fourth one?"

I can see her eyes get a little wider and shine in the street-light coming in through the blinds. Then she puts her head back down on my chest. And I feel warm, wet tears. I don't know what to say. I don't know what she's thinking. She sniffs a little, under control again.

"Four," she says, without lifting her head. "Four is me. Four is you looking all the time. Four is you growing tired of me, finding something better, running away from me. Escaping. That's four."

It surprises me. I never thought she felt that way, that she was that worried about me. It makes me love her even more.

I squeeze my eyes shut, hold them closed with my fingers, make sure nothing can escape. I don't know what I can say. I would love for Ellen to explain me, to understand me, to fix me. I sure can't.

objects in mirror are closer than they appear

Ellen needs the car so she can go see her parents. I catch Metro-North out of Grand Central Station, taking the train to Tuckahoe, a nice town in the Westchester suburbs north of New York City. It's a little more than a half hour ride. Sully's getting his gear at his folk's house, and he's going to meet me at the station.

The initial clutter of people in front of the station slowly clears as they get into waiting cars. When I'm the last one, I check my watch. It's 5:45. We're supposed to be in Mount Kisco in fifteen minutes. It'll take us more than twenty. I'm standing at the pay phone fishing for change in my pockets when I see the Striped Tomato, Sully's red '76 Ford Gran Torino, at the light. I grab my pack and when he pulls up, I open the door, lift the front seat out of the way, and wedge my pack in the back seat. Then I get in.

"C'mon, Mike, c'mon."

"Where were you?"

"Had to do some things. Picked up something new." The light changes and Sully drops his foot hard on the gas. This thing's got no air bags and a very hard dashboard. It's a relic.

And Sully doesn't want to get to Zander's house much after six.

He coasts through stop signs, runs another red light. "Why couldn't Zander get you in Mount Kisco?"

I laugh. "Zander? You know who you're talking about, right?"

"Why couldn't you get an earlier train?"

"You wouldn't have been there anyway."

The Bronx River Parkway is two lanes in each direction separated by a metal rail, no shoulders. It winds under old stone bridges through lower Westchester. No trucks are allowed on it because of the low bridges. There are too many cars. Sully dodges the slow ones or gets up close behind them and flashes his brights to make them change lanes. He's driving like he's on a racetrack. The road is so old that the curves are not banked and every one we drive through makes me slide on the seat. I try to forget where I am, except that I'm gripping the door handle hard and slamming my right foot into the floor.

"This is going to be great, Mike. The Syndicate, together again."

I'm about to tell him how wrong he is when I remember the talk I had with Ellen last night. I look at him. He's scanning the road ahead, the cars around him, using the rearview and driver's side mirrors. He's ignoring the speedometer.

His speed limit is simple: faster than everyone else. He does check to see what's behind him every so often.

We pass a white car with blue stripes parked next to an exit ramp. Sully sees it too. I watch it in the passenger side mirror; it doesn't move. I'm surprised. The Striped Tomato is bright red—Sully washes it often—with a white stripe zipping along each side, from back to front, like the very end of a lightning bolt. We used to pretend we were Starsky and Hutch after he rebuilt it. It stands out. It's a cop magnet.

"I know. I saw it," Sully says.

Sully shouldn't pay any attention to what's behind him anyway. He should worry more about what's happening in front of him, around him.

We all should.

The world comes rushing at you all the time. Sometimes you can see something coming and you can prepare for it, react to it. But when it gets here there's nothing you can do. It's coming at you so fast that when it happens it's a blur. Then you can look at it in the rearview mirror, you can study it, while you steer straight off the road and into a tree.

"You hear?" Sully says. "Chuck Walters is being a little bitch."

"Why?"

"He came into my office today."

Chuck Walters is Sully's boss at Williamson, and the manager of the Williamson softball team. I wish I could get Sully to focus on driving. I wish I could forget where I was as easily as he can.

"What did Chuck want?"

"I'm not sitting out, Mike. I'm playing."

"Chuck asked you to sit it out?"

"No. Not directly."

"What, then?"

Sully gets busy with driving, doesn't have the time to answer me right away. Then he seems to forget what he was talking about.

I know Chuck a little. He probably just pointed out to Sully that it wouldn't look good, Sully playing against his own company's team. Left it up to Sully to decide what the right thing to do is. Sully won't do it. And I don't blame him. He's always played with KM, just like me. He wants to play. That's all. There's no room for him on the Williamson squad. It won't make him any friends with the people he's got to work with. But if they know him at all, this one little thing isn't the deciding factor.

We get to the top of the Bronx River Parkway, near Kensico Dam. Sully accelerates, whipping the Tomato around the traffic circle before veering right, toward the Saw Mill Parkway. We're still at least ten minutes away from Mount Kisco. According to my watch, it's 5:57.

"Why don't you let up a little? There's no way we're going to make it by six."

"Zander said six."

"Zander can wait a couple of minutes."

"What's up about Alison's dad?"

He's driving right on the bumper of a big Chevy Suburban. The bumper is practically on our hood. The Suburban is massive and totally blocks our view of the road ahead. There's no way to tell what's in front of it. If the guy hits his brakes, we're going to be inside his car. Or all over that bumper.

"Sull, let up."

"He's not even doing fifty."

"That's the speed limit."

"We're going to hear it from Zander all weekend."

"We're going to be picking our teeth out of your dashboard all weekend."

"Pussy."

A whole weekend of this. On the other hand, I could be getting psychoanalyzed by Ellen. Maybe we'll get lucky and my brains will be all over the Saw Mill Parkway and everyone can pick at them as long as they want.

Sully's not going to let it go. "You gonna tell me? You said you would tell me. He was a drunk. What'd he do, molest her?"

The Suburban moves over to the right, and Sully has some open road. The reason the Suburban moved over and slowed is there's a State Trooper HQ here. We speed past the building and keep going. Sully gets lucky again; there are no troopers waiting by the side of the road.

"Does Zander know? I'll ask him."

"You're like a little kid. Everything's gotta be now, now, now."

"You're just pissed everyone knew about you and Allie. You're making shit up about her father."

"That's right."

But instead of this being the end of it, he only starts to work himself up.

"You want to start with me, don't make shit up like you're protecting her."

"Whatever."

"She doesn't need any protection. And she has zero honor for you to defend."

"Shut up."

"No, *you* shut up. She's a manipulator. A real bitch. She used you, back then. You were seeing her and you couldn't fire her, no matter how many times she screwed up. I'm glad I avoided her claws. She's going to screw Pete out of his money. Literally screw him out of it."

"Now who's making stuff up?"

Sully laughs. "You think you're the only one with secrets? I know about her, Mike. I know."

I refuse to ask. That's what he wants me to do, and I won't.

"Wanna know how I know?"

I look out the window and then at my watch. We're passing Chappaqua. It's 6:10.

"She leads everyone on," Sully says. "She was leading us all on. Did you ever stop and think there might be someone else?"

"You?"

"A-hole. I could've messed around with her but I'm your friend."

"How was I supposed to know?" What Sully's saying doesn't make sense. He's remembering it all wrong. Probably the same reason he doesn't remember about Allie's dad.

Sully smacks the steering wheel with an open palm. "You could've asked."

"I don't remember us ever setting up rules for that."

"You betrayed one of your own. You could have had anyone. Anyone else. They were always falling all over you."

"Just because she ran with us, didn't give you exclusive rights. Or me. She's her own person. You know the rules."

"And she always hides behind her dead drunk dad who couldn't hold a job. Still does."

I roll down the window and adjust the side mirror so I can get a better look at what we've been passing. What the hell, Sully wasn't using it anyway. Around the mirror, the place we are right now is a blur of green and gray. But in the mirror it reappears, captured in the frame of the mirror, receding but understandable, smaller but in focus.

My first year or two in college, I would go out nights for a run at the high school track. This was Alison's junior and senior years there. If she thought I was coming to the track, Alison would show up, sit in the bleachers, watching others run, waiting for me.

It would be like we just bumped into each other, didn't plan to meet. But she planned it, she put herself there to wait for me, and I grew to count on it.

After the thing with her father, I offered Allie a job at the movie theater where I worked. She was a terrible employee. She couldn't keep her drawer even; she'd show up late or not at all. But she tried, when she did show up. And she was fun, smiling no matter what. Even after all that happened. That smile of hers made you forget everything else.

I'd drive her home sometimes, and sometimes we would stop at Friendly's on the way and get ice cream. At some point it turned into dating. It was nobody's business what we did. I was her boss and I thought keeping it quiet would be better. Anne found out anyway and was furious at both of us, giving us even more reason to keep it a secret. Or try to.

We're almost at the Mount Kisco exit. I want to get this over with before we reach Zander.

"When was the last time you talked with Alison, Sull?"

"I don't know. The other night."

"Before that?"

"I don't remember."

Everyone knew about Allie's dad, but only in the limited way that Sully put it. He was a drunk. Alison couldn't do this or that thing because of her father who was, you know, sick.

When Allie was in high school, the problem kept getting worse, and it affected her—her mother was busy caring for him, and not able to pay attention to Allie when she had trouble in school, or with guys. And Allie's dad was a violent drunk. He hit her mom, and he hit Allie.

Sully's dad was a drinker, too. He died in his early fifties, when Sully was in college. You'd think Sully would be more sensitive about Alison's situation. Instead, he's bitter and he blames her for making it an excuse. But I don't think he knows the whole story. I know he doesn't. And there's part of it I won't tell him, or anyone else. Ever.

"You know how her dad died, right? You went to the wake. What was everyone saying? Drinking finally caught up to him."

"What I said." Sully turns right and we start up the hill into the cluster of townhouses where Zander and Anne live.

"But you don't remember the details."

"No. What details?"

"He came home one night. Probably blind drunk. Something happened. He shot himself. That's how he died."

"Oh. Shit. I remember now. Everyone knew that."

"Alison was home when it happened. Imagine that. What she had to see."

"I had no fucking idea. I totally forgot about that."

"Forget it again. Don't bring it up. Just think before you say anything stupid."

"Shit. All right. I had no idea."

"So we're okay? Now you understand why I got mad?"

Sully nods. "Good. Looks like we beat Pete."

With that, for all I can tell, we never had that talk. Sully amazes me that way. Drop something like that on me, and I'd be moody for hours. And I didn't tell him the whole story. I just told him what everyone else knew. I didn't tell Sully that Allie called me right after it happened, that her father was threatening her with the shotgun, that Allie's hands were on the gun. She was struggling to get control of it when it went off. No one knows that part. Not even the police. Only Allie and I know this secret. Just telling Sully the part I did tell, just watching it roll off him, will probably wreck the rest of my night.

Parking around Zander's townhouse is tough. Too many cars, not enough spots. We stop in front of the mailboxes, making our own parking space, and get out. We don't see a silver Jaguar. We're glad to get here before Pete. It'll be Pete that Zander attacks for being late. Zander must be inside, probably on the phone leaving nasty messages on our answering machines. We get out of the car.

"Hey, Mike."

"Yeah? What?"

"I guess I really was an asshole the other night."

Sully has no idea how much better this makes me feel, that our talk did in fact register inside him somewhere and that it matters to him. I had pretty much given up on him as a human being. I shouldn't be so hard on him. Whatever his faults, he's my friend. I'm closer to him than I am to Zander or Pete. And I've known him longer. That would make him my best friend.

"You had no idea, Sull. You didn't know. You couldn't help it."

"She alright? It didn't upset her? What I said?"

"She was fine."

We're at Zander's front door. I ring the doorbell.

"It didn't bother her?"

"Nope."

Zander, somewhere inside, yells, "Get the door!"

"You know why it didn't bother her," Sully says.

My heart suddenly feels heavy. "Why's that?"

"Because she's too busy thinking about how she's going to suck Pete dry."

The door opens with a sucking sound of tight insulation around its edges. Anne DiNapoli—I will never think of her as Anne Lombardi—is there on the other side of the screen door. She looks frightened to see me. Surprised, just like I feel. But we both knew this was coming. It's nothing, it's just that we haven't seen each other in five years.

"Yo, Annie," Sully says over my shoulder.

"Hi, Thomas. Hi, Michael. Come in." She steps back away from the door, as if we're contagious.

I pull on the screen door. "It's locked."

"Here." She fiddles with the lock on the other side of the door. I don't want to look at her face, so I look at her hand, which is very close to mine except for the screen. Her wedding band is smooth, plain. I held it, once. I was best man at her wedding.

I pull again and this time the door opens. Sully and I step into Zander's house. I've never been here before.

Sully gives Anne a kiss on the cheek.

"Zander's downstairs," she says.

Sully steps around the corner and down the stairs to find him.

"Nice place," I say.

"Thank you."

I point. "Downstairs?"

"How are you, Michael? What have you been up to?"

"I'm fine. You?"

She shrugs her shoulders. "Good." Her hair, which is long and black, is tied back and shines like her eyes under the hallway light. She's still got her fantastic bangs. But there's something wrong with her makeup.

She's wearing a dark blue Yankees t-shirt and faded blue jeans with a torn knee. All these details come slow, in waves.

"Since when did you like the Yankees?"

"Zan." She shrugs again.

"Sure."

"I hear you're a computer guy now."

"That's right." I'd rather not go into the details of my unemployment with her.

"You fix them?"

"No. I break them."

"Santino!" Zander yells from downstairs. "Get your ass down here!"

"You better go."

When I get to the top of the stairs, I turn and go back. "You look good."

"Thanks," Anne says, and smiles. "You too."

"What happened to your eye?"

"This?" Anne gives me a little laugh. "Yeah. You should see the other guy."

Zander is putting a little black leather case into his pack when I get downstairs. He's gotten larger. Not fatter; more substantial. Wider. His hair is thinning on top and he's trying to cover it. The basement is finished, all paneling and flat gray carpet with an exercise center in the middle of it and a sofa facing a big TV and stereo at the back. Sully's flipping through the channels looking for weather.

"How much you pay for cable?" Sully asks.

"You gotta be kidding me," Zander replies. "The guy next door pays for it. I split my signal off his line."

"What about the box?"

"Got one from a friend. Two hundred bucks, that's it—never have to pay for HBO again."

Zander hefts his pack. It looks like he's loaded for more than a one-nighter. He looks at me. "What's with the sneakers?"

Sully's in his socks; so is Zander. I remember this now. This is the way it always was at Zander's house: his father insisted everybody took their shoes off when they came in. Now Zander has established the same tradition in his own home. I kick my sneakers off, pick them up, and put them near the stairs.

"You miss your train?" Zander says.

I look at Sully. He looks away.

"You're not even ready yet," I tell Zander.

"I've been ready."

"You're still loading your pack."

"I was showing Sully something."

Sully jumps in. "Tell Zan we should take my car."

"Mike doesn't want to die either."

"C'mon, Zan," Sully pleads. "The Striped Tomato."

"Ever throw a tomato against a wall? Splat." Zander slaps his hands together. "We're all set. Let's get going."

"What about Pete?" I pick up my sneakers and squat to put them back on. Taking them off for that short a time seems silly to me now. Zander likes to play head games. "Aren't we going to wait for Pete?"

"Pete's not coming," Sully says.

"The prick called a little while ago." Zander bumps me with his pack as he goes up the stairs past me, nearly knocking me down. "Said he had to take care of something, couldn't get away."

"Damn. I was really looking forward to this trip," I lie. "To the four of us getting together."

"Yeah, well."

Sully grabs his sneakers and goes up past me.

I finish tying my laces. Then I go upstairs, too. "We'll just have to reschedule," I call up the stairs as I go.

"Fuck that. We're going."

Now I'm upstairs, we're all in the hall by the front door and the kitchen.

"What do you mean? We can't go without Pete—he's the guy who came up with the idea."

Sully says, "Forget Pete. He's got more important things to do. Forget him."

"What's the point of going without Pete?" I try with Zander.

"Pete's been bailing on us since he went to MIT."

"Let's go," Sully says.

"Wait a minute. I have to make a phone call."

"Go ahead," Zander says. "Use the phone in the kitchen. Right behind you."

I pick up the phone and dial home. I take the phone around the corner into the dining room to put some distance between me and the guys. Anne is sitting at the dining room table with some books. There's a computer on the table. It must be new; there's a couple of big boxes with cow spots on the floor next to the table.

After four rings the answering machine picks up. I hang up.

"You know anything about America OnLine?" Anne asks.

"I stay away from it."

"What about the Internet?"

"Sure. Yes." I dial the number again, hoping that maybe Ellen just wasn't able to pick up.

"My AOL crashes when I try to download a website. Do you know why that might happen?"

I get the answering machine again, and I hang up again. "You don't download—no, I don't know. Maybe you can call tech support."

"I tried, but they suck."

I can't remember her cell phone number. I could try Ellen's parents but I don't think she's there yet. Anyway, I don't think I know *their* number. I could try Pete.

"Mike! C'mon, let's get out of here," Sully shouts.

The books aren't all computer manuals; some look like textbooks. "What are those?"

"I'm getting my real estate license. The market is so hot right now. I've been wanting to do it for a while."

"You'll be good at it."

"Hey! Moron! Let's go!" Zander comes into the dining room from behind me, goes around the table, bends down, and gives Anne a kiss on the top of her head. "See you Sunday," he says.

She looks at me while he kisses her. "Sure. See you."

heart of darkness

The stereo in Zander's black Ford Expedition is blasting. I can't hear a word of the conversation Zander and Sully are having in the front seats. It's dark and roomy in the back and I get comfortable but as soon as I shut my eyes the music cuts off.

"No sleeping!" Zander shouts.

I sit up and the volume goes back up but every now and then Zander turns his head to check on me. Zander's got a big head. He's got a big ego and of course the big car. And a loud voice. He tells big stories with his loud voice, stories you're compelled to listen to, because he's so loud and the stories themselves are big, about big things he's done, big scores on the Street, his big-breasted blonde secretary, and the big beatings he puts on people. Most of it's a big lie, but it's usually entertaining. Only I can't really hear what's going on up front because the music's so loud. I need to call Ellen. I need to talk to her, to make sure she's nowhere near Pete.

Zander lowers the volume. "Sully wants to get the Syndicate back together."

Sully turns in his seat to look at me. "That's a good idea, isn't it, Mike?"

I lean forward between the two front seats. "And what are we going to do?"

"I don't know," Sully says. "Hang out more."

"Sounds like a shitty idea to me," Zander says.

Sully turns back in his seat. "C'mon, Zander, stick with me on this. We could meet after work."

"What about those of us who don't work?" Zander looks at me in the rearview mirror.

"What about Pete?" I say. "Are we going to leave him out of everything?"

Zander says, "Pete's too unreliable. He's on the pay-no-mind list."

Funny. The 'pay-no-mind' list. We're replaying our greatest hits.

I'm hoping Pete is reliable enough.

"What about you, douchebag?" Zander asks.

The trick is to not answer him.

"I already said it was a great idea," Sully says.

"I was talking to Mike, dick."

"He'll show," Sully says. "You'll show, Mike? Right? We could hit Atomic Dive Bar."

"That place is too crowded. We're there all the time, let's go somewhere else." I know too many people there to risk introducing Zander.

"Where?"

"It's New York City, Sull. There are other bars."

"Listen to you two bitches," Zander says. "Let's see how this little trek goes before I decide I want to hang out with you again. By the way, my answer is trending toward no."

"C'mon, Zander," Sully pleads. "You'll see. It'll be good."

"I'll pick the place," Zander says. "I don't want you embarrassing me in front of dudes I have to work with."

We come to the exit for Warrensburg. At the bottom of the ramp there's a couple of gas stations and an intersection. We go left, and are soon in what looks like the center of town. There's a pizzeria, a Chinese take-out, a run-down super-market and strip mall, a laundromat, a couple of bars, a post office, and a motel. We check in to the motel.

Sully and I split a room while Zander gets his own. We settle in, Sully turning on the television set and me laying on my bed. I can't remember Ellen's cell phone number so I call home and fail again to reach her.

"Why did you tell Zander I was the one who was late?"

"No harm no foul," Sully says. "He never lets up on me for things like that, but he goes easy on you."

"And you told him I wasn't working."

"You never said that was a secret."

"Who else have you told?"

"No one! I swear! Just Zander."

"You have a big mouth, Sull. That's why I don't tell you things."

Zander pounds on the door.

He barges his way into our room and goes over to the bed nearest the door. Sully's bed. He unzips his pants and pees a little on the pillow and the bed and next to the bed.

"Mark your own territory," Sully laughs.

"Already did. Just emptying my bladder."

Sully laughs again. He's slept without pillows before. This is what he wants: the full Syndicate experience. I don't let Zander near my bed.

"Let's get something from the Chinese place," I say.

Zander disagrees. "Empty stomach, quicker buzz."

Sully pipes in. "Cheaper, too."

I grab my wallet and the room key. This gives me the option to leave earlier, and it relaxes me a little bit. I'd rather be in control of something like that, especially around

Zander and Sully, especially if they're going to be drinking all night.

The bar we pick is walkable from the motel. That's better than driving, given how much we're planning on drinking. It's not like we're planning on it, exactly; it's more inevitable than that.

There's less than a dozen people inside. They look at us as we come in. This is upstate New York, and we're strangers here. They're probably thinking we're New Yorkers, as in *from the city*. Otherwise they'd recognize us.

I put a twenty on the bar to get the bartender's attention, but Zander hands the guy a credit card. "Tonight's on me, guys," he says. "I'm buying."

We start out with a round of Budweisers. These go down fast. Zander calls for another round, and three shots of Jäegermeister. Then he tells the bartender to have one too.

There are six guys and three girls at the bar. The guy closest to us leans over and says, "Where you from?"

"New York," Zander says, and he holds out his hand. "I'm Alex."

Alex? That's new. That's what his teachers called him. His parents called him Alexander. But to us it was always just Zander. I can't recall him ever telling anyone else to call him anything but Zander.

I get off my stool, step around Zander and shake the guy's hand. "Mike," I say, and point. "That's Sully."

"I'm a Mike, too," the guy says. "You can be Other Mike."

"Sure. I'm Other Mike."

Zander calls the bartender over. "Pour a shot for Mike, too," he says, and nods at his new friend. The bartender says, "I'm Jim," and shakes Zander's hand.

I can see this is going to be a long night.

I clap Zander's shoulder. "What about everyone else, Alex?"

He looks at me, with only the faintest sign of a smile. "Jim," he says, "line up some of these for the bar." Then he turns back to me. "That better, 'Other Mike'?"

Sully finds the pinball machine and pulls me over for a game. Someone puts money into the jukebox and the party starts. When I turn around after my turn, Zander is carousing with everyone in the bar. He's telling a story and they're all laughing.

"There he goes," Sully says. "A natural communicator."

"A natural bullshitter."

Sully and I listen a little bit, and Sully says, "Let me translate: Lie, lie, truth, major lie, bullshit, major lie, lie."

"You got just the right amount of truth into that," I laugh.

If it was just me and Sully, we would have sat there quietly enjoying a couple of beers before quietly going back to the motel. But Zander is in his element. The beer and the Jäeger shots keep coming.

When I go back to the bar to grab a couple of fresh beers, I hear Zander finishing a story. "So this guy has a black eye, it's already swollen shut. He's bleeding from his nose and his mouth, and he finally says, 'you're right,' to me. Then he asks me to help him find his tooth. I tell him to find his own fucking tooth." I don't know where this story started or what it's about, but everyone else laughs. We're best friends with the locals.

I find myself standing next to a high table talking to a girl whose boyfriend is at the bar, getting smashed. Zander starts up a sing-along with the jukebox and soon everyone is shouting out the words, but it's one of those songs I never could make out the lyrics so I just stand there, grinning.

"Your friend is funny," the girl says.

"Don't you think he's funny looking?"

"Not really. I'm Charlene."

"Mike. I mean, 'Other Mike,'" I say, keeping an eye on her

boyfriend, who's at the bar with Warrensburg Mike. I don't want trouble. Sully has disappeared. He's not in the bar. Last time I checked he wasn't in the men's room.

"You guys going up to the caves? I've never been."

"You've never been up to Chimney Mountain?"

"No. I go fishing with Steve. On the lakes. He's my boyfriend."

Steve's not going to be happy tomorrow morning. He's going to wake up with a massive hangover. Jäeger does that to me, so I'm trying to avoid the odd-numbered rounds.

"It's beautiful up there, Charlene. Even if you don't go into the caves. You should go up there with Steve. The chimney is fantastic."

Steve has finally noticed me, and he keeps looking over. He's got a rough beard and it looks like he ripped the sleeves off his jeans jacket to make it a vest. Without tools. I tap bottles with Charlene and go back to the bar. Nights like this, I end up watching Zander's show but keep to myself. I start playing with a cocktail straw.

Sully comes in the front door.

"I was starving, man," he says. "Pizzeria down the street. But it's closing."

We usually eat after the bar. But up here in Warrensburg, we might be out of luck. Dinner might end up being one of the energy bars I have back at the motel.

Then a guy comes in with four pizza boxes. He brings them over to the bar and Zander pays him. The delivery guy is surprised at the size of the tip. Zander's got a lot of money and you can say this for him: he's not cheap with it.

"Damn," Sully says. "I should've known." But apparently he's still hungry.

I grab a slice with everyone else and try not to drip grease on myself.

Zander's spending a lot of time talking with one of the

other girls. He's so preoccupied he's totally forgotten us. She must be fair game because there are no objections.

Sully and I end up playing on the pinball machine, looking at our watches, and waiting for last call. That's another of Zander's things. Closing bars. But he surprises us, and tells us to beat it, he'll see us in the morning. I know where this is going, so I corral Sully and help him stagger back to the motel.

In the morning Sully's hung over. We don't say much to each other. We repack and check our backpacks. From our gear you would think we were going on a multiple week trip into the mountains. Most of the stuff we're carrying won't come out of the pack this weekend.

We toss our stuff into Zander's Expedition and drive to the trail head.

I'm feeling pretty good—my head is clear because I avoided half of the shots—and I'm looking forward to seeing the chimney and Eagle Cave again.

Then Zander says, "Fucking Pete is missing all this fun." This reminds me that Pete's not with us. He's somewhere behind us, in New York City. Doing what? What was so important? Zander won't let anyone use his cell phone to call their girlfriend.

Sully says, "You know he's been to that place in Chile? And he wants to try Everest?"

"No shit. We must be beneath him. What place in Chile?"

"Argentina. Patagonia," I say.

"He was sucking wind last time he came here with us," Sully says.

He was not. Pete's always been in almost as good shape as me, especially for hiking; he was shit at softball. With Patagonia behind him and training for Everest, he might do this hike without breaking a sweat.

When we get to the parking area I switch from sneakers to hiking boots and heft my pack onto my back. There are two other cars parked there, next to each other. One of them has a bumper sticker in the shape of a bat and the other has one that says, 'I'd Rather Be Spelunking.'

The logbook at the trail head shows there's a group going to Eagle Cave. There's a golf pencil that's mostly blunt. I take out my utility knife and whittle a better point on it. Then I sign us in and list our destination as Eagle Cave as well.

It's a steep climb from the parking lot trail head to the chimney. There's no rock climbing involved, just hiking. I take the lead on these hikes. Being in front and uphill is the only way to avoid the farts. It's painful that that's still a thing. I walk as fast as I can to lose them behind a bend. If I can get far enough ahead I won't hear their panting and chatter and I might get some of that feeling of being alone out here. The trail is a narrow one. It sometimes disappears over rock scrambles but the blazes keep me from getting lost.

When I need a break I find a boulder by the side of the trail that puts me in a commanding position, and sit there and wait for them to catch up. In a few minutes I hear them swearing and struggling up the hill.

They stop for a break, but I'm rested and ready to go.

"Fucking yak," Zander says.

"Yak, yak, yak," I say. "No wonder you can't keep up."

I leave them there, wheezing.

We get to the top and find a place off the trail to make camp. It's just a day hike, but we make it a two-day thing. Gives us more time to explore the area and to play with things that otherwise would remain in our bags.

First time we got into camping, toward the end of high school, we geared up as if we were going to walk the Appalachian Trail. Whenever possible we went with ultra-light things: sleeping bags, tents, the rest of it. We counted ounces going into our packs. But our bags were always too heavy. Each of us tried to be more prepared than the others so we ended up with a lot more gear than we needed. Yet we've never been out together for more than three nights.

As we're taking things out of our packs and pitching tents, Sully pulls out this neat camp chair that uses his sleeping pad like a hammock. We like this: seeing who can one-up the others with the gadgets that we brought. Sully peels the plastic off it. It's something new.

"Let's see how that works." Zander takes the chair from Sully. He puts it on the ground and sits on it. "Almost comfortable," he says. He starts adjusting the straps.

Sully sits on a nearby boulder, happy to surprise Zander, maybe even impress him. Now he's waiting his turn for his own camp chair, which may never come.

After setting camp we scramble around the chimney for a bit. The chimney is a tower of rock on the edge of a small cliff. One of the wonders of the Adirondacks. It stands out from everything else up here, its slabs of red and orange and gray rock like something from the Grand Canyon, but shaped from glaciers and weather. There are a couple of deep crevices to avoid when walking around on the top of the cliff. We have the place to ourselves.

Sully tries to whistle. "You can see for miles up here."

I give him a little nudge while he's stepping over one of the crevices so he almost puts a leg into it. "But you can't see where we parked," I say.

"I don't even know which way to look."

"Well, you can't see the chimney from down there," I tell him. "The car is probably on the other side of the mountain."

The chimney looks climbable. We've never gotten around to it. We're more interested in the caves.

I look for a place to sit and just enjoy the view for a while. If they weren't here, it'd be better. I sit to the left of the chimney with my legs dangling over the cliff and chew on a piece of beef jerky.

Zander comes over, sits next to me. We look out over the treetops at the ridge across from us. Zander and I have a few things in common, and appreciating a wilderness that hides any signs of people is one of them. For me it's because I like what looks like pristine nature. For Zander it's because he hates humanity. We sit together quietly and breathe in the warm air. We can't see any roads or buildings. I'm not saying there aren't any. If there's anything man-made it's hidden by rolling waves of green treetops.

There's a couple of lakes glimmering silver in the distance. I wonder if Steve and Charlene ever had a view of the chimney from those lakes, and just never looked up. But then I realize the chimney is really not that large and wouldn't be noticeable from that far away.

I debate whether I should ask Zander what happened last night. I decide not to. It's bothering me, though. Does he cheat on Anne all the time like that? I don't want to know about it.

"Spectacular." Zander can modulate his deep booming voice when he wants to.

"I missed this place. I never know how much until I see it again." I offer him a piece of jerky.

"Thanks, slacker."

"What did Sully tell you?"

"That you haven't worked in months."

"Almost a year."

"He also says you hooked up with a hottie. Says she hasn't kicked you out yet."

"She's great. She's good with it for now."

"Unemployment?"

"No. Savings."

"Better than being a burden on society."

"Yeah, well."

"Savings won't last. Fucking get a job already. Before your ass is on the street."

Sully sits down on my other side. He takes a piece of jerky for himself without asking. "When do we go to the cave?"

"What's your rush?" Zander says.

"Enjoy the view," I say.

Sully stands up and hurls his piece of jerky toward the opposite ridge. It doesn't go far. "C'mon. Let's go."

Zander and I don't stand up. Sully never gets to tell us what to do. He goes away.

"I like this," I say, nodding at the treetops. "All the animals in the zoo should feel like this."

"The fuck you talking about?"

"So they don't know they're in cages."

"We're all in cages, dude. Stop fighting it."

"You're not in a cage."

"Hell I'm not."

After a little bit, I say, "What happened to Anne?"

"What?"

"Her eye."

Zander scowls. "She hit her face on a cabinet door. Stupid bitch."

I don't know how to challenge him on that. The way he said it lets me know he doesn't want me to ask again.

A couple of minutes later Zander stands. "Can't keep the child waiting. He's going to throw a tantrum."

We go back to the camp. Sully's sitting in his lounge chair, pouting, his back to us. Without saying anything, Zander and I get our caving stuff together. Helmets, flashlights, rope. Then Zander says, "Let's go."

Sully jumps up. "I need a minute," he says, and scrambles to put his gear together.

"Why are you taking so long?" I say.

Zander joins in. "Thought you were ready, you little prick."

I start pushing Sully. "Let's go, let's go." Then I let him alone so I can gather small stones to throw at him.

Sully's ready now. "Bastards," he says.

I hate this thing I just did with Sully. Getting on his case for no reason. Zander didn't make me do it, but I only do it around Zander. It's one of the things I used to do, and I'm surprised it came back to me so fast. I don't know why Sully thinks he wants to go back to that.

We descend into the shaded vale between the chimney and the other ridge and explore there below the cliff. It's a hot June day so there's a thin coat of sweat on me, which the mosquitos love. Down in the vale there are boulders with pockets below them and cuts into the cliff. The last ice age had its way with this place. Descending into these pockets hits me with chill air, my breath suddenly visible. But no more mosquitos or sweat.

There are pockets like this all over, exhaling cold air from deep beneath the surface. Crawl down by the cliffs and in the dark spaces under overhangs and deeper you can find caves with ice in them.

There are a number of openings that could be caves, and we shout to Sully, who's willing to explore anything, "Does it go?" Does it go deep; is it a cave entrance? Most of these are a no; we've been here before and we don't expect to find anything new.

We do find one cave. It's more like a tunnel. The opening is small enough and in such a position, squeezed between two big rocks, that we don't have to worry about waking a bear. Sully goes first, and he goes head-first. There's no room to turn around so he'd have to back out if it's a dead end, which could be difficult.

"We're going to have to pull him out by his ankles," I say.

"No. Just leave him. I'll take his chair. You can have his boots."

Sully's boots disappear. I imagine a large rabid raccoon dragging Sully by his face deeper into the hole.

It gets quiet, and I say, "A cabinet door?"

Zander doesn't answer me.

"Really?"

"You're going to run into a cabinet door too, if you don't shut up," Zander says. It takes me by surprise. It makes my speculation real.

Sully comes out head-first.

"It's a corkscrew. There's a small chamber where you can stand up and turn around."

"Anything else?" Zander asks.

"A human skeleton." Sully laughs. "Nothing."

"So, no human skeleton?" I kick the dirt. "A waste of time."

Zander has to see it for himself, and then so do I. We take turns because there's only room for one of us at a time. There's nothing to see. There's just the feeling of being a worm working your way through the earth. After, we shake grit and dust out of our clothing.

We climb out of the pocket depression this hole is in and it's June again. I take out a Nalgene bottle full of water and hand it to Zander. He takes a swig and passes it to Sully. When Sully gets it he chugs hard at first, then settles into a nice, slow rhythm. My hand is extended. I've only brought three of these thirty-two ounce bottles. Sully's eyes are closed. A slow grin creeps onto Zander's face, growing with every one of Sully's swallows. Sully finishes, sighs, opens his eyes, and hands me the empty bottle.

"Way to go, Sull," Zander laughs. "Leave nothing for the next guy."

Serious cavers—spelunkers, as they prefer—don't reveal

the locations of wild caves, to preserve their natural state from too many visitors and to keep amateurs away from danger. Years ago, Zander had been looking through an Adirondack trail book and the listing for Chimney Mountain mentioned unusual rock formations and caves. Then Pete found something in a caving magazine.

The first time we came here we wandered around the area for a few hours looking for the entrance. We know it's on the opposite side of the ridge across from the chimney. Exactly where, it's hard to say. There are no landmarks. We've lost its location again this time. Finding the right overhanging ledge after so many years is a little tricky. It's not obvious, it doesn't look like anything special, just a place where you might get a little shelter from the weather.

We finally run into the other group. They look at our helmets and rope.

One of them says, "You looking for the cave?"

"We could ask you the same thing," Zander says.

We all laugh, then there's an awkward pause.

A different one of them says, "You're close." They turn and disappear in the underbrush.

It's up to us to follow them discreetly, so we can't see each other but we can still hear them. They eventually stop and from the sound of it have a lovely lunch. Then their voices seem to fade away.

We scramble quietly to what we think was their last known position and find some of their gear beside a low overhanging rock that I had already passed a couple of times this morning.

There are voices coming from under the overhang. We can see no obvious cave entrance but we know it's there.

We climb around the overhang and find a position above it from where we can see their gear on the ledge outside the cave, but they won't be able to see us. Then we wait.

Sully, impatient as always, says, "Why don't we just go in behind them?"

"We want the cave for ourselves," Zander says. "Does any of their gear look useful? I like that pack over there to the right."

"Why don't we go and pee and shit on all their stuff?" Sully asks.

Zander leaves us. He reappears by the other group's gear. I watch him zip open the top of one pack. He fishes out a wallet, opens it. He takes the cash. With the wallet in his hand, he zips the pack closed, and goes to another pack. He zips open a side pocket and puts the wallet in that pack. Then he comes back to us.

This bothers me. "Why?" I ask when he settles in next to me.

"It'll fuck them up," he says. "They'll be at each other's throats. They won't know who to trust."

I wish I could say this is a new side of Zander that I haven't seen before.

They take only about an hour in the cave. When they come out they pack their stuff, and no one notices there's a misplaced wallet. After they leave it's our turn.

Exploring the back of the overhang looks promising but you don't get too far before the ceiling meets the rock floor at an acute angle, which is why I missed it the first time. But a short way in, invisible from outside or even directly below the ledge, there's what looks like a keyhole in the rock, and if you stand in it and lay back toward the wall, and scooch down and look left, you can see a small crevice that maybe you could slide along, and there might be more cave beyond that. Pete found it the first time, but he's not here now, I remind myself. Maybe he's with Ellen right now. I turn my headlamp on and lie back, turning my head to the left, into the cave.

The floor of the crevice—really the lower side of it—is a

flat sheet of rock. The ceiling is inches above me. They're not very far apart and the whole thing is at around a 45-degree angle. I inch along on my back. I could slide down into the unknown darkness but I'd probably get wedged in before falling too far. Getting unstuck could be a problem.

Once I go in I can't look up or turn my head back toward the light of the entrance for comfort because there's not enough space for my helmet and headlamp to turn. I can only look to my left and keep squirming in that direction. I can't retreat if I get claustrophobic because Zander's coming in behind me, too close.

"Move it, slacker," he says.

It's only a small stretch but I can't help thinking that if the walls of the crevice decide to have a reunion I would end up like a slab of butter between two hot pancakes.

After what feels like a hundred feet but is probably only thirty, I come out the other side of the crevice where I can sit up and look around. My headlamp lights up a big room. I'm able to stand and scramble out of the way so Zander and Sully can come through as well.

Zander hands me the coiled rope. "Here. You don't have a job, so you're the porter."

The air is cold. Moving ahead, I scramble over some rocks and come to the next obstacle. There's a pile of boulders blocking the way.

"I remember this," Sully says, and he tries to push past me to lead the way. I block him. There's a small opening you can wiggle through to get to the other side. It's not bad, just a couple of twists and no tricks. I get through and wait for them again. Now Zander takes the lead.

We come to a drop that requires about thirty feet of rope and some decent climbing skills.

Zander squats. "Let's go, porter. Set up the rope."

Going down the rope puts us in the biggest room. It's like

a cathedral. The darkness at the top of the big, vaulted ceiling absorbs our lights. There's ice down here, lots of it. We don't speak except to warn each other of tricky spots.

Zander says, "Turn off your lights," and flicks his headlamp off. Sully and I follow suit and it's suddenly pitch black. Every now and then we hear a rustle. Bats.

"This is fucking beautiful," Zander whispers. "Black hole dark."

Sully turns his headlamp on, blinding us, and we yell at him to turn it off again. We have another moment in the absolute dark underground.

"Hey Zander," Sully asks. "What happened last night? With that girl?"

"What girl?"

"Good question," I say. "Do you do that a lot?"

"I deny everything," Zander says.

Sully isn't done. "Has Annie ever caught you?"

"When I'm out of my house she stops being my parole officer."

It's better if I don't say what's on my mind.

But Sully pushes on. "So last night wasn't the first time."

"Shut up. I want to hear what silence sounds like."

It's eerie, but it's spoiled a little by a high-pitched whine that's in my head and seems to be coming from everywhere. Tinnitus? At my age?

Zander turns his headlamp on, and so do we.

"It's fucking awesome," Sully says.

I'm shivering. Now that I notice that whine, it doesn't want to go away.

We explore the cathedral room and find a couple of passages to other, smaller rooms.

Sully says, "I wish I had infravision."

It doesn't take me long to answer him. "Would it be that

great, being able to see in the dark? But never being able to *be* in the dark? Would you notice that it's gone?"

Would you miss it, the way I'm missing silence?

We want the experience to last longer, so we squat and eat energy bars. We don't say much to each other. There's nothing to say. Except, maybe... no. There's nothing to say, and saying anything would spoil the moment. Even we know that. Even Sully.

It's much easier coming back to the campsite from the cave. You just point yourself at the chimney. It dominates the landscape up here, its rocks layered like an unbalanced stack of books at the edge of the cliff. The whole thing looks like it might slide right off.

We follow a trail along the back of the chimney uphill from the right and come to a place where the slabs and boulders of the chimney look like they're being held up by a head-sized rock. It's wedged in there good and it makes a little window that looks out to the ridge that holds the cave.

"Hey Sully, stick your head in there, see if it fits," Zander laughs.

"No fucking way."

"Do it," Zander says, and he grabs Sully by the neck and forces his face into the rock window.

"Cut it out!" Sully yells.

Zander relents, lets go of him, and we keep walking.

When we get back to camp we boil water and prepare a meal of reconstituted freeze-dried food. It's Zander's stove so we must have his favorite, beef stroganoff.

"Still the best meal in a pouch," he says.

"I don't remember trying anything else," I say. "How old was that package?"

"This stuff lasts forever."

"There's gotta be an expiration date on that somewhere." Sully turns the empty package over. "Oh. This stuff is good until 2006. So it's fine."

"It's no good now," I say. "It expired the day it was made."

Then we have dessert in the form of freeze-dried ice cream. It's like eating insulation.

As the sun sets, Zander collects all our food and puts it in a bag which he hangs on a tree off in the woods. Even the freeze-dried stuff. Just for practice, really. We tell each other some old stories, things about Pete we can laugh at. Then we settle in for the night. It's all a little bit anticlimactic, the whole thing. The trip, the hike, the cave. Being together again.

Still, I'm glad I came. Yes, it is just like it was, just like I wasn't looking forward to. But it feels good, or anyway not bad, to know I was right all these years. I've grown out of this.

Growing up, I didn't know what to do with my life, and I didn't like being lonely. The Syndicate could have been a way to fix that. But all it did was make me feel more alone. It didn't create the kind of close, lasting friendships that it should have done. At least not for me. Maybe that's my fault. And that's what made me want to avoid this trip. I didn't want to face myself, at least not the me from back then.

I'm afraid that maybe, I haven't changed at all.

I'm in my own tent, but there's no avoiding Zander's snoring. How does Anne live with this? I don't get how Sully can sleep through it. And I'm annoyed that Pete isn't here to share in my suffering. It starts with a slow grinding rumble that rises in volume and gets deeper in pitch and ends with a slight whistle on the exhale. I've called it many things in the past. It's a bear or a lion (Zander liked those), or whale noise, or heavy machinery. You have to try to fall asleep fast, before Zander, if you want a chance to get some rest.

The horror of Zander snoring drives me into action. I grab my flashlight, unzip my tent, get out, and stand up. It's a beautiful night. The moon is rising, crescent, with Venus nearby like the radiant point of an arrow extending from the bow of the moon, as the poet says. I have no fear of wandering animals. They're afraid to come close to the sleeping Zander-beast. I make my way up to where the chimney is and sit care-fully on the edge of the cliff, where I sat in the sunshine earlier, legs hanging out and down again.

You can still see the Milky Way here, far from city lights. It stretches across the sky like a brush stroke. In spots there are so many stars that it looks like clouds of stretched out cotton balls. It reminds me of nights growing up, playing hide and seek in the dark around houses in the neighborhood.

One night I was hiding behind an air conditioner at the side of a house and I heard footsteps in the grass behind me. It was Anne. Her black hair was cut short then. She joined me behind the air conditioner, out of breath and laughing. She lived next door to me forever, and we were in the same grade in school. She was like my sister. If you can have a crush on your sister.

"Shhh," I told her. "Sully's coming."

Sully was walking down the middle of the street. We watched him turn the corner and Anne grabbed my hand and ran for the bushes behind the Haney house. The branches scratched us as we settled in. She didn't let go of my hand. Instead, she leaned over and kissed me. Her mouth was open and then so was mine. After we stopped kissing she looked out of the bushes as if nothing had happened. But we held hands a few more seconds. We were fourteen. It was my first kiss.

Sitting here with the dark below the cliff and the black sky above me, I wonder if anything was supposed to happen with us. It didn't matter, because I met Zander in high school, and through me, he met Anne. And she fell for him hard.

I get up and walk quietly back to the campsite, but not quietly enough. Suddenly there's a flashlight on me. Sully's holding it, and through the glare I can see Zander standing there holding something else. It's a gun.

"The fuck you doing?" Zander hisses.

"I was communing with nature. What's with the gun?"

"Self defense. Could've wasted you just now."

"Is the safety on, on that thing?"

Zander fiddles with it. "Now it is."

I get back into my tent and lay on my sleeping bag. My heart's racing. A gun. In Zander's hands. I'm no expert, but it was a semi-automatic. He always talked about owning a Beretta. He could've put a lot of holes in me just now. I don't think I can sleep the rest of the night.

I try reading. I take out my *Seven Habits* book and a small headlamp. It runs off watch batteries and has two LED bulbs. Not strong enough to use in a cave, but perfect for reading in the dark.

It doesn't work. The lamp works, but the reading doesn't.

Part of it is the thrill of actually still being alive. This must be what they mean when they say 'I dodged a bullet.' But I know I would have dodged nothing. My mouth is dry and I get this itch in my throat and soon I'm coughing, a dry cough that should work to clear whatever it is but doesn't. My imagination turns the dry cough into something in my lungs, rubbing against one of my ribs. It makes me cough some more. Soon I'm coughing uncontrollably. But I can't cough it out.

"Shut the fuck up over there," Sully says, but he says this over Zander's snoring. Zander has had no trouble falling asleep, after that. He must be used to sleeping well, after all the stuff he's done.

The coughing stops. "Did you know Zander brought a gun?" We're rasping to each other through our tents, as if we're trying to maintain the natural silence of the world. It's pointless.

"Sure. He showed me before we left."

"You couldn't warn me?"

"Never had the chance."

"Does he have a license for that?"

"He said he does, but you know Zander."

"Doesn't it make you a little nervous?"

There's a brief stop to the snoring, and when it resumes, Sully says, "No. Zander's not going to shoot me."

"Not on purpose, maybe."

"Shut up and go to sleep."

"I want to leave first thing. Pack up and head for home."

"Go to sleep."

Sully's usually the jumpy one.

I open the book one more time, and the picture of Anne and Alison falls out, reminding me why I'm carrying it. I'll show Sully tomorrow. There's no way I'm getting out of my tent again tonight. I start reading from the first page. Again.

The trouble is, the first habit is to 'Begin With the End In Mind.' You're supposed to know where you're going first, then all the rest of the habits will effectively get you there. That's why I'm not making any progress with this book, or with any other self-help book I try.

I have no end in mind.

I can't make it through three pages before I start thinking about what Ellen said about jobs and careers.

All I know is that I want to write computer programs. I don't know how that translates into a goal or a job or a career for someone with no experience and no computer science degree. There's a lot of talk about Y2K ending the world anyway, so maybe I shouldn't bother worrying about the future.

I wake up, but only after I missed the sunrise and killed the batteries on my headlamp. The cover of the book is now creased where I rolled over on it.

Before we break camp we have breakfast. Zander boils more water; scrambled eggs from powder are coming our way. It's not as appetizing as it sounds. I settle for more beef jerky.

Sully looks up from his eggs. "See, Zan? This was good."

"Maybe because fucking Pete's not here. And Mike is only good for target practice."

"Hey Zan, did you hear that Pete's going to do a Super Bowl commercial?" Sully asks while we're packing for the hike back to the car.

"No fucking way."

"Way."

Zander reaches into his bag, comes out with the black leather case. He unzips it and takes out the gun again. "Check this out," he says, and he flicks the safety off and pulls back the slide. He points it at a pile of rocks a dozen feet from us, fires the full clip. I move over and stand right behind him. There's the bang bang bang of the gun and the tinkle of spent cartridges spitting out the side, and what sounds like the wind zipping through the leaves of the underbrush around us. Then everything gets quiet, hushed. He ejects the clip and puts it into his left pocket. Fortunately he's decided he's shown off enough. It's impressive, and I'd like to try, in safer circumstances.

Maybe that was Zander's answer to Pete's Super Bowl spot.

My pack is leaking; a ricocheting bullet shattered one of my Nalgene bottles. I was standing right there when Zander started shooting, before I stepped behind him. I want to get as far away from Zander as I can.

out of the frying pan...

We get to Zander's place late Sunday afternoon. Zander pulls up to the Striped Tomato and pops the back of the Expedition.

"You guys bore me," he says.

For some reason I can't fathom, Sully suggests, "Let's do this again."

I want to tell him the Syndicate is dead. But I can't, not in front of Zander. I don't know why.

"We'll bring Pete next time," Sully says.

Zander shakes his head. "Fuck Pete." He makes it sound like it's been settled. That's usually how things go around him.

Sully and I grab our packs and boots and throw them into the trunk of the Tomato.

Anne comes out to see us. She's wearing grey sweatpants and a faded baby blue tank top that has 'Sexy' written across it in balloon letters and patchy glitter. Her bare arms are folded across it, but I know the shirt. It's old. I can't believe she still has it. Her hair is tied in a loose bun, frizzy and out of control, a dark cloud framing her pale face.

"You boys have fun in the woods?"

Zander takes his sweaty Yankees cap off and puts it on Anne's head. "Tons," he says.

Anne reaches up delicately with her middle finger and tips the cap so it falls off her head. Zander doesn't notice, or pretends he doesn't; he's got his pack on the pavement in front of him, and he's bent over it, fiddling with the top pocket, the one with the Beretta.

"There's something wrong with the new computer," Anne says.

Zander still doesn't look up. "So call tech support."

"I did, all weekend. I was on the phone for two hours with some guy. He wanted to charge for the support and he didn't even fix it."

"Two hours?" Zander scoffs. "Tell him you're charging *him* for phone sex."

Sully snickers.

"If it's under warranty they should handle it no charge," I offer.

Zander straightens up and snorts. "Not if it fell off the truck." He grabs his pack by the top handle. "You ladies still here? I'm going to take a hot shower and wash your stench off me."

"You think *you* can take a look at it?"

It takes me a second to realize Anne is looking at me, asking me. The black eye is still there, ugly even on her face. There's a couple of seconds of silence. Zander stoops and picks up the Yankees hat, puts it more forcefully on Anne's head. She cringes.

"Sure."

"Not today," Zander says. "I'm beat. Later, girls." He goes into the house.

Anne stands there for a moment facing me and Sully. She shrugs her shoulders, takes off the cap, twists it in her hands. Sully is looking at me.

"Uh, give me a call. Here's my number." She writes it down. I look at Sully; he's smirking again.

"Yeah, I will." She smiles. "I will." Her whole face brightens when she smiles. All of it except the bruise. She looks from me to Sully, back to me. "Good night."

"Nite."

"Let's go," Sully says to me. "Nite, sexy," he grins at Anne.

She smiles at him. "Nite, Sully."

In the Tomato, Sully's thinking. I can smell the wood burning.

He finally speaks. "She's still got it going on, don't she?"

I look out the side window, pretend not to hear him.

"I said, she's pretty hot, still."

"What? Anne? Yeah. I guess."

He snorts. "You guess."

"What's wrong with you, Sully? Why do you always have to start shit?"

Now he laughs. "I knew it, man. I knew you still had the hots for her. Ever since you went all whacko over that stripper. Montana."

"Her name was Dakota."

"Same thing. You remember her name. You're fixated, man." Now he gets serious. "You better not mess with Anne. Don't even think about it."

I can't show him the picture now; he'll make a bigger deal out of it. Anne hasn't changed that much so it doesn't matter anyway.

My beeper goes off. It's Ellen. It's her cell phone number. She's not home.

I finally get back to my place around 10 pm and Ellen's still not home. There's a message on the answering machine.

"Hey. I'm leaving mom and dad a little late, probably going to get stuck in traffic. Don't wait up. Hope you had a good time. Tell me about it in the morning. Love you."

I throw my backpack into the closet, don't even bother unpacking it. Then I head for the shower. I need to wash this weekend off, too. Zander and Sully. Me, back in the Syndicate. The stink of it all. I take a long, hot shower. Half hour. Hoping she'll come home. After, I pace for a while, drink a beer. Now I can call her.

She answers on the third ring. Sounds like she's driving.

"Hey, El. It's me."

"You home?"

"Yeah. Where are you?"

"Exit 9. Lots of traffic. How was the trip?"

"Remember *Lord of the Flies*?"

She laughs. "It couldn't be that bad."

"Zander doesn't like Pete very much."

There's a long, staticky pause. Maybe Pete's sitting there right next to her and she can't say anything. I can't believe I'm playing this game. This is the girl who gets upset every time she catches my eye wandering. The girl who is probably the best thing in my life; she deserves better than me. And now I want to keep her. Now, after playing games all this time, this matters to me.

"Really," she says, after what seems like too long.

"Yes, really. You should've seen the two of them."

"Um. I'll see you later."

"Yeah. Drive safe."

"*Drive safe?* What's that, a public service announcement?" There's an edge in her voice, one I rarely hear.

"What's wrong with that?"

"Drive safe?" She says again.

"Why, is there something wrong?"

"You sound different."

"I've always wanted you to drive safe."

"It's the traffic. We're both tired. Maybe it wasn't such a good idea to see your friends. Maybe you were right."

"I'm always right."

"Go to bed. I'll be home soon."

I hang up before she does.

She took too damn long to answer me. She knew Pete wasn't with us. She didn't know what to say. Without lying to me. But I lied to *her*, telling her Pete was with us. And she *knows* I lied. She knows *why* I lied. *She knows I know.*

Or maybe she had to pay attention to the road for a few seconds. Maybe I'm reading too much into it. Maybe I should stop thinking so much. I have to do something. I have to fix this. We never fight. Not even when we talk about whether we might get married or just keep living together, or how many kids we might have. But now we're fighting. About what? I don't know yet.

Ellen gets home after one, tries not to wake me but I was never asleep. She slips into bed very quietly. Puts her back to me. I roll over, fling my arm across the bed so it's lying on her. I pretend to pull her close to me in my sleep. But she knows I'm not sleeping.

"Em," she sighs.

"Glad you're home." I pull her closer, cuddle, spoon. A little closer.

"Em, I'm wiped out. It's late."

"Uh-huh." I freeze, unwrap from her, roll so we're back-to-back now. "Me too."

"Michael."

I don't answer her.

We don't talk much in the morning. There's something toxic brooding in the air, something that won't go away, even if we wanted to get rid of it. It wants to sit there between us and not let us talk. She gets dressed, I stay in bed.

"Let's have lunch. I'll call you later," Ellen says, and gives me a peck on the cheek.

. . .

I get out of bed around eleven. The house is quiet; that uncomfortable presence is gone. I wait for Ellen's call. There's nothing good on TV so I try to get absorbed in a video game. When the phone rings, I play it cool, let it ring again before I pick it up.

"Hi, Michael." It's Anne. "Are you busy? Should I call back later?"

"No. I've got all the time in the world."

"It was nice to see you."

"Same."

I look around the living room. No one is there to look at me, no one is there to listen in on this call.

"Think you can help me with this computer?"

"Where did Zander get it?"

"He said the company had some extras for home use."

"That's bullshit."

"That's Zander."

"Yeah. That's Zander. What's wrong?"

"I think it's AOL. It won't connect to the phone."

"Maybe it's the modem."

"See, you know all about this stuff. You were always a brain."

"Can you try to connect?"

"Can't you come over and take a look at it?"

I take another quick look around the room, finally coming to the picture of Ellen that's on the wall. I remember taking that picture, but I can't remember where or when. She's smiling at me. The background has docks, boats. It's black and white but you can tell she has beautiful eyes. They're almost transparent in the photograph. Her hair is loose, strands of it grab the sun and turn blonde, some of it is blowing across her face. Look at that smile. She makes me so happy. It's me that's the problem.

"Sure. I can come over. I'm going to be busy all week though." That's a lie. I'm hoping she can't wait a week. She'll have to get someone else. I realize I'm afraid to be around her.

"Saturday then?"

"Um."

"Is that okay?"

"Can you call me Friday afternoon, just to make sure?"

"Michael, if you don't want to do it, just say so. Don't wait until Friday to come up with an excuse."

What is it with the women in my life? When did they start misunderstanding me so well?

"No excuses. Just call to confirm the time."

"You sure? Do you have plans? Are you seeing someone?"

"Yes, no, and yes," I say, and a door closes.

"Is it serious?"

"Very."

"That's nice. I'm happy for you. I'll call on Friday."

Well, that's that. She's happy for me. That should lower the odds of me getting shot by Zander.

Ellen calls and says she's going to be in meetings until three o'clock. She asks for a dinner instead. I go out, thinking maybe I can buy something for her. A peace offering. Something nice, something she'll like. Something different.

I end up someplace looking at 'women's fancy undergarments.' This is not our thing. I never bought anything like this for her before, and maybe this isn't the best idea for a peace offering, but I see this black camisole with a frilly trim. I know it's a camisole because it says so on the tag. It's so unlike Ellen. She's always been happy in my old shirts but this would be a nice thing; it's not too lacy or racy.

I can't decide but after a couple of minutes I start to feel uncomfortable standing there in front of it. I grab it. She'll like it. Then I forget the bag on the train.

Which is fine, because Ellen has left another message on the machine. She's gotten caught up in meetings with the creatives over the Super Bowl spot, and Pete's headed over to look at storyboards, and she won't be home until late. What's that mean? How late? She asks for a rain check on the dinner.

I go out and get a couple slices of pizza and a six-pack. I figure I'll celebrate what I did earlier. I didn't lie to Anne about Ellen and me. Which I might've done last week. Not because I *wanted* something to happen. Just that I wanted the *possibility* of something happening to be greater than zero. This is a big step for me.

The message light on the answering machine is lit when I get back with the pizza and beer. But there's no message; just a hang-up. I sit down to watch *Treasure of the Sierra Madre* and work through the six-pack. They say Bogart wore a wig in this one. Maybe, but it doesn't matter, it's still a great movie. After three beers, the phone rings.

"Lose something?"

Oh, great. It's Olivia.

"I thought you were through with me."

"I am. Just calling to check in."

The beer. I swear it's the beer. That's why I don't hang up right away. And why the hell should I, I've got nothing better to do tonight.

"What's up, Mike?" Olivia says. She's the only woman in my life who doesn't call me Michael. It's a relief because I find that the way a girl says 'Michael,' the way her tongue catches on her teeth on that 'L', is irresistible.

I decide to try to have a conversation with her. "What do you do for a living?"

"I stalk cute guys."

"Really."

"Not really. But cute guys think I do. I don't know what's worse."

"Actually stalking them."

"So if they don't *know* I'm stalking them, but only *think* I am, then it's okay?"

I lie down on the sofa with the phone. "Yes. I suppose it is. It's flattering."

"How can I get them to think I'm stalking them, if I'm not?"

"I don't know. Hey, this is how *you* make a living, not me. You have to figure these things out. Maybe, like you said, you know someone who can get you inside information. Like tracing licenses to phone numbers."

"I can do that. What are you doing right now?"

"I'm lying on the sofa drinking beer."

"Where's the old lady?"

"She's working late." Telling the truth is safe. Second time today.

"Poor boy."

"Yes."

"Poor, cute boy."

"Hah. You're pretty funny."

"Flattering, too. I'm the best non-stalker around."

"I don't really care for it. You're wasting your time on me."

"No I'm not. I've got you just where I want you."

"We live together. My girlfriend and me."

"Doesn't matter. You're going to do whatever I tell you to do."

I turn off the TV. This is getting interesting. "Like what?"

"Like, why not come out and meet me, and find out?"

I start to say 'no' but it comes out "Now?"

"Sure. Your old lady has blown you off for the night. Come out. We can talk. Face to face."

This is getting a little too dangerous. I realize that we've crossed a line. I don't remember where, but we did. "I don't think that would be right."

"Come out for a drink."

I've got three more beers left, but drinking beer at home isn't really satisfying. This is tempting. *Way too tempting.* This is not looking. This is something else.

"I don't think that's a good idea."

"Your old lady won't let you go out by yourself?"

"Stop calling her that."

"Okay. Ellen."

I sit up. "How did you know that?"

"I'm a stalker, remember? Come out."

"Where?"

"East Side," Olivia says. "Safe for you. Know where the Lantern is?"

"Is that the one on 71st Street?"

"Meet me there in half an hour."

"No." I shake my head, not that she can see it, but to try to clear it. I must've drunk those first three beers too fast. I'm a little cloudy and not thinking straight. That's it; it's the beer. "Look, I don't think so."

"I know. You don't want to do anything bad. You don't want to cheat on your old—Ellen."

"No, I don't."

"I just want to meet you face to face."

"I don't think that's a good idea."

"Yes. Yes you do. I *know* you do. I *know* you want to meet me."

"Why, because we're talking on the phone?"

"No. Because you're not afraid of me. And besides, you want to get back what you left on the train this afternoon."

Now I'm standing up. I look around for the bag.

She chuckles, low and with confidence. "Half an hour at the Lantern. See you there." And she hangs up.

...into the nuclear reactor

The Lantern is a small pub on the upper East Side that always seems to be empty. Ellen would never come near the place. It's Monday but it's not football season so there are only a few older guys hanging out, watching the Yankees game. The jukebox is on but the volume is down, like it's saving itself for a bigger, noisier crowd. I grab a spot at the bar and look around, order a pint of Guinness. I don't see anybody who could be Olivia. I don't really know what she looks like now that I'm looking for her. She didn't tell me how I was going to recognize her. But she knows what I look like.

Maybe she's going to stand me up. This is some strange game. How did she know Ellen's name? How did she know I lost a package on the train? Unless she was on the train. Did I see her on the train?

After ten minutes I order another pint, my fifth beer of the night. Getting more light-headed. Not bad enough that I can't get home, but enough to keep me here, sitting in an old man's bar, waiting for Olivia the Stalker.

Then she's there. She comes in, she's about—well, not as tall as Ellen, maybe a couple of inches shorter; and younger.

She has curly brown hair. It's braided into a loose ponytail. She's wearing a sleeveless black button-down collared shirt and tight blue jeans. Black sandals with sensible heels. I'm sure it's her. No one would come into this bar looking like that unless they were meeting someone. Olivia's drop-dead gorgeous. She's got my bag, and she sees me and gives me a small smile, and comes over and stands next to me.

"Hello, Mike."

"Hi, Olivia."

"Just 'Liv.'"

"Hi, Liv."

Now she has a bigger smile. "At last."

"Whatever."

Her smile goes away. "Why 'whatever'?"

"Nothing. This is a little weird."

"Maybe. Interesting."

"Okay, interesting."

"Buy me a drink. Gin and tonic."

I signal the bartender. Olivia sits down at one of the high tables by the window, on one of the stools. Her jeans wrap tight above her ankles. She puts the bag on the table. I sit down across from her.

"Now what?"

She shakes her head, sighs. "No, no, no. You're supposed to say, 'nice to see you.'"

I play along. "Nice to see you."

"Same." She smiles again.

"I think my memory isn't working right. You're not what I remember."

"Better, I hope," she says. "I thought I'd dress up a little for this go-see."

"What's a go-see? That's a funny thing to call this."

"It's an appointment. You should see me in a showroom."

"You sell cars?"

"I could."

I have no idea what else I'm supposed to say.

"All I wanted to do was thank you for helping me and my friend that night."

"You're welcome. Did you call the other guys, too?"

She takes the bag off the table. "No, I did not."

"I see."

"I had *your* license plate number."

"I'm the lucky one."

"You don't know how lucky."

"I think I do."

She puts the bag back on the table. "I've always been curious."

"You know what curiosity did to the cat."

She gives me a deadpan stare and says, "Meow." Her eyes are hazel. Not brown, not green, not gray, something in between. Wild. Prehistoric. Where Ellen's eyes are like open skies, Liv's are like the jungle. I do not want to start comparing her to Ellen. I get caught staring and look up at the ball game. The Yankees are winning.

"Cats have nine lives," she says, drawing me back.

"Not really."

"Do you want to know what I'm curious about?"

"First, I'm curious about something. How long have you been following me?"

"Just today."

"Just today. Right."

The bag comes off the table again. "You don't have to be so hostile. I'm not going to bite."

"I'm not afraid of a kitten's bite."

"I scratch, too."

"What are you curious about?" I offer.

The bag is back on the table. "Guys," she says. "What they think their girlfriends want."

I remember what's in the bag.

"Do they ask, or are they pre-programmed to buy certain things? And where does that come from?"

I try to remember other things I've bought for Ellen.

"Is it in their disposition? Is it genetic?"

She's right. This time, anyway.

"Does Ellen have a preference?"

I'm glad that she's talking about Ellen. It makes me feel safer, but I haven't stopped trembling. "No. She never said. I never asked. It wasn't important to me."

"*To me.* Why would it matter whether it was important to *you*?"

"You win," I say. "I'm just like all the other guys."

"Maybe you're better than most. What *does* Ellen like to wear to bed?"

"Whatever she wants. Mostly my t-shirts." Maybe that'll work. I'm trying to think strategically. Let Olivia know I'm in a long-term, stable relationship; that she can't change that. T-shirts sound long term to me.

Olivia looks down at the bag on the table. "Get me another G&T," she says.

When I get back with her drink and my beer, Olivia's fingers touch mine as she takes her glass. I pull back like I've been shocked and almost spill the drink.

"What were you doing on that train? Why are you following me?"

She gets a little flustered and talks fast like she did on the phone. "I *wasn't* following you, but I saw you. And I *was* going to say something. Say hello. But I was afraid. I was afraid you didn't want to talk to me. And then I saw you forgot your bag. And I wanted to give it back to you."

"Now you've helped me. Now we're even."

"Yes, I think we are." She smiles, looks me in the eye. She looks relieved. I'm the one who's on edge.

From the way she slipped into the fast talk, I get the feeling she's acting. All the seductive stuff is an act. She's really just a confused girl pretending to be a sex kitten. A very pretty one. I don't have to worry; I'll be able to resist her.

"What do you really do?" I ask.

"I'm in school. College. I'm going to be a physical therapist."

"Of course you are. If you don't mind, how old are you?"

"Twenty." She says it defiantly.

"Drinking age is twenty-one."

"So?"

"So you're… I don't know. Too young to be responsible." I look at the bartender. He's talking to some of the regulars at the far end of the bar. They're all watching the game. "You're very forward for someone so young."

"I was in drama in high school. I do a little modeling. I work part-time as a receptionist. I like people. Want to know something else about me? I'm *not* too young to be responsible."

"Twenty's young."

"I lost my virginity when I was *twelve*. But I can't *drink* yet?"

"That's *young*."

Olivia looks past me, over my shoulder, at nothing. "Yes, it was." Then, back at me: "Are you still nervous about being here?"

"Me? No." But I'm still shaking.

"Good. Me too." She smiles. Her teeth are perfect. She's got a pretty smile. She's got a pretty everything.

We sit quietly for a while. We don't know each other well enough and it gets uncomfortable.

"You didn't ask me what kind of modeling I've done," Olivia says.

"Are there different kinds?"

"Some models are only used for certain things. You know, hand models. Legs."

I look at her hands, which are nice, a little small, nothing special. I make a show of looking under the table at her legs, which look like they could be alright.

"Lingerie."

My eyes involuntarily dip below her neckline. I try to wash the lump in my throat away with my beer, but it's going nowhere; it's going to choke me. It must be obvious now, how much I'm trembling.

"Nothing like 'Victoria's Secret.' Other catalogs."

I nod. I have no idea what else to do. We get quiet again.

After a minute, I say, "Maybe I should get going."

"Not yet," she says right away.

"Liv, it was nice to finally meet you."

"Same, Michael. I *knew* it would be. I *knew* you'd be okay."

"But I should go. My 'old lady.'"

She makes a face. "She's not home yet."

"Maybe not yet, but soon. Can I have the bag now?"

Olivia pulls the bag toward her. I reach quick and grab it. There's some crumpled up tissue paper, but nothing else.

"There was something in this bag. Where is it?"

"Think for a minute. You know where it is."

"No, I don't—Liv, that's not yours."

"It's pretty."

I take a deep breath. "Okay. You can have it."

"It's soft."

"It was meant for someone else." Funny, I can't say Ellen's name.

"No it wasn't. You gave it to me. Just now, and on the train."

I'm a little drunk. Maybe I should just leave. I should have never come. But Ellen isn't home. Ellen stood me up. Ellen's with Pete. Probably had dinner with him after the meeting. Probably won't let me touch her again tonight.

"Liv, I'm sorry. I don't know what you want."

"Yes you do. You want to see what it looks like. On me."

"No. I can't."

"You shouldn't, but you will." She is so sure of herself.

"No. No. No way. I can't."

"Yes. *Yes* way. You *will*. You *want* to, anyway. Don't lie. So I'm saying, you can. Just look, okay? Will that make you feel better?"

"No. It won't be just look."

She thinks. "Maybe. But you can *say* it was just look."

"It has to be."

Olivia opens a button on her shirt. "See? That's just look. But you want to see the rest."

My heart is thumping so loud that I wish the jukebox was blasting. I look quickly over my shoulder at the bar. Nobody saw that.

"I have to make a phone call."

"Do you need permission?" Olivia laughs.

There's a pay phone outside the bar. I call home. The answering machine picks up. She's still not home. I hit the pound sign and punch in the secret code and check the messages. Ellen left one, saying Pete is very happy with the storyboards, he's taking them all out to dinner. She says she'll be home after eleven. It's only 8:15.

Olivia's standing by our table, holding the empty bag. "Ready, Michael?"

Her place is only two blocks away. I'm a step behind her, following. Being led. It's the East Side. Chances are Ellen is somewhere on the West Side, farther downtown. We don't pass any restaurants, but I find myself scanning both sides of the street. Olivia doesn't seem to mind that I'm looking all over, trying to make sure I'm not seen walking with her.

I wish she would walk faster. She's strolling, putting one foot in front of the other, deliberate.

My mind is wandering. It's been wandering for a while, fueled by the beer, like it doesn't want to be here right now.

If she walks faster, we'll get to her place sooner, and I won't have to be worried about being spotted. But that won't give me time to think about what I'm doing. I should stop, right here, and do that thinking before taking another step forward.

There's a couple of guys on the other side of the street, just standing, talking. As we pass, they stop talking and watch us. I realize they're looking at Olivia. I imagine she looks as good from across the street as she does up close. I know I'd look, if that was me over there. Even with Ellen standing next to me, I'd look. I wouldn't be able to help myself.

One of the guys calls out. "Hey beautiful, drop that loser. Come over here."

I'm thinking of something to say but Olivia laughs and yells back, "Leave him alone. He's mine." They laugh, and Olivia takes my elbow and we walk faster, and leave them behind.

"Thanks," I say. "I could've handled that myself."

"I'm not afraid of them. I'm safe with you."

Things rush over me, one on top of the next. What she said about feeling safe with me. How hard it must be to walk anywhere with her. Olivia is trouble. Ellen would've ignored them, but let's not think about Ellen right now.

We stop at a crosswalk. "I'm on the next block," Olivia says. I find that I'm watching myself. I've been this way before. When it really matters, when I need to be inside myself and know what it is I'm feeling and be in full control of my actions, I'm looking on, like a bystander, an observer, an audience. Am I in control? No.

She is, though, so there's really nothing to worry about.

Olivia stops in front of her building. She turns to me.

"Last chance," I mumble to myself.

She smiles. "That passed a while ago."

She waits for me to say something else. But my mind has gone blank. She's thinking, though. Tilting her head, squinting a little, watching me. Her index finger traces her neck along her collar, she undoes another button on her shirt, traces a little farther down. Watches me some more. I try not to look, but that just means I have to stare into her eyes. She lifts her fingers to my lips, grazing them. Damn, she smells nice.

Olivia smiles again. "Let's go inside."

eleven
situation comedy

I get home a little after one. Ellen's asleep. I stink of beer and betrayal. I have to take a quiet, quick shower. There's no way I can get into bed next to Ellen like this.

When I shut my eyes to rinse the shampoo out of my hair, I see Olivia. I see myself sitting on the edge of her bed in her small, cluttered bedroom. There are things on the floor: clothes, books, magazines. There's a stuffed toy octopus on the bed by the pillows, very furry and purple. An Erica Jong book on the table next to the bed. The bed's not made. She moves around the room, lighting candles. Lots of candles. She comes and stands in front of me. Asks me if I want to see, now. I nod. I can't speak.

I turn off the shower, breaking the memory. As quietly as I can, I slip into bed. But Ellen's awake. She snuggles close to me.

"Mmmm. Where were you?"

"Out. Drinking. Smelled like beer and cigarettes."

"Hate that." She puts her head on my shoulder. I hear her breathing get regular. She's got an arm across my chest. I'm surprised she can't feel or hear my heart pounding. I'm staring up at the ceiling, terrified of falling asleep. What if I talk in my sleep? What if I say something, replay tonight while I'm dreaming? The darkness swirls in our room, creating monsters out of shadow. I'm still a little drunk, and wired with guilt.

I shut my eyes and Olivia's there. She takes off her shoes, then slowly unbuttons her shirt and slips it off. She unzips her jeans, bends at the waist, pulling them down to her ankles. I can see her smooth back, the curves of her, in the candlelight. She's very athletic, balanced. She straightens up and steps out of the jeans. I'm no expert, but she could be a leg model too. She smooths the camisole. It's very pretty, she says. I nod. She steps toward me. Steps between my legs, where I'm sitting on the bed. Close, way too close. I can smell her. Whatever she's wearing, it's exotic, like jasmine and... silk? What does silk smells like? She puts her arms on either side of my head, balanced on my shoulders, and I can't help it, I put my hands on her waist, I touch the camisole, I smooth it against her skin, I feel her curves. Nice, she says. That feels nice. Yes, I manage to croak. She takes my hands. This is called jacquard, she says, and traces my fingers over the flowery pattern sewn into the cloth. Did you know that? When you bought this, did you know that? I shake my head. See, here, she says, and runs my fingers vertically on the seams. This could be like a corset. Ribbed. I like that too. She guides my hands all the way up over her breasts. And these are princess seams, she says. Along the shoulder straps, to her neck. My fingers reach into her hair, feel her braid, play with it. She bends her face to mine.

Ellen whispers in my ear, "Can you go to the gym late tomorrow?" Startling me. Did she see what I was seeing? Of course not.

"Why?"

"Let's sleep in."

When I was in the Syndicate this was one of my crowning achievements. Two girls in the same night. Something to brag about. But now I don't feel so good about it. I feel wrong. I feel sad. I know I have to be here, go through with it. Anything else would be further betrayal. It was one night. It's over. Put it behind me and get on with Ellen. Like I started the night doing.

"We'll sleep in," I whisper back. I'm glad I took a shower.

"Good." Ellen's palm drifts along my chest, down. "Later, I'll make breakfast."

"You're too good for me."

"Then we could talk."

Oh. Talk.

What about? About where I was? About where *she* was? I'm distant, and she feels it and becomes distant too, and after a while it gets mechanical. It's as if neither one of us is there. It's just something our bodies are doing so our minds can go somewhere else away from this bed and this person. When it's over it's a relief and we roll apart. We don't cling together like we usually do. We roll apart and go back to back and fall asleep until our alarms start buzzing and we turn them off but we can't sleep now, this is when we normally get out of bed.

I get up to pee and when I come out she's up and heading for the kitchen to make eggs and bacon and toast. I sit down at the table and wait, watching her.

"No shower this morning?"

She brings the plates to the table and sits down, takes a bite of bacon. "Took one last night when I got home."

Did she have to wash betrayal off too? "We're making new habits."

"Aren't we."

I'm more than a little hung over but the eggs are good, and who doesn't love bacon? I get the coffee for both of us from the Mr. Coffee machine. She stares out the window, holding her mug with both hands, blowing on it to cool it off.

When we're done eating breakfast, Ellen takes the plates

and puts them in the dishwasher. Then she comes and sits back down at the table and holds her coffee again, staring out the window.

"We going to talk?"

"Yes." Ellen puts her coffee down. "We've been together a couple of years now," she says.

"Three."

"Three. That's a long time."

"Not really. Lots of couples—"

"Break up."

"Or—"

"Yes, or."

We've been here before. Ellen thinks her parents would be happy to see us get married. I can't imagine it. Maybe if I was a Kennedy. We've always settled on leaving things as they are: we're together, we're going to be together. That's it. I don't want to break up.

"Okay," I say, and entirely too lightly add, "this is the marriage talk."

Ellen glares at me and stands up, frustrated. "No, this is not the marriage talk." She puts her mug in the dishwasher and goes into the living room and throws herself on the sofa.

I leave my mug on the table and follow her. She's sprawled on the sofa, legs straight out, head resting on the back cushion, looking up at the ceiling. I can't help it, but I see Olivia lying on her bed, the camisole long gone. I have to squeeze my eyes shut to make it go away.

Now Ellen sounds concerned. "You're hung over."

"A little."

"Michael, you can't keep drinking like you're still in college."

"Hey, I know."

"You know I care about you."

"Me too."

"Don't 'me too' me."

I'm silent. She gets silent, waiting.

"I care about you too, El."

She exhales loudly. "This is not the marriage talk."

"What is it then? The drinking talk?"

"Not the drinking talk."

I sit on the edge of an armchair, kneading my eyebrows. The headache is coming from my forehead. I think I can crush it.

"Take some aspirin."

"I did."

"Mike. This is difficult, and it isn't easier when you're not looking at me."

The headache somehow disappears for a moment, as if it knows something else is about to screw my brain.

"I need to say this," Ellen says.

"*Mike,*" I say.

"What?"

"You never call me Mike."

She rolls her eyes.

"You just never call me Mike, okay? I don't have a problem with it or anything."

"Maybe I'm just used to hearing Pete tell stories about you."

My stomach suddenly sinks, settles on the ocean floor. The wave of nausea passes. But the headache is back.

"That so."

"I need to say this."

"You said that already."

We're getting a little louder, and now she lowers her voice and gives me not the business Ellen, but one I don't think I ever heard before. Monotone, rehearsed. "We never had to set ground rules before, and I think we should, now."

"Ground rules for what?"

"For handling a situation."

I move over to the big chair, the leather one. But I can't relax; I sit on the edge of it. "What's a situation?"

"*Michael*, please. Don't interrupt me. This is hard enough."

"What's a situation?"

She sighs and sits up. "A situation is when one of us finds themselves doing something not in the best interests of us as a couple, of staying together."

"That's a situation?" How did she find out? How did she suspect? What stories has Pete been telling her? He wouldn't. But he would. He would tell her things about me to wheedle his way in. He was always above Syndicate rules.

"Yes. That's a situation."

"You want ground rules for that? I thought we had them."

"Yes. But I think it would be best if we just say out loud what we expect of each other. And what we wouldn't appreciate."

"What are you trying to say?" I don't want an answer.

"I'm just saying that maybe it's important for us to *know* what's important for us. Where the boundaries are."

"Boundaries to what?"

"Between being a couple, and not being a couple."

"El, we're a couple."

"Are we."

"Yes, I like to think that we are," I say.

"Are there things we can or cannot do?"

My brain might feel better when blood is rushing to it, so I flip on the chair and dangle my head over the edge, my legs hanging over the back of the chair, looking upside down at Ellen. She's waiting for an answer.

Wait a minute. This is not about *me*. This is not *my* indiscretion she's talking about.

"I'm not going to make this easy for you," I say.

"I can see that from the way you're sitting."

"Can we not talk about this anymore?"

"No. We *have* to talk about it."

"Why? Were you in a 'situation' recently?"

"Michael."

"Planning on being in one soon?"

She shakes her head like she's annoyed at the question. It's not an answer.

"So why do we need more ground rules?"

"What about you, Michael? Been in a 'situation' lately? Last night?"

I let my eyes close. The blood is pounding in my head; this isn't working. I find myself trying to get dressed in Olivia's dark bedroom, tripping over things.

"Michael?"

"What? No."

"But let's say you find yourself in a situation," she says.

"No."

"Are you saying it can't happen?"

"Yes. I mean no. I mean yes."

"Yes it can? Or no it can't?"

"It can't."

"Well, I can see it," Ellen says. "I can see it happening to one of us. Not that we want it to happen. Not that we're looking for it. But it could happen."

I let myself slip from the chair until my cheek is resting on the rug. My neck is twisted, and I'm looking across the floor at Ellen's feet in front of the sofa. If I shut my eyes, I could probably fall asleep like this. And wake up very painfully. I feel a twinge in my shoulder. Oh, great.

"*You* can see it happening?"

"Yes, I do," she says.

"I don't."

"You don't?"

"No, El, I don't." I somersault out of the chair and almost fall over. "Are we done? I'm going to the gym."

She doesn't answer. A little later she follows me into the bedroom to get ready for work. I'm already dressed, waiting for her. She doesn't say another word. It's not like her. Usually she tries to finish the thing, solve the problem, get the last word in. It's like she gave up. It's not fun.

When I get back from the gym there's a message from Chuck. He wants to talk about this week's game.

He answers the phone on the first ring. "Williamson, Chuck Walters."

"Hey, Chuck. Mike Santino. You called."

"Mike. Thanks for getting back to me. How's it going?"

"Good. Already in the playoffs. You?"

"Not yet. You know we have a problem on Thursday."

"Kraven Morrisey is going to knock you out of the playoff chase?"

"Funny guy. No. *We're* not getting knocked out. *You* might, if you end up forfeiting."

"Come on, Chuck. Sully joined you guys mid-season. He never had a shot at making your team. Let him finish out the year with KM."

"It's not Sully I care about. It's the shortstop and the center fielder."

Scott, and me. Our two best players. Our ringers.

"Who's playing third for you these days, Chuck?"

"Not a problem. I'll sit Derrick. Look, I know it's the core of your team. I know KM doesn't have a shot without its ringers. So give me one."

"I'll think about it."

"If both you ringers play, I'm going to the league."

"That's nice, Chuck. Good to see it's still just a game for you."

"It's not a game, Mike. I'm trying to get into the playoffs." Chuck hangs up.

He's got a point. A weak, overly competitive point. I would never bench Scott. But I hate the thought of not playing in the last game of the regular season. I'll call him, see what he thinks.

I've got his number scribbled somewhere on a sticky note on my desk. There's a whole pile of them, no longer sticky, under the monitor. Looking through these, I find one that says 'Saturday—Annie—Computer'.

I'll call Scott later. I pick up the phone and dial Ellen. Ask her if she can get out for lunch. And finish the talk from this morning.

We're sitting on the steps of the New York Public Library, looking out at Fifth Avenue and the people walking by. Eating a sandwich (me) and a salad (Ellen) we bought at the gourmet deli across the street. It's a beautiful, cloudless, perfect day. The traffic noise seems mellowed by the sunshine. No one can work hard today. Not bad for a summer Tuesday in New York.

My plan was to have this talk she wants to have, and to tell her all about what happened last night, and she would forgive me and understand, and everything would go back to normal.

Maybe I could tell her I don't want her to seek revenge, especially not with Pete. I could tell her some nasty things about Pete. But I can't: Syndicate rules.

I'm not sure I could listen to her tell me about something that already happened with him.

But now that we're here, I've forgotten my words. I don't want any of those things.

Ellen sits quietly, done picking at her salad, and waits for me to start. I feel her watching me as a rollerblader goes by. Tall, graceful, long legs, incredibly short shorts. I look away, and I can feel Ellen relax.

I don't want more rules. I don't want to make what I did real. I want to deny it.

"El, about these situations."

"Yes, Em."

"Do you think *I'm* going to need these rules, or are you?"

She doesn't answer.

"I'm uncomfortable about this, El."

"I know, Michael. I am, too."

"Has... there already been... I don't want to know."

"No, Michael. There hasn't."

This makes me feel a lot better. "Same here."

The sky is clear, so it won't be a lightning bolt. Maybe I'll spontaneously combust. Maybe my nose will grow. Nothing happens.

"I want us to be together, Michael."

"Then why are we doing this?"

"I don't know. But we have to." Ellen stands. "Come. Let's walk around for a while."

We get up and throw our lunches into a trash can, and start walking up Fifth Avenue, uptown. Back toward her office. Slow. Not wanting to get anywhere fast.

Ellen nudges against me and makes me lose my balance for a step. "I think it's because I love you. And I don't want to lose you. I don't want you to think there's anything better out there."

I nudge her back, just a little harder than she did, but she's ready for it. "There isn't."

She holds my hand. "You're always looking for something better," she says. "Things can always change. You can feel like you're in a cage, that you want to escape. Michael, you attract women. You can't help it. People get tempted. Then they start keeping things from each other. Then they start to resent each other. They start to mistrust each other. Then they break up."

"How is seeing other people going to keep us together?"

"That's not what I had in mind."

"Then what?"

"I don't want to know about it. If something happens, don't tell me about it. And I won't tell you."

I feel like hurling my lunch on the sidewalk.

"Is that okay?"

"Do I have a choice?"

"I don't like this myself, but I don't know what else to do. I want you to see this works both ways. This looking you do. And whatever else it might lead to. Just respect my feelings. That's the rule. Think about how *you* would feel if the roles were reversed. Maybe that'll save you. Maybe, *if* something is about to happen, remember us. Don't hurt us. Remember that it can still be good. If that doesn't stop you, I don't know. Be discreet. Let it play out, if you have to, then come back when it's over. But no lying. No two-timing. Respect each other. Something like that. Just don't do anything stupid. Just don't do *anything*."

This is so unlike Ellen. I can't tell if she wants an open relationship, or something else. It seems like *she* doesn't know what she wants, and is trying to put it into words before the thought is ready. That's usually me, not her.

If it's an open relationship, I see how this all works out for me, saves me from the guilt I'm feeling. But I don't like how it works out for Ellen. I don't care if that sounds like a double standard. Anyway, the thing that happened last night will never happen again.

No. I don't like this at all. I don't need more rules. No open relationships. I need Ellen. I don't want to share Ellen with anybody. I guess I really do love her.

But why did it have to take that thing that happened last night to prove it?

I know what I have to do.

We're on the corner of 47th and Fifth.

"C'mon." Instead of walking uptown, I pull on her arm and we cross Fifth Avenue.

"Where are we going? I have to get back to the office."

It's a block we usually avoid. A block that causes trouble. That has led, in the past, to the marriage talk. It's the Diamond District.

"What are you doing?"

"Something crazy. But I think you'll like it."

I drag Ellen past the windows where the marriage talk usually starts, and through the door of one of the shops. We have to knock, and then someone on the inside buzzes the door open.

The place is crowded. We stand in front of one of the glass cases looking at the rings.

A man finishes a transaction with another customer and stands across the counter from us.

"Can I help you today?"

"Yes, you can." I'm not letting go of Ellen's hand. "We're looking for a diamond, and hopefully also a mount."

The man pulls out a laminated sheet that shows the different shapes and cuts of diamonds. Before he can start describing them I point at one. "That's called brilliant, right? The round one? Ellen, is that the one?"

"Brilliant. Yes." She sounds stunned.

The man puts the sheet away and lays a piece of black velvet on the counter top.

"We're looking for clarity and color over size," I tell him. Ellen and I have looked before, and know all the terminology. He gives us some prices so we have an idea of what we should be looking at. It's more than I expected, but this is for Ellen. She deserves it.

While the man gathers a few diamonds to show us, I see Ellen's biting her lower lip. She does that when she's thinking. "You okay with this?" I ask.

Ellen nods. "Are you? How are you going to pay for it?"

"Don't worry about that." And I really don't want her to worry about it, because it's going to burn through the rest of my savings and push me into getting a job sooner than I thought.

"Make it a simple mount. Nothing fancy."

"Whatever you want." We haven't stopped holding hands the whole time, and now Ellen squeezes mine again.

The man suggests a diamond. "You're looking for a solitaire mount. This one is elegant, classic. You can go for four or six prongs."

"Six," Ellen says.

The man puts the other diamonds away, leaving the one we picked alone on the black velvet. He takes out a pad and starts writing the order down.

We're getting engaged.

The whole thing, the whole life change, happens in a flash. Ellen's excited, happy, overjoyed; I know she is, but she has to get back to the office because she's late, too. So she's not showing how excited, happy, and overjoyed she is. I'm feeling things, not observing myself. It's me standing there with Ellen.

Then she lets go of my hand and takes a step back from the counter. "No, Michael. No. I'm not ready."

life after ellen

We're playing in Central Park. The team's playing. I'm not. I've done something to my shoulder while sitting the wrong way in a chair and I hope rest will make it go away. This has worked out great for Chuck Walters and Williamson, and I didn't have to decide between benching me or Scott.

I'm sitting alone at the end of the bench along the third base side of the field. Williamson is winning, 5-2 in the sixth inning. If I was sitting near the other KM bystanders, I'm afraid I'd ask about Ellen, or they'd just tell me. I'm still managing the team. I'm responsible for pinch hitters and position changes, but I feel helpless. Watching the game is not as fun as playing—but I've already explained that. Chuck looks over at me every so often, his smile telling me how satisfied he is with my discomfort.

I keep toying with the new cellular phone I picked up yesterday, flipping its cover up and down like I'm Captain Kirk calling the Enterprise.

Sully's playing centerfield instead of me. Other than that one ball that got past him and scored three runs, he's not doing a bad job. It's not his fault we're losing. It's mine.

No one approaches me. I'm glooming heavily; feels like I haven't smiled in a week. But it's only been 48 hours. How fast does gossip move? Does everyone know already?

After we lose, we head to the bar.

Atomic Dive Bar is more crowded than usual. The league has scheduled extra games today to make up for rainouts as the season winds down. It's thrown the logistics here all out of whack. Sully squeezes through the crowd with a round of beers. We tap bottle necks and drink. He's being unusually polite tonight.

"Sucks. Your shoulder," Scott says. "How do you think it happened?" It's not the first time I've had to answer that question.

"Maybe on that throw I made last week, the off-balance one."

"It's not like you threw it that hard, or far," Phil jokes.

Sully stays quiet. Phil punches him in the arm. "Hey, it's not all on you, man," he tells Sully. "We made the playoffs anyway. Mike couldn't have caught up with that one that got by you."

"You think so, Mike?" Sully asks.

"Nobody was going to catch that ball," I lie.

I'm not in the mood to drink, but I'm on Sully time.

I'm trying to stay on his good side. I'd like to keep my crash landing on his sofa as short and friendly as possible. I have the feeling he would, too; it's been a couple of days and he still hasn't made a duplicate key for me. It's not like I have someplace to go, other than the gym, but his apartment makes me squirm. And I don't have my programming books with me, and that feels weird.

When no one is looking I corner Phil. "Got a minute?"

"Sure, shoot, Mike."

"Are you aware of anyone looking for a roommate, or with an apartment they're renting out?"

"Is it *that* serious?"

"I don't know. I'd like to avoid signing a lease."

"I'll ask around."

After Scott and Phil leave, Sully leans in and asks, "How're you holding up?"

There's plenty of time for this kind of talk, especially since he wants to talk about it all the time. I shrug and take a sip of beer. Someone elbows me and I spill some on myself.

"Can't catch a break," Sully laughs.

"Not one," I say. It feels like nothing is going right for me anymore.

"I'm going to try to hustle up a game of nine ball." Sully heads for the back of the bar.

The redhead, Rebecca, slips through the crowd toward me. "Hey, Mike. Sorry about your arm."

"Shoulder." I'm relieved she didn't say 'sorry about Ellen.'

Eventually she says, "I hear you know Pete Sera. One of our clients."

"Yeah, I do. We go back to high school."

"Do you talk to him a lot? Are you close?"

"No. The opposite. For some time."

Rebecca hesitates, and then says, "Was he always so creepy?"

"What's he up to?"

"He's one of those 'hands on' sort of guys. Too touchy."

"You should go to HR with that."

"I can manage. He's a big account and I don't want to mess that up."

"Do what's best for you, not what's best for the agency."

We stand there awkwardly for a while, talking about nothing and anything. Then she pretends she sees a friend. "It's never that bad," she says. Before I can ask what she means I'm left there standing alone in the crowd again.

I'm not surprised about Pete. He was always holding

himself above everyone else, privileged, treating others like objects. It seems to have gotten worse.

In the back, Sully's on a winning streak, and he's going to keep playing until he loses. I lean against the wall, not watching because pool bores me. I never learned how to play. There's a baseball game on the TV over the bar. I make a point of looking at my watch from time to time.

Sully comes back to me, says, "I'm on a roll, Mike, and you need a new beer. Say hi to my partner."

Olivia steps out from behind Sully. She's got a red KM hat on her head. It makes her look cute, like a softball groupie. While Sully heads toward the bar, Olivia smiles and looks up at me. "Hi, Michael."

"What are you doing here." I say it the way a guard might say it if you were trespassing.

"I wanted to find someplace new. What a coincidence!"

Even dressed so casually, just a t-shirt and jeans and the hat, she looks good. Real good. I start looking around for anyone watching us. Is it obvious, what happened between us? It feels like I have no place to hide. The bar smells like a bar, but she smells delicious, and I'm suddenly hungry.

"Where did you get the hat?"

Her eyes bounce from left to right, then lock on mine again. "Here and there. It's Thomas's."

She takes a step in, closer to me, and I slide backwards along the wall.

"This is not right."

"Oh, stop. This is nothing. Just someone you and Thomas met at the bar."

"Leave Sully out of it."

"Is that what you call him?" Olivia laughs. "Oh, he's not getting in."

"Don't tell him anything."

"You think I tell every strange guy I meet in a bar about my other lovers?"

Sully's back. He hands me and Olivia a couple of beers and taps necks with us. "This girl's a shark, Mike. We're unstoppable."

"Okay... but it's getting late."

"Let's go already," one of the other pool players calls.

Sully puts his beer down on a booth divider. "I gotta break," he says. As if he needs to explain this to Olivia, he adds, "Mike's crashing at my place."

"Oh?"

"Yeah. Of all the nights, right?" Sully grabs his stick and makes for the pool table.

"He is so sadly hopeful. What's going on?"

"Nothing. It's temporary."

She laughs softly, low purring that you feel more than hear, even through the noise of the place. "You've got better options, you know."

I don't know what to say. Olivia baffles me with her directness.

"It's not like you don't know where I live."

Sully taps Olivia on the shoulder with his stick. "You're up." When she's out of range, he smirks. "What do you think?"

"About what?"

"She's a hot little firecracker."

"Sure."

"Listen, this is real inconvenient," Sully says. "Anyplace else you could stay tonight?"

"You're that sure of yourself?"

Sully nods. "Heck, you could still crash on the sofa, if you don't mind the noise. This one looks like a screamer."

I look at my watch. "Alright, it's only seven. I'll go catch a movie or something, give you time to have some fun. But then you have to let me in. Around midnight."

"Deal, pal. That's a deal."

I walk around for half an hour and then walk toward Olivia's apartment. It's so easy. She's standing out front of her place, waiting for me. As if we planned it.

It's after three when I get back to Sully's place. Getting in the outer door is easy; it doesn't lock so there's no need to get buzzed in. When I get to the apartment door I realize I'm just too tired to have to deal with him, and I sit on the floor next to his door and try to catch some winks. But I can't. It's like Olivia is burning herself into my brain.

Eventually, the sun rises, and I stand up. Sully answers the door after I knock on it a couple of minutes. "Hey, what are you doing out here?" He's still waking up.

"I went to a movie, remember?"

"Oh yeah. That chick. She left around midnight."

I can't call him on this lie so I let it go. "You getting me a key today?"

"That reminds me, I have one already. I'll get it for you."

It's not the sort of thing I'd forget, but this is Sully. Maybe he didn't expect me to be here more than a night or two.

After he gets ready for work, we walk to a nearby diner for breakfast. Then I go back to the apartment to get some sleep. I wake up around ten, shower and get dressed, and head out.

I wander around looking for a park, a quiet place I can sit, and maybe write. I find myself drifting toward Central Park. I don't stop there; I keep walking until I'm in front of the Library. It's a long walk but such a nice day I don't mind. I sit in the same spot Ellen and I sat a couple of days ago. I just sit; I don't take out my notebook or pen. My head is full of thoughts but nothing I could write down. I didn't bring a book to read. The sky is cloudless again and the air is warm; it hasn't got sticky yet. I replay what happened one more time, then again, and again. I keep looking for a point where I could've stopped what was happening, or at least slowed it down. Every time I run through it I end up in the same place: here, on the steps of the New York Public Library. Was it the rollerblader? Was that the last straw?

What Ellen meant to say was *I* wasn't ready. I'm sure of it.

Ellen said we had a good thing and she didn't want to let that go, but we needed some time.

"You could have all the time in the world," I said.

But she said, "That's what we've had so far. That's what I've given you."

I tried to deny it, but she was right. And I felt so, so guilty. She suggested we take some time apart. It's not what *I* wanted, I thought it was just a negotiating point we would get past, but she insisted on it. That was the change she was looking for. We needed some time apart. Now it seems I really do have all the time in the world.

Maybe time will let me wash off the guilt. Maybe with time I could forget what I did and she would never have to know. But just two days into it I slipped again. It was just an awful coincidence, Olivia showing up at Dive Bar. I felt so lonely, and it was such an easy thing to do.

I have to decide what it is that I want. I want Ellen. But I keep doing stupid things. Is Atomic Dive Bar now a place I can't go? All I have to do is avoid Olivia. This is not the sort of separation that's going to end well.

I take out the phone and call Ellen at her office. "I've got this new cellular phone. I wanted to give you my number. In case you want to talk or anything."

"Yes. Sure." She repeats the number back to me after writing it down.

"I'm crashing at Sully's."

"I heard."

"Already? News gets around fast."

"You know agencies. Everybody knows everyone else. Or talks about everyone else. And Sully's involved."

I sense awkwardness, like she doesn't know what to say.

"How long does this have to last?"

"Don't do that, Michael. There's no time limit. No deadline. It's just... life. It'll happen if it happens."

"Is that it? Can I get a presidential pardon?"

"It's not *for* life, Michael. It's just life. You have to decide what you want."

"What if I know what I want?"

"What if you don't?"

"What do *you* want?"

Ellen sighs dramatically. "Don't put this on me, Em. I'd *love* it if we could be together."

"But you don't love me?"

"You're doing it again. Look, I have a meeting in a few minutes."

"But you don't *trust* me?" I know I have no right to ask for that.

"Get a job, Michael. Start there. You don't want to be living with Sully."

"You want me to get a place of my own."

There's a pause. "That might be a good idea."

"Is it going to take that much time?"

"Gotta go, Em. Thanks for your number."

This getting my own apartment thing makes it sound like I have a long way to go before I'm eligible for parole.

The afternoon is placid. The warm air doesn't sit on me; there's enough of an intermittent breeze so all I want to do is shut my eyes, maybe lay down on the steps of the Library and take a nap. But I can't help thinking about this mess and how I can't get out of it. I'm also worried that someone's going to step on me. The nap lasts a minute, then I grab my bag and walk down the stairs. There are things I must do.

I take a cab back to Sully's place, where I left my laptop. Borrowing his DSL connection, I look up the Monster Board, this website where you can go search for jobs. Within minutes I'm frustrated. Everything sounds the same. All the programming jobs are out of reach without experience. Everything is Y2K and COBOL. No one knows COBOL anymore. So I leave the apartment, and start walking toward the subway. There's an employment agency in mid-town that has found temporary gigs for me in the past.

I walk right past the waiting room full of people carefully filling out forms and go to the front desk, and ask if Emily Clark is available. Emily has found me work with business magazines. Always part-time. Desktop publishing, that sort of thing. Maybe she could help me land a programming job. I'm hopeful she can find something full-time. Hopeful? Full time? Not really, but if I'm going to get an apartment, if I'm ever going to get back together with Ellen, I have no choice. I wait twenty minutes before I get called into her office.

"All your experience is writing copy," Emily says after I tell her what I'm looking for. "It would have to be very entry level. Let's see what we can scare up."

She looks at her computer screen, then gets up and leaves the room. She comes back with a file folder. "How much programming can you say you've done?"

"C, C++. I taught myself and I'm a fast learner."

"COBOL?"

"No."

"Too bad. There are *so* many openings right now. Old programmers are coming out of retirement to help with this Y2K thing. Do you have any Perl? Java?"

"I've looked at Perl. It's so much like C that I don't think it would be a problem. Java? How much Java?"

"Two years."

I laugh. "Nobody has two years of Java experience. Maybe only James Gosling."

"Oh, that's right, it's new. I have a *lot* of openings for it. Some of these are for more senior programmers; that would be a hard sell."

"I've done some desktop publishing," I offer. "But I really want to go for one of these programming jobs."

"Okay." She pulls one sheet out of the folder. "Do you know what HTML is?"

"Yes. That's an easy one."

She dials a number. "Hello, it's Emily Clark from Wonder Jobs. Have you filled the web programming position yet? Good. I have someone here who checks all the boxes."

I can't hear what the person on the other end of the line is saying.

Emily covers the handset. "When can you start?"

"I'm available immediately."

"He'll have to give notice, if that's okay... great."

When Emily hangs up I've got an interview with Mega Group scheduled for next Monday. "Never say you're available immediately. It means you're unemployed," she reminds me. "Red flag."

"Thank you. I won't let you down."

I'm going to need a suit so I call Ellen. "Mind if I drop by the apartment and get some stuff?"

"You can leave it here," she says.

"I have a job interview next week."

"Oh, that's a good thing."

"So can I come by?"

"Well, don't take everything. Not until you have a place of your own."

I swing by and grab my blue suit, a shirt, a tie, and shoes. Also a couple of programming books. I put everything neatly into my suitcase. On my way out, I take the house key off my keychain and put it on a napkin on the kitchen table. When the door shuts behind me, it's with a soft shush.

Maybe I shouldn't have left the key. I don't want to rush into this life after Ellen too fast. I don't want to get too far away. But I think this is the right thing to do.

dongling participle

A few days later, around six o'clock, my cell phone rings. It's Ellen. There are no opening pleasantries. "Another one of your 'little friends' called. She said something about you getting together with her tomorrow."

What? Anne. The computer. Oh, shit.

"I can explain—"

"Don't bother."

"No, really. I gave her my number while we were still together—"

"Together? Does that make it better?"

"Really, Ellen. She's married to my friend Zander."

"The mysterious Zander. I gave her your new number. Good luck."

"No, Ellen, it's not—" but she hangs up.

That 'another of your little friends' bit sticks in my head. Has Olivia called there again? I have no idea. But it sounds right. Why would Olivia do that? Is she sabotaging me?

Or is it Pete? Is he telling Ellen stories about me, getting her to not trust me?

A short while later, Anne calls.

"Michael, is everything alright?"

"Yeah."

"I called your number. Someone answered. She sounded annoyed."

"She is, but it's at me. You just got caught in the crossfire."

"Are you still able to come tomorrow?"

"Yes. Sure. Is noon okay?"

"Zander's playing golf. He won't be back till five."

Great. I should be done and gone long before then. "I just need a ride from the Metro-North station."

We settle on plans. Then it hits me that I'm going to be alone, with Anne, in her house. And Zander won't be home all day.

Anne picks me up at the train station on Saturday. She's wearing cut-off denim shorts and a pale yellow t-shirt with some frittery art that reads 'Ziegfeld Follies of 1916.' The shorts are short. I'm curious what the white fringe feels like against her skin. The shirt seems to have shrunk. I try to focus on the dashboard or out the windshield. It's the safest thing, and it's something I've been doing with her since high school.

It's just a few minutes from the train station to Zander's house. Annie's house. Goddammit. There's just no way to avoid looking while I follow her into the house.

"How was the woods?" Anne says.

"It was what you would expect."

"After such a long time, did it feel normal?"

"Nothing's normal around us. Remember?"

"Stop it, you were always having fun together."

"You were away, in college."

The computer's set up now on a coffee table in front of the couch in the living room. Anne sits on the couch, I kneel down in front of the screen.

"It's just not connecting to AOL. Zander's computer is fine, but he doesn't want me using it."

"Powers up normally."

"Here. Look." Anne leans over my shoulder unnecessarily close and takes the mouse, opening AOL. She clicks on the button to connect. Nothing happens. She smells like coconuts and clean sheets.

"How's this plugged in?" I look around the back of the box, find a phone cable and trace it back to the wall.

"I see the problem. There's no DSL filter on this line."

"What's that?"

I try to keep it simple. "Since it's a phone line, it needs to be filtered." That's too vague but it works. "You should have one of these... dongles..."

"Does Zander have one?"

"You should know," I say, but she's outgrown my juvenile sense of humor. "His computer should, if he can use AOL."

"It's in the bedroom."

The bedroom is immaculate and soft; Zander must have nothing to do with it. In fact, the whole house is decorated like a magazine. Big, welcoming pillows cover half of the bed. There's a computer sitting under a desk in the corner. I check behind it, come out with a dongle. "This is it."

"Can we use that one?"

"Sure. But it's got to go back later. Better, see if you can find another one. They usually give you two."

"Would it be with the other phone stuff?"

"Sure." I stand up. Anne doesn't move out of the way.

"Um," is all I can manage. I hand her the dongle. I can feel the heat coming off her legs searing me. "See if you can find another one of these."

She takes it from my hand but doesn't step back.

"Where's your phone stuff?"

"It's in the kitchen. I'll go look."

This breaks the spell. I go back to the living room and kneel in front of the computer again. Anne goes into the kitchen; I can hear her rummaging around in drawers. "No luck," she calls. "Want some iced tea?"

"Sure. Thanks."

Anne comes back with a glass in each hand and the dongle hanging between her pinky and ring finger. There is no ring there.

She notices I'm aware of that, and that's what she planned. "Zander and me are splitting up," she says, as if she's talking about the weather, slipping coasters under our glasses. "Did he say anything last weekend?"

"Nope." I try to act normal. I plug the dongle into the wall, and then plug one end of the phone cord into it and the other end into the computer. "Let's see if that did it." And it works. AOL says, "You've got mail."

They always give you two filters. I wonder if Zander has hidden the other one so Anne can't use her computer. It was working fine when we showed up at the house that day for the camping trip. I should be getting out of here as quickly as possible. But there's the iced tea to drink, and the next train is an hour away. I kinda want to stick around and see if something might happen with Anne. No, I don't. I don't know. Maybe.

Anne moves over a little, pats the couch. "Come sit. We haven't talked in years."

I get off the floor reluctantly and try not to sit where she wants me to. There's an ugly yellow bruise on her left thigh.

"Tell me about this girlfriend of yours. I bet she's nice."

"She is."

"How long have you been with her?"

"Three years."

"That's a long time."

"You've been married what, five years?"

Anne shrugs. "It feels like forever. When I called yesterday... it sounded like something was going on. Are you two fighting?"

"I wouldn't call it fighting."

"Why did she have to give me your cell phone number? She called it your 'new number.' Are you still together?"

"Um. No. We split up. But it's just temporary, I think. There are some things we have to work out." That's the way Ellen said it to me. I don't know if it's better to be honest or to lie. "But I'm sure it's nothing," I try to convince Anne—and myself.

"Zander and I aren't fighting either. It's like a cold war. He doesn't want to talk about it. So it's hard to make progress."

"I can imagine." I look down, at the bruise on her thigh. "What happened? Cold war?"

Anne shrugs. "This is nothing. Fell down the stairs. Got rug burns, too. Wanna see?"

"Ouch. No." I try not to imagine where they are, given how much of her skin is already showing. "Are you sure?"

"What, about falling down the stairs?" Anne laughs. "Yes, I'm sure. I was there."

"Where was Zander?"

"It's nothing, okay?"

"Did he make you fall? Did he push you?"

"Please, Michael. Don't make a big deal out of it."

"I don't like it."

"Yeah, but you're not here, so don't worry about it. I'm okay. I can take care of myself."

"Annie, if he's hurting you..."

"What are *you* going to do about it?" It looks like she wants to cry, but she doesn't. "Let's not talk about it, okay?"

I think of staying here, waiting for Zander to come home, confronting him. How much worse that would make things. Just finding me here alone, with Anne, would be bad enough. I've tried to avoid getting into a fight with Zander my whole life. Even when we were just kids, horsing around. I try to bury the thought that Zander might be hurting Anne, bury it somewhere deep where it won't trouble me. I try hoping there's nothing to be worried about. I try to switch myself off.

"What happened to you at the wedding?" Anne asks. She really does want to change the subject.

"What do you mean, what happened?"

"You disappeared."

I try to look everywhere but directly at her. "Did not."

"You said you would be right back. To dance with me."

There's nothing wrong with her memory. I can't think of an excuse that would sound real. "Oh. I don't remember. It's been years."

"Yes you do. I know you left. Figured it out after standing there a little while. And you came back for Allie."

"You have some memory."

"It's not a hard thing to forget, when the best man and maid of honor disappear in the middle of your wedding."

"Honestly, you were having so much fun, I didn't think you would notice."

"Again. Best man? Maid of honor? Isn't that trite?"

"You never did like it when the two of us were together."

"No. I did not."

Anne traces her finger along the rim of her glass, watching little droplets of condensation go racing down the side. She shakes her head. "Our timing was never right."

Funny hearing that from the girl who grew up next door. Our timing was always right. And then Zander showed up.

"Annie, you're like a sister to me. You're family."

"Don't say that. I *hate* it."

After a moment she says, "What's going on with Pete? Wasn't he supposed to go with you last week?"

"Something must've come up."

"Zander was pissed. It was almost like he wanted Pete there more than you and Sully. You should've heard him after you guys left."

"I don't think he wanted any of us there. I don't think he wanted to be there himself. Probably blamed Pete for setting it up and then not showing. Mind if I ask, what happened? With Zander and you?"

Anne shrugs. "Mostly, it's me. I'm sick of staying home. He's always out, working, and after work. And, well, you know. He's out a lot. Late. Or early. Depends on whether you're an owl or a rooster. Anyway, it's not like we have kids. You know how Zander feels about kids."

I nod. "So mostly it's him."

"That's why I'm getting my real estate license. So I have somewhere to land."

"You're ahead of the game." I look at my watch. "Annie, I've got to get to the station."

I stand, and when she does, again it's too close. Then she does something expected. Anne kisses me on my mouth. She hesitates for just a moment, her lips close to mine, and then goes for it. I'm startled, but I had a feeling something was going to happen. I don't stop it at first. I've always wanted this. I can't help returning the kiss. I want to hold her but my hands are hovering around her waist, not touching her, as if she were on fire. I stay inside myself, in control, feeling everything, not just letting it happen. When she starts putting her arms around my neck, I gently reach back and untangle us. I kiss her bangs, still holding her wrists in my hands.

"I'm sorry," she says, into my chest.

"Don't be. I'm not. But this can't happen."

"Why not?"

I shake my head. You can count on one hand the number of times I've felt this courageous. Or maybe this is cowardice. "There are other people involved," I tell her.

"Zander's not a person."

"It's not right."

"Will it ever be?"

"I don't know," I say. It's an honest answer.

Growing up I spent many lonely nights thinking about something happening with Anne. After the wedding it stopped. Just now it all came back and I almost went with it, almost let it happen. But I can't do it. It's not fear of Zander that's holding me back. I just don't see how it could end happy for anyone. And it's wrong. I love Ellen.

When Anne drops me off at the station she kisses me on the cheek. It's tentative and proper. I'm almost in Grand Central when I remember that we were supposed to put the dongle back.

Zander calls a little after six. "How the fuck would you like it if I dropped in on your girl when you weren't home?"

"I was just helping Anne out with her computer."

"Stay away from my wife."

"Did you hurt her? I swear, Zander—"

"And what? What the fuck are you going to do about it? Stay. The. Fuck. Away."

Before I can answer, he's gone.

That didn't sound good. What did she tell him? Anne was never a very good liar. Not that there was something to lie about; whatever happened was nothing. Just that this is the kind of thing I was always afraid of with Zander. When we were in high school, it wasn't a problem. We thought it was fun trying to get him to blow up. I could hide behind the others. He wasn't as scary. But from the moment they got engaged, it seems, I've been waiting for something to happen. Between me and him, over her.

I'm worried about Anne. I know Zander. I hope she's alright.

Right after that Ellen calls. This time she's talking almost in a whisper. "Em, is everything okay?"

"Yeah. Why?"

"Someone who said he was a friend of yours called here looking for you. Or rather, 'that little piece of shit.' He doesn't have very nice phone manners."

"Now that you gave him this number, that'll be on me," I say. "If he calls again, just hang up. He's trouble."

"Are you getting yourself into something with someone you should be leaving alone?"

"No, it's not like that. Anne needed help with her computer. Before, you know. Before we... split. I forgot she was going to call."

"And the other one?"

"Zander."

"*That's* Zander. I get it now. Why didn't you ever mention Anne?"

I'm stumped. I never wanted to talk about the Syndicate with Ellen. I rolled Anne and Alison into it without thinking. They were part of a different life, one that I was trying to forget. The only time they ever came up was in the bar with Pete and Allie the other night. It would be hard to talk about one without the others. And old flames don't make good conversation with current partners.

"I hope you're not angry at me for that," I say.

"Oh, I'm not angry at you," Ellen says. "Not about *that* call."

"Then why... why are we apart?"

"Again, Em? We need more time. That's all."

"And what if... 'situations' come up?"

"Are you planning on that?"

"Not for me."

"You're not chasing Anne?"

"No. For real." There's an empty space. "How are you?"

"Don't worry about me, Michael. I'm fine. I'm just crazed over this thing Pete wants. I didn't realize he was so... pushy. Eccentric."

"I can see why you'd say that. He thinks different. He was always the smartest one of us." I wish I could take that back. I wish I had said he was the slimiest. "I'm the best one."

Ellen laughs.

I remember what Rebecca told me about Pete harassing her, and I want so badly to bring it up with Ellen. But there are Syndicate rules. I can't talk bad about Pete. It's not a rule I think he follows. I don't know why I still do.

I spend the rest of the weekend playing video games with Sully. We only stop to get pizza and beer. It's like we're back in college.

Sully's place looks like his room when we were growing up. In one corner there's his softball glove, a bat, a hockey stick, and a basketball. He's never been a football fan. There are a bunch of New York Mets caps, all different.

"Hey Sull, where's your KM hat?"

"What KM hat?"

"The one you wear at—wait a sec, you *always* wear a Mets cap."

"I wish I had a KM hat. Never got one. I wish I still worked there."

"How are things at Williamson?"

"Too many projects with Gretchen. And Chuck likes to needle me. He's always telling me to fix this, change that, there's always something."

"Can't you go back to KM? Or find another agency?"

"I've thought about it. More than thought. There's nothing open right now."

"Why did you leave, anyway? Was it Gretchen?"

"Yeah, mostly, and now she followed me to Williamson. That's my life. All I got was a tiny bump in salary. Same hell."

Monday's the day of my big interview. It goes over very well. They give me some programming problems and I don't have any trouble with them. I make a joke about the Java requirement and get a laugh from the three guys on the panel doing the interview. I didn't expect to be able to walk into a web development job with so little experience. There's a big demand for people to fill these jobs these days. Everyone else is working on Y2K. Within an hour I get a call from Emily at Wonder Jobs. I can start in two weeks; I'll be on a trial period for the first two months. I realize I'm going to miss the easy life I have now. I can use the two weeks. I call Ellen.

"Hey El, what's up?" I say, all bouncy and free.

"Michael? You sound different."

"I am, babe, because I'm a working stiff now. Nine to five. Got a *real* job."

"What agency?"

"Mega Group."

"Never heard of them."

"It's a technology analysis and consulting company. They're a big deal for other companies. Of course you never heard of them."

"It's not a copywriting job?"

"Nope. Uh-uh. I'm going to be paid to program. It'll be HTML at the start, so it's not really programming, but I'm hoping I can join the back-end team soon."

"I don't know what any of that means. Is all that tinkering finally going to be useful?"

"Hell yeah. Isn't this great news?"

"When's your first day?"

"Two weeks. Hey, now that I have a job... can we..."

"You haven't even started it yet, Michael. Relax. Get on your feet. But it's a good first step."

I guess I can't complain about that.

The sky is clear and blue as it's been most of the month, but it feels brighter. If I knew it could be that easy, I would've done this a while ago.

you're out!

Chuck Walters calls me. "How did it feel, benching yourself?" is how he starts the conversation.

"Felt pretty good just not being you."

"Ha ha, funny. You lucked out. See the playoff brackets?"

"Not yet."

"You're gonna love this. Guess who you play in the first round."

"Shit."

"Same deal, sit one of your ringers or else. But this time *you* can play. Bench Sully."

This is starting to feel like what it is: blackmail. Chuck is as bad as Zander when it comes to playing games with people.

"He works for one agency, plays for someone else. He's going against his co-workers. Doesn't seem right. Agency morale, you know."

"Fuck you."

"If you don't like it, you can forfeit. Don't matter to me. I'll beat you on the field, or off. Either way, Williamson's going to win it all this year."

I wonder if Chuck knows Sully and I are best friends. Sadistic son of a bitch.

"You're not going to beat us. I'm not benching Sully."

"Then you *and* your shortstop sit out. Your choice. Sully, or the two of you. Figure it out. See you at the game."

I'm benching Sully.

I haven't told him yet. It's just an idea floating around in my head. It doesn't have to happen for a few days. I've got time to come up with a solution, like my shoulder tweak. Maybe I can push him down some stairs. Or make him trip over a power cord. Something minor, but temporarily crippling.

Maybe the idea will disappear. Just a passing fancy.

But a forfeit hurts the whole team. Benching Sully will only hurt *him*. The needs of the many outweigh the needs of the one, I tell myself.

I should talk to Scott about this. He's been around. But he doesn't care about anything but playing. He won't care for this drama.

Phil. That's the guy. He'd get the problem I'm facing.

I call him, ask if I can buy him lunch, we have to talk.

Phil's concerned with what I'm going through, says he's still asking around about that apartment. After the small talk, I change the subject. "I have to bench Sully for the playoff game."

"Is he hurt?"

"He's going to be when he finds out."

"Why?"

I tell him about Chuck's threat. "If I don't bench Sully, I have to bench me and Scott. If I don't do *that*, Chuck's going to the league."

Phil thinks. "There's no way we can win. We can't replace both of you."

"It would be that or a forfeit."

"This isn't on you. It's on us. The whole team. We've had it good, gotten spoiled, never looked for a shortstop or outfielder in the company to replace you two."

"Sure, I would understand if it comes to that, but I don't know what I'm going to do if I can't play softball with KM next year."

"Let's not worry about that now. Have you told him yet?"

"No. I can't tell him the reason. Imagine his reaction? He'd get himself fired from Williamson."

"It's a pickle," Phil says. "We should ask the team. Not put it on you. Ask everyone but Sully. Vote to forfeit, or to play without Sully."

"That would get me off the hook, but it's unmanageable. There's no way you can get a vote from everyone without Sully thinking something was up."

"You forget, Sully doesn't work at KM anymore. It'll be easy," Phil says.

"Then who will tell Sully what the team decides to do?"

"That's tougher than figuring out what's best for the team." Phil thinks again. "It'd have to be you. You're the manager. You're his friend. I know it's tough, but it's the only way."

Phil's right. Let them decide, and if they decide to bench Sully, I'll tell him.

The team votes to bench Sully.

The game is on Tuesday. It's a week away. I'll tell him tonight.

Thursday night, I figure I'll tell him on Friday, to start the weekend.

On Friday I decide to tell him on Saturday so he'll have the whole day to absorb it.

I'll do it Sunday night. Don't want to ruin his weekend.

No, that would give him too much time at work to get into trouble with Chuck.

Monday's out too, then.

It has to be Tuesday.

After work.

Right before the game.

I make sure I'm the first one at the field. Sully shows up after half the team is already there. He comes over to me.

"Playoffs, Mike! It's that time of year." He stretches his arms out. He's got a pretty good wingspan.

"Got a minute?"

He stops, his arms falling slowly to his sides. "No way I'm batting lower than six."

"You're not starting tonight."

"What do you mean? Damn right I'm starting!"

I wait for it to sink in.

"What for? Why the fuck?"

"We're going to give Alan Linnel a shot, to start the game. He hasn't had much playing time. He did fine in right field last week when you were covering for me in center. Don't worry. You'll get in."

Sully comes around eventually and agrees, grumbling, to go with my plan.

Crazy that somehow the right words came out. But they weren't the right words. All I did was avoid, or just delay, a dramatic event.

Chuck keeps looking over and smiling at me. The game is tied, 8-8, in the bottom of the sixth. We're the home team. Sully's pacing back and forth behind me. "Now would be a good time," he's muttering. There's not going to be a good time.

Melissa's up, and she's the pitcher. I can't pull her. Then me, Phil, and Scott. The big hitters. If we get farther down in the order, I'm going to need another excuse.

Melissa singles and advances to second on a bad throw to the infield, giving me an opportunity to drive in a run and take the lead.

I foul off the first pitch. They're playing deep to take out the threat of a long ball. I'm looking to smack the ball into right field. I swing late and don't get much of the ball. It pops into the air behind first base, and I'm out.

Phil's up next. He hits a worm killer to the shortstop who bobbles it, but holds Melissa at second and throws the ball to the first baseman. Phil's out.

It's Scott's turn. He's money. He's a guaranteed hit. He's played a little minor league baseball, and he can crush the ball. They play deeper for him than they do for me, but they leave the short fielder in close to the infield, knowing Scott can hit the ball anywhere he wants to. I nod at him. "Let's go, Scott. Get a run in."

He hits a screamer over second base. Melissa runs for third, and should get home on this one. The short fielder just happens to be standing in the perfect spot and puts up her glove and the ball hits it and bounces onto the grass. Everyone on the Williamson side yells, "Throw it home!" The short fielder throws it as hard as she can and the catcher blocks home plate and tags Melissa out.

Great. Our three best hitters, and we couldn't get a run.

From the outfield in the top of the seventh I can see Sully's still pacing, bat in hand. The whole team, having voted on this, knows what's going on, and everyone's avoiding getting into a conversation with him. He's so wrapped up in his own head that he doesn't notice the shunning around him. Even if

I gave him a chance to hit in the bottom of the seventh, he'll be too agitated to trust at the plate. And Chuck will call the league office tomorrow. That's what I tell myself, but it doesn't make it better.

They get a runner on first. Then their ringer, Derrick, comes up. He's hit a couple of homers against us so we play him very deep.

He swings, and slashes the ball into right field. It gets to Linnel quick. Then it skips past him and rolls a long way. By the time Linnel runs it down, Derrick has circled the bases. Suddenly we're losing, 10-8.

We get out of the inning without any more damage.

It's our last shot, and we need around two runs. Not two runs; a tie means extra innings and finding more excuses to keep Sully benched. I just want it to be over.

First up is Laura, then Linnel, followed by Andre.

Laura swings at the first pitch and chops the ball to the second baseman. He tosses the ball to first. One out.

Linnel looks at me, and I wave him to the plate.

Sully is standing right next to me, clenching his bat. "I would've fielded that ball. Pull him," he snarls.

"I'm going to let him hit," I say into the air in front of me.

"What the fuck, Mike?"

"Giving him a chance to make up for the error. Saving you for the right time."

Linnel taps the ball and it starts to roll toward third base. But it rolls slow enough, and Linnel is fast enough, and he beats the throw. So he's on first.

"Okay, now, right?"

"There's only one out. Andre gets on, you'll get a shot at a game-winning homer." I have no idea what my next excuse is going to be.

Sully turns around and starts pacing along the first base

foul line, swinging his bat back and forth, like he's sweeping dust off a wooden porch.

"You have this, Andre," I shout.

Andre looks at me, nods. He swings. He tips the ball straight back.

He takes a couple of practice swings, gets back into the batter's box.

Linnel takes a couple of steps toward second.

Andre swings again. He hits a soft line drive right at the first baseman, who steps on the bag, doubling up Linnel.

Game over.

There's a loud gong as Sully hits the fence post with his bat.

Playoffs over.

I sigh with relief that my ordeal's over. But it's not over yet, not really. I still have to face Sully.

The team is quiet. They're all stunned at the sudden end of the game. It's going to hit them soon that besides this loss, they are going to have to bear responsibility for benching Sully.

Maybe. I sure feel it. I'll forget the loss. I won't forget I sacrificed Sully. For nothing. He probably won't, either.

When we get to the bar to drown our sorrows, Sully doesn't show. That's probably for the best. I pull the team together in the back by the pool tables.

"That was a tough loss," I tell them. "I'd rather have a chance to win, than no chance at all. So don't blame yourselves." I mean this two ways, and hope it doesn't sink in too painfully.

"We had a great season. There's always next year, right?" I take a deep breath. "But you'll need a new manager."

I can hear them saying 'no,' 'what?', and 'you can't go,' so I quiet them.

"I can't say I'm not playing with you guys anymore,

because I'd miss it too much. But I'm done being manager. You know, lineups, administrative shit like that." They know exactly what I mean. "So don't wait too long, find yourselves a manager for next season.

"And one more thing." I raise my bottle. "This is for Sully."

That doesn't go over as well as I expected. There's a long groan from all of them.

"He's a good guy, and a good friend," I interrupt. "I've not been either one."

Then Williamson shows up. I get down from my chair and we all try to not look at them.

It doesn't take Chuck long to find me.

"Hey, Mikey, no hard feelings, right? I'm just trying to make it fair for my guys."

"Sure, Chuck. Just making things fair. Next year, get yourself more ringers. You're going to need them."

"I can't help it if KM can't find enough actual employees to field a team." Then Chuck tries to tap my bottle neck with his. I pull mine away.

I'd like to smash my bottle into Chuck's face, but Phil and Scott are suddenly on either side of me, hands on my shoulders.

"C'mon, Mike." They pull me toward the back of the bar. We don't stay long; nobody's in the mood. Now I have to go back to Sully's place. I have a bad feeling about this.

I'm walking from Atomic over to Sully's when my cell phone rings.

"I like your new phone," Olivia says. "I don't have to make sure someone else isn't picking up. Or... you know what I mean."

"How did you get this number?"

"Got it off your phone that night."

"I'm having a bad day."

"Poor boy. Come home."

"Home?"

"Come over."

"I wish I could. I don't want to go where I'm going."

"Don't."

I think for a moment. "I have to. It would only be worse if I didn't."

"Go do whatever this bad thing is, and then come here. I'll make you feel better."

"I don't know. This could take a while."

"Don't make it forever."

I unlock and open the door to Sully's apartment.

"The fuck you doing here," he starts. "You fucking benched me. You were going to do it from the start, and you lied."

"Sorry, man." I can never tell Sully the reason. Not as long as he's working at Williamson with Chuck.

"Sorry? Fuck. You lied to my face."

When I was outside the door I was ready to explain it to him, and for him to understand. I was ready to blame Chuck. Now I'm stuck thinking what I can say.

"I was sure Andre was going to get a hit."

In fact I was hoping for the double play, so I'd be done with the whole charade.

"He's one of our weakest hitters."

I don't know if it's good or bad that he blames Andre. I don't want to be let off the hook like that. So I say, "No, it's my fault."

"Fuck you."

"I'm sorry I didn't bat you for Andre."

"Get the fuck out."

"Sully, please. I said I'm sorry." I want to make things right, but I won't grovel.

"What you did isn't just softball, fuckface. You stabbed me in the back. And I don't even know what I did to deserve it. Get out."

"Where should I go?"

"I don't care. How the fuck am I going to sleep with a backstabber in my apartment? No fucking way."

I start picking up my stuff. Spare clothing and laundry both go into the suitcase. My sports bag gets everything else.

"I can't believe you're doing this," I say.

He crosses his arms, waiting. "You wear out your welcome quick. Wonder what you did for Ellen to kick you out."

I've got everything but my suit. Now that the suitcase is full the suit's got to be carried separately. At least it's in a garment bag. I figure out a way to carry everything.

Let's see if he'll go through with it. "Can you get the door?"

Sully stomps over and opens it.

I step out of the building, onto the sidewalk. I start walking. I know where I'm going. I know it's not right. But I've got nowhere else to go. I've got no one else.

a normal day

Olivia answers the door wearing nothing but a short red silk robe, her dark curls cascading over her shoulders. I'm standing there in my grimy softball clothes with a suitcase, a gym bag, my day pack, and a suit. I feel awful.

"Interesting," she says.

God, she's good looking.

"Sorry. I don't want to assume anything."

"You're really having a bad day."

"Is it okay if I spend the night?"

"Here, put your bags down and don't worry."

She smells sweet when I hug her. Vanilla and another spice I can't identify. The hug starts turning almost immediately into something more. I can't stop myself.

"Game tonight? If I had known, I would've met you at that bar again."

"Didn't go well. You shouldn't go there."

"Why? Because you're there?"

"Yes. And because of everyone else who's there."

"I like how you think you can avoid me for a week, and then show up here and tell me where I can't go."

Maybe I should find a hotel. Anything but this. Why didn't I just do that? She's pulling on my arm, dragging me toward the bedroom. This should be humiliating. Instead, it feels so, so welcoming.

Next morning Olivia gets up and takes a shower. Then she lays out what she's going to wear, drops the towel, and starts putting things on. A black g-string; a lacy bra. There's no shyness about her. She can tell I'm awake; my eyes are open but my head is still on the pillow. She dresses careful, deliberate, and slow. Like she's putting on a show. Watching me the whole time. Like she did that first night, when she was getting undressed.

She puts on a garter belt, black stockings. She covers herself with a conservative skirt and blouse.

"Do I look professional?"

"You look great," I say.

"Just keep thinking about what's underneath this. I'll be back around four. You can stay here."

I can't stay here. I can't allow myself to settle in. This is wrong. But I can't drag my stuff all over the city. I need different living arrangements. After Olivia leaves, I take a quick shower. I'm amazed at how many hair and skin products are in Liv's bathroom.

Dude! You hooked up with a model! The voice is a combination of Zander and Sully and Pete. Almost like they're waiting for me to high-five them. Then I remember what Sully sounded like last night. If he had plans to reunite the Syndicate, they're off to a terrible start.

But I didn't just betray *him* yesterday. I keep betraying Ellen. I don't mean to. I'm not trying to, not intentionally, but events are happening that I can't stop.

I need alternate living arrangements, fast.

I can't sit here and wait for Olivia all day. It's like I'm in a cage. I go out and find a little park tucked between two skyscrapers and there are benches there. I sit on one and take out my phone.

"Hey Phil, what's going on?" I start.

"That sucked yesterday, Mike. That really sucked. Did you talk to Sully?"

"I did. It didn't go well. That's what I'm calling you about. Any news about that apartment?"

"Holy shit, Mike. That bad?"

"That bad."

"Did he kick you out yesterday? Where did you go?"

"I crashed at a friends' place. But it's very temporary."

"Who?"

"Nobody you know."

"...okay... I'll ask around, call you back."

A little bit after noon, he gets back to me.

"Good news, Mike. Friend of mine knows someone who's got a sublet and the dude needs a roommate. Rent's a lot less than anywhere else. It's upper East Side."

"That's great news, Phil. When is it available?"

"Right away."

"How upper?"

"Eighties. I'll give you the guy's work number. Say you're my friend. You know, pretend. His name is Kyle."

"Sweet, Phil. I owe you big time for this."

"Better than knowing my buddy is out there on the street."

Kyle doesn't get off work until five, so I wander around the city, gradually working my way toward the upper East Side. I meet Kyle out front of his building. He's a short guy, losing his hair early in life, working for an accounting firm in the city. The building looks fine. He's five floors up but the elevator's unreliable. We go upstairs and he shows me my room.

"It's an illegal sublet, so just give me cash before the first of each month," Kyle says. "For this month, it'll be pro-rated. Before you move in. When do you think that'll be?"

I shrug. "Tomorrow?"

"Fine. That's seventy-five percent of the month you owe. You could bring it tomorrow. Keep it clean and quiet, we don't touch each other's stuff, but don't be surprised to see a roach. It's Manhattan."

We shake on it. Kyle takes a key out of a drawer. "I'm trusting Phil on this," he says.

"You can trust me too."

As I'm leaving my phone rings.

"Just wondering when you were coming back," Olivia says. This place isn't far enough away from hers. That might be a problem.

Olivia opens the door dressed as a schoolgirl. White blouse, pleated plaid skirt, saddle shoes, black hose, and, I can imagine, the garter belt and the rest of it. "Where were you? I ordered Chinese."

"I got a lot done today," I tell her. "I didn't expect you to be wearing that."

"I couldn't wait for you. Come inside."

There's a low coffee table in her living room. There's no TV, nothing else but a stereo and speakers, a yoga mat, a couple of small weights, and a VersaClimber. And candles. Lots and lots of candles, on small dishes and plates, all around the room.

I sit cross-legged on one side of the table. Over the white cartons, in the candlelight, wearing that outfit and with her hair in pigtails, she looks so young. She said she was, what, twenty? Remarkable, and a little bit scary.

"How old are you really, Liv?"

"Stop asking me that."

"How do you afford this place?"

"I told you already."

The subject is dropped.

"What's all this you did today?" Liv asks.

"I found a place."

"You found a place?"

"Yes."

"Just like that?"

"I got lucky."

"You got lucky."

"Hey, what's the matter?"

"Nothing." Liv stuffs some noodles into her mouth. We eat the rest of the meal in silence. Maybe I should've told her tomorrow, when I was ready to go.

But after we eat she perks up. "You're staying tonight?"

"...yes, if that's okay with you." I can't say no to her.

She grabs some things and brings them into the kitchen. I follow with the rest. There's a lot of dishes in the sink.

After we clean up, she spins around. The skirt blossoms out. Sure enough, there are the garters. "Do you want me like this?"

"You look so young in that."

"Some guys like it."

"Not me."

"We'll have fun taking it off me."

I should consider myself lucky. I found a job on my first serious try, and an apartment almost as fast. There's a beautiful woman who's trying to make me a better man. And there's a beautiful woman who's trying to make me... I don't know what. Her pet? I just need to decide which way I want to go.

Maybe I'm not so lucky. These kinds of decisions

shouldn't be put in front of a guy like me. I'm not known for good decisions. I don't have family I can fall back on for advice. I don't have friends I can talk to about this. Pete? No fucking way am I telling Pete any of this. He's been known to swoop in on relationships that are on the rocks, and he may have already swooped.

Zander? That's laughable. Sully? Not even if we were on good terms.

Phil? I know him mostly through work, but he's too nice a guy for me to expose to all this messiness.

The one person I can think of who could help me out of this situation, who would know what's best for me, what I should do, is Ellen. And she's part of the problem.

I'll just have to figure this out on my own.

I call Ellen in the morning, ask if I can come get some things.

"You didn't need to leave your key. I'm not afraid of you."

"I wanted you to see I'm taking this separation seriously."

"You're going to have to wait until tonight, then. I'll call you when I'm home."

"Thanks, El. So... now I've got my own place, I start the new job on Monday. How am I doing?"

"Let's see how this works out."

"Works out? How long?"

"As long as it takes."

"I bet your parents are thrilled you dumped me."

"I didn't tell them. It's only been a couple of weeks."

This is the first positive sign I've had. If Ellen hasn't told her parents yet, it could mean she's not planning on this lasting too long. But why did she make me get my own apartment? Do I smell, or something?

"You mind if I ask... when did you decide we were going to do this?"

"When we were looking at diamonds," she says.

"I should have never proposed."

"You didn't."

"That whole thing when we went to that store... that wasn't proposing?"

"That wasn't a proposal. I stopped it before we did something foolish. I'll call you tonight, Michael. When I get home."

I don't want to sit around all day in Olivia's apartment. I'm starting to pace. I'm getting tempted to snoop around. I leave my suit and things in the apartment, and it's only after the door shuts that I realize I could have done this without having to deal with Olivia again in person. My new place isn't far away and I already have a key. I wonder if I did this so I would have to see her again. So I could say goodbye, like a gentleman. I head over to the West Side. There's a couple of friendly spots where I can sit down, maybe read a little.

I spend the day in coffee shops and bookstores. The McGraw-Hill bookstore on Avenue of the Americas has an incredible collection of technical books, so I spend a couple of hours in there, browsing. Ellen calls after six, telling me she's home.

This will be the first time I see Ellen since we separated. The first time since I dove into cheating on her. That's not true, it started before we split. Although that first time was really out of my hands. At least that's what I tell myself. I'm filled with nervous energy and anxiety. Ellen's sharp. I wonder how she's going to figure out what I've been up to. Not if. How.

Ellen answers the door fully dressed. Because that's what normal people do.

"Hello Michael," she says, and gives me a polite kiss on the cheek. I just want to hug her. She lets me, but she's stiff. I breathe her in, then I gently kiss her neck. She pushes me away.

"Please don't make this harder than it has to be, Em. We're

going to start something, and then we're never going to get this right."

"...okay." I let go of her. Then we both run out of things to say. So I say, "May I...?" and she steps aside. I grab my camping backpack. Toss in a couple more pieces of clothing.

"How's Sully? Is he glad you're moving out?"

"Sully's great." What are the odds she knows what happened with the softball game? I think I'm pretty safe.

"I would've thought you two would've got along famously."

"Maybe you don't know me well enough. I thought I made it pretty clear how I felt about the guys."

"The... Syndicate."

"Whatever. At least now I'm not around so you can't force me to see my 'friends'."

"Are you still upset about that camping trip?"

"If you knew how upset it would make me, maybe you wouldn't have insisted. Or maybe you would, anyway. Maybe I didn't explain it right." I realize I'm just looking for excuses to fight, so I shut up.

"Sorry about that."

I don't answer.

"Why are you just taking your backpack?"

"I have no furniture." I don't want to explain what I plan on doing. She doesn't need to know. I'm not looking for her pity. I heft my pack onto my back, grunt a goodbye, and don't wait for her to close the door. I start walking fast toward the East Side, across Central Park.

That didn't go well. Yes, I know it was my fault.

I hit the buzzer for Olivia's apartment and at first she doesn't answer it. Finally I get buzzed in. I knock on her door. When she opens the door, she's wearing a pink bathrobe. A big, soft thing. It must be the most unsexy thing she owns, but with her wearing it, maybe not. I can see that her eyes are red from crying.

She throws her arms around my neck and buries her face in my chest.

"What's wrong?" I put my backpack down on the floor inside the door.

"I thought you weren't coming back."

"But I left my stuff here."

"Is that the only reason you're back?"

"…No," I say, not because it's true but because if I said 'yes' I'd be a monster.

"Why the backpack?"

I try to explain without mentioning my apartment. "I need my sleeping bag."

"You're still going."

"Hey. I'm here now." I offer a hug.

Olivia wipes her nose on my shoulder. Then she brightens. "Is there enough room in your sleeping bag for two?"

"It's not that kind of bag."

"We can make it that kind of bag. I'm just having salad tonight," Olivia says, as if she's forgotten the previous moment. "But I'll make something for you, if you want."

I don't want to owe her anything else, so I tell her I'm fine.

While Olivia eats her salad I look around her living room. "Liv? Why don't you have a TV?"

"No," she manages to say between crunches. "Not interested."

"Not even for the news? The weather?"

"Not interested."

"What *are* you interested in, then?"

"You."

"What did you do before me?"

"Waited for you."

I laugh, a little bit uncomfortable. Liv's harmless.

"What about before that?"

"I knew I'd find someone like you. Handsome. And nice. You're a nice guy. You know that? You won't hurt me."

There's nothing but vegetables and the leftover Chinese food in her fridge. I grab a bottle of water. "Do you mind if I lay down?"

"Mind? I'll be right there."

An inconvenient logistical problem comes into my head. Now I have the backpack, my suit, a sports bag, a suitcase, and my day pack. I'm trying to figure out how to get all this stuff to my new place in one trip, without help. One trip, so I don't have to do this again tomorrow night. Without help, so I can be sure she doesn't know where I'm living. Then, all I'd have to do is get a new cell phone.

But Olivia would still have our—*Ellen's* phone number. And I can see now it's not going to go well. How much of a hard time would she give me? There's no way to tell, but from everything that's happened, I could be in trouble.

Olivia comes out of the bathroom wearing one of my t-shirts. I can't tell if she's wearing anything else. "What do you think?" she says, pulling on the bottom of the shirt with her fists in front of her and twisting from side to side demurely.

I'm speechless. I remember telling her that's how Ellen dresses for bed.

"You don't like?"

"No, no, it's okay. It's just a… surprise."

"I don't get dolled up every night. But for you, I might. How's this?" She picks something up off the floor and puts it on her head. It's Sully's KM cap.

No it's not.

"Where'd you get that cap from, really?"

"I told you, I got it from your friend."

"No you didn't. He never had one."

"There were *so* many cute boys there. I'm *sure* I got it from one of them." She takes the hat off and flings it into a corner. "There. No reason to get jealous."

"Sure," I say, and there's little to be said after that.

Until later. Then Liv says, "I don't want this to be our last time together."

"I really appreciate you letting me stay here the past couple of days, Liv, but we should look at this for what it is."

"And what's that?"

"A mistake. I can't see you while I'm trying to get back together with my girlfriend."

"If you stay with *me*, *I'd* be your girlfriend."

"You know what I mean."

"No, what do you mean?"

"Look, you're the one who started this."

"You had no problem coming out to see me when you were still with *her*. No problem at all. Not at all."

"Liv, I—"

"What, Michael? What do you want? Are you just going to use me when it's convenient? Just because you need a place to stay? What is it you want from me?"

"Nothing."

"Nothing more? You've had your fill?"

"Please, Liv, don't make this harder than it has to be."

Olivia sits up in the dark. "No, *I* won't. *You* will."

"Come here. It's been nice."

"Nice?" Olivia starts to cry.

I've got to get her to stop, so I sit up and hug her. She pushes me off.

"You don't know anything about me."

"You haven't wanted to tell me too much."

"You want to know who I am?"

The correct answer should be 'no,' but that's not polite. "Yes."

"No you don't." She lays back down facing away from me and puts a pillow over her head.

I lie down and put an arm around her. I say the hated words: "We can still be friends."

Her body stiffens.

"I don't want a friend."

"No, I know. That's not what you want to hear. But friends are good. You're allowed to have more than one without getting hurt."

"What does that mean?"

"Someone I know. Someone who needs a friend. But she's looking for trouble. Tell me something about yourself."

"Do you think I'm pretty?" Olivia sniffles into her pillow.

"Very."

"People always said that. Since I was very young. My mom would take me for modeling jobs and beauty pageants. In Ohio." Olivia sits up but hangs her head so her hair covers her face. I can hear my watch ticking between her sniffles.

"It's not a very pretty life. You get treated like a piece of meat. That's what they say, but it's not, it's more like a piece of fruit. Fruit can be bruised, but you can hide it. I was bruised a lot."

"Physically?"

"First verbally. Mostly by my mom."

"First."

"Then, like a bunch of grapes. Everybody wants a taste."

This is the part where I know to shut up.

"I should've been home playing with dolls."

It sounds rehearsed. Like she's told it many times. But the way she's sobbing as she tells it makes it so sad. There's no reason to believe it's not true.

"My mom... she would ignore when someone who didn't belong was in the dressing room with me."

"Where was she?"

"She was there. Outside. She'd say tough it out. Don't burn bridges, she'd say. She'd tell me I brought it on myself. That I led them on. That it was *my* fault. I believed her."

"That's got to be confusing."

Now she sounds almost defiant. "By the time I was fourteen I was no longer a minor, really." She looks up, looks across the room.

I rub her back lightly as she talks. "How long did this go on?"

She uses her forearm to wipe her nose, then cradles that arm with the other. "When I turned sixteen I ran away from home. Got emancipated. My mother told me I'd end up a street walker. A whore. Said that's what I deserved for leaving her. But that didn't happen. I didn't let it happen. Now, here I am." Olivia looks at me. Her eyes are red. "I'm old enough to make my own decisions. I know how to survive. I know how to use the tools I've been given. But I keep getting hurt." She starts to lose it again.

She leans on me, tries to compose herself. "I'm not going in to work today," she says.

"Why not?"

"So we can have more time together."

"But Liv—"

"You'll give me that, won't you, Michael? Before you go?"

I have no choice, after that story.

"Please, let's just have the day together. Pretend we're a normal couple."

"What do normal couples do?"

Olivia has stopped crying but it takes a while for her to breathe regularly again. "I don't know. Go to the museum? Go out to lunch? Go shopping together?"

"Okay. We can go to the museum. We can do all that." I carefully leave out what I was going to say: 'then I have to go.'

Olivia's excited now. She bounces on the bed. She throws herself at me, knocking me back.

Olivia dresses up all bohemian, long flowing skirt, embroidered vest, frilly peasant shirt, straw hat. With her wild dark hair, she looks like she belongs in a Renaissance fair. Like she should be telling fortunes. Not what people are wearing these days, but she looks great. She's going to draw attention to us wherever we go.

First, we go to the Metropolitan Museum of Art.

Olivia bounces from painting to painting, carrying the straw hat in one hand. She doesn't have a museum whisper. People keep turning their heads. I start looking over my shoulder to see if there's anyone I recognize. She stops in front of the painting I'm looking at, a couple running in the rain. It's *The Storm*, by Pierre Cot.

"Why does she have to be practically *naked*, but the guy doesn't? Those wispy garments... *veils* she's wearing... they're running in the *forest*—oh, and *barefoot*..."

"You figure they'd get scratched by branches, have bleeding feet," I say, using my proper museum whisper, hoping she picks up and imitates it.

"I guess this is supposed to be idealized. Romantic. Running in the rain. Never done it."

"Everyone's been caught out in the rain."

"Not dressed like *that*." She eyes me, smiling, head tilted.

I get the feeling Liv would like to run in the rain with me, dressed like that, and I'm glad the day is sunny.

She moves on to another painting. "This one looks like I was the model."

"No. The hair is wrong."

"*I* can do that."

"What, with all the ringlets? That seems like a lot of work. Also, she's too pale."

"*All* these naked women are too pale, Michael."

"Well, it's not you."

"Which one is me? Is there one you like more than the others?"

"That one. *The Storm*. That's my favorite painting."

"Is that long-term, or just today?"

"Long-term. Practically the first one I want to see when I come here."

"I want you to pick another one. Your favorite painting when you go to the museum with *me*."

"Why can't it be the same one?"

"Another one," Olivia insists.

"Can it be a sculpture?"

"You mean *statue*."

"Isn't that the same thing?"

"I don't know. But yes, it can be a statue."

"Well, okay. Come on. I'll show you one I can make my favorite."

We work our way through the museum until we come to *Ugolino and his Sons*.

"That's hideous," Olivia says.

"Here, read the description."

"Why would you pick *this* to be our work of art? It's morbid. There's so many that are prettier."

"I like how Carpeaux captured the agony of the moment. Look at the details. The gnawing of the fingers; look at his face. Veins on the forearm there. The boy's hand clutching his father's leg. Look at that. It's beautiful, in a way. Plus, it's from Dante. Sort of appropriate for me, right now."

"Agony. *That's* what you think about today."

"I'd like it if it was happy, but sculpted the same way, with the same attention to detail."

"*Sculpted.* I guess you can't say *statued.*"

"I suppose you can't."

"Pick something else."

"I'd pick a pretty one for you, but they're all headless or armless. I like you how you are."

"Pick something *else.*"

"I'm not picking anything else."

"Then let's go. I'm hungry."

We find a cute bistro and even though it's a fine day I ask that we sit inside.

"I know why you did that," Olivia says as we sit down.

"I don't like street noise."

"You want to hide."

"We're just having a normal day."

"No we're not. Instead of lunch I want some pastries. And a cappuccino."

"Sure."

We order and when the dessert and coffee come Olivia says, "What's she like?"

"Who?"

"You know who."

"She's taller than you. Blue eyes. Light brown hair. But I don't want to compare."

"Don't worry, you won't hurt my feelings."

"She doesn't have your extensive wardrobe."

"You think she's beautiful."

I nod.

"People are beautiful in different ways."

I nod.

"*Everyone's* beautiful."

I nod at what she's wearing. "You're a hippie."

"I *could* be."

"I thought I saw some magic crystals in your apartment."

"Don't make fun."

I signal the waiter for the check.

"How do you know she wants you back?"

"I don't."

"Did you tell her about us?"

"No."

"What happened? To get you thrown out?"

"I proposed."

"Oh, I'm sorry. I didn't know it was *that* serious."

"I guess she didn't either." I pay, and put the change and another couple of singles next to my mug. "Would you have stopped calling if you knew?"

"Yes. No. But I'm not a home wrecker. Not deliberately."

"I suppose not."

"I don't have to chase guys, you know."

"I can imagine."

"I'm just very selective; only the best-looking and sweetest guys. Like you."

"Let's go."

"Shopping?"

"That's what you want to do."

"Yes it is."

We go window shopping, then into one of New York City's fine department stores.

"C'mon, Michael." Olivia drags me toward women's clothing. She tries some things on, asks for my opinion. It's like a private show, just for me. Soon we're in the lingerie department.

"Mmmmm," Liv sighs. "That was nice."

My brain is starting to come back to me. I'm in Olivia's bed again. There's been sex going on here. I'm pretty sure I was involved.

Liv is curled up alongside me in the most comfortable,

delightful way. I wish I could put it into words. From her toes to her eyelashes, she's embracing me. Every bit of her feels right. I can't help kissing her.

I need to be moving on. Even if it means dragging a pile of stuff to my new apartment. As long as Liv doesn't see where I'm going, I'm safe.

I'm not sure I'll ever be safe. This is something beyond my comprehension. This is otherworldly. It's fantastic and terrifying, and a good thesaurus will tell you exactly what I mean.

I'm not sure why I was thinking of moving on.

life after olivia

When I wake up the next morning Olivia's gone. I sit up, alone and surprised, and look around. No sign of her. My watch says it's 9:30. That's some confidence Liv's got. Then I fall back on the bed thinking *that's because she knows she has me.*

Most of me just wants to lie there in satin sheets and let it happen. Part of me doesn't like the feel of satin. A small part of me doesn't want to surrender. It's the contrarian part. It usually goes against common sense. It's got grudges; it loves underdogs. This morning it's actually the voice of reason.

Its tiny little voice tells me to get out.

I open my eyes, try to raise my head, and fail.

My eyes stay open, unfocused, seeing me on my feet and racing out the door. My imagination escapes. I haven't moved.

I focus on this big y-shaped crack in the ceiling. How much time do I have to make this decision?

The little voice starts using four-letter words.

You don't have all day, shithead.

What if I don't make a decision?

Not deciding is still a decision, you dumb fuck, the voice barks.

What if I acted without thinking? What if I left it up to momentum and gravity?

Sure, if you let me do the driving, the voice coos.

I try to think. When I look at Olivia, I'm almost frightened by how pretty she is. But my heart doesn't hop skip and jump like it does when I'm with Ellen. There's a lot more to Ellen that I have to consider. The way she smiles at me. The way I can make her laugh. Her voice. The way she lets me know I found the right spot. I never grew tired of it. I miss it. Our memories together. Our traditions. Heck, even her parents. There's so much we share, it doesn't seem like an easy surgery to separate us.

I sit up and start looking for my clothing.

Once I'm dressed, I take a look around the bedroom to see if I forgot anything. I repack my suitcase so I can fit my suit without too much damage. Then I try a few variations of slinging my backpack and my gym bag on my back, what kind of shuffle I should walk with.

I give myself one full circle of the apartment to make sure there's nothing left. There's something handwritten on a sheet of paper. It says 'You looked too cute, didn't want to wake you' followed by a quickly drawn heart.

Maybe I should leave a note, but I have no idea what to say. Just about anything I write will make it worse.

I put things down to open the door, transfer them to the other side, and shut the door, making sure it locks. Well, this is it.

I shuffle my way out to the sidewalk.

At the corner I wait for a taxi. It's a short trip, but I can't carry all these things that distance. When I get to my building I let myself in the front door and drop everything by the stairs. The elevator's not working. I have to shuttle everything up to the fifth floor and drop it all in the hallway in front of the apartment door. It's a workout. I wiggle the key into the lock and open the door.

The apartment has a long entry hallway that would make a lane at a bowling alley look spacious. But it's my apartment. Well, Kyle's and mine. I move everything inside the entry hall and let the door shut, then I bring it a bag at a time into my bedroom.

The room has spotty gray wall-to-wall carpeting. There's a coaxial cable coming out of one wall and coiling on the floor. The walls were once white. You can see where posters and paintings had previously been hung by the lighter rectangles. A yellowed overhead fixture broods over the space. There's a small closet.

I'm not sure when this rug was last vacuumed but I fall face-first onto it. The rug smells of beer, maybe smoke. I can make this work. I can be safe here. It's not as bad as my first apartment.

I open the backpack and start taking gear out, just as if I was camping. I won't have to use my stove so I set that aside. The tent is also not necessary, but it makes a fine pillow. That self help book is in there, too. I unroll my mat and sleeping bag and set them up in the far corner of the room, diagonally so my feet will be pointing toward the doorway.

I poke my finger through the little hole in my pack where the bullet went in. I feel around inside and find a small misshapen piece of metal. This thing bounced off a rock and could have killed someone. It could have killed me. I put it next to my sleeping bag. Maybe I could get it framed or mounted or something. Or maybe I should just throw it out.

I clean my camp dining ware in the kitchen sink. Next I check the refrigerator. The grocery store on the corner has everything I need: a carton of milk, cereal, a six-pack. I'll ask Kyle if he needs anything later.

I take a walk around the neighborhood. See what there is to see, which is not much. Besides the grocery store, there's a florist, a barber, and a coffee shop with fresh coffee and cinnamon rolls. It's not even twelve o'clock.

I go back to my apartment and sit with my back against a wall in my bedroom and pick up the self-help book and start again. Maybe the little voice is going to tell me what my goal in life is. I'm just not sure the book is going to help. I know Ellen wants me to read it, but I'm not going to get any more out of it than the chapter titles.

It's a best-seller. This book has sold millions of copies. Maybe it works for a lot of people. But it doesn't work for me. I never made it through the entire first chapter. I toss it across the room. Not hard; not to damage anything. It hits the base of the wall, putting a small dent in the drywall, and the picture of Anne and Alison falls out. I leave the book and the photo where they fell and pull out my copy of *Programming Perl*.

My phone rings a little later. "Ice cream?" Alison says.

It's been years since we've gone to Friendly's.

"I'd love to, but Ellen has the car." I don't think Alison knows about my breakup.

"Take the train. I'll pick you up."

"You drive?"

She laughs. "Can you believe it?"

"What's this about?"

"I wanna talk."

"Is there a problem?" Is Alison going to tell me about Pete and Ellen?

"You're the problem. Can you meet me?"

She picks me up at the train station and drives us to Friendly's. She orders a hot fudge sundae; for me it's a root beer float.

"Look at you," I say. "You're like a blonde Joan Jett."

"What? Oh. It's been a while since I did this. It's starting to grow out."

"You look good."

"You too. You haven't changed. What have you gotten yourself into, Michael?"

"Nothing. What?"

"*She* told me."

So Ellen knows.

"I really want to get back with her," I say.

"You can't. Stay out of it."

"What do you mean? What do *you* know about it?"

"Don't be stupid."

"But I've stopped it. I cut it off."

"That's not what Anne says."

"Wait a minute. What's Anne got to do with it?"

"She thinks you two are getting together. Says you've already been messing around."

"First of all, that's not going to happen," I say. "And I did see her, but it was just to fix her computer."

"She told me about what happened. Why did you do that? I don't care about Zander, but why take advantage of her? Don't get in the middle of it. You don't want to be the one he comes for."

"I'm not. Seriously, Allie. Nothing happened. I don't know what she told you. There's nothing going on between me and Anne. There never has been anything."

"That's a lie. You always wanted her."

"That's different. That's something I dealt with a long time ago. Nothing happened the other day. I mean it."

"Just stay away from her, Michael," Alison pleads. "He hits her. I don't want her to get hurt. I want her out of there, before he explodes."

"I know. I counted one black eye and some bruises."

"She lies about how they happen."

"I really hope she gets out of there," I say. "I've seen what Zander can do."

"Let *me* take care of it. I'll talk to her. I'm trying to get her to get some help. You… you would only confuse her."

"Does she have someplace she can go?"

"She doesn't want to go home. Says she'll feel like a failure if she does that."

"She would be safe there."

"I tried. But she won't hear it. I told her she could stay with me for a while. She doesn't want to go to a women's shelter. She won't let go of the condo."

"She's not going to be able to kick him out. He won't let her. It's Zander."

Alison stirs her sundae. She loves mixing everything together, letting it melt. But she's working frantically at it; she's frustrated.

"He scares me, Michael. You haven't been around. You haven't seen. He keeps getting worse."

"Does she have a lawyer?"

"She said it's not that bad yet. But he's hurting her."

"Not that bad?"

"Michael, please. Stay away from her. I'll take care of it. Just promise you'll stay away."

"Alright. I won't go near her. But I'm worried. I don't like this at all."

"Me too." She puts her spoon down. "So. Why do you sound so guilty?"

"What?"

"You didn't think I was talking about Anne."

I shrug.

"You were talking about someone else. Ellen…?"

I want to lie to Alison. She's the person least likely to pass judgment on me, most able to keep a secret. She's the best person to confide in about my mess. But I want to lie to her anyway.

I can't.

"It's over."

"What happened? She was so nice."

"I did something stupid."

"What did you do, Michael?"

"I thought... well... I'm convinced there's something going on between Ellen and Pete."

"I think not," Alison says. "What makes you think that?"

"Nothing. In hindsight, nothing. My imagination. He's around her all the time. He's been avoiding me. I've been avoiding him. Haven't talked in weeks."

"Don't you think I'd know about it?"

"What? Why? Are you and Pete...?"

"Yes. I thought you knew."

"When?"

"Some time now, but it took him a while to admit it. What is it with you guys?"

I shrug. "There's power in secrets. Safety. You know."

"Yes. I know." She reaches across the table and grabs my straw. She starts drinking her sundae.

"So, you and Pete are tight." I wonder if I should mention what Rebecca told me, about Pete's roaming hands. But I don't want to spoil Allie's happiness.

"Yes. Don't try to change the subject. What did you do?"

"What? Nothing."

"There you go again." She twirls some stray whipped cream with the straw.

"There's no fooling you."

"You should've learned that by now."

"I don't want to put it into words."

"Just say it once. To someone you trust. Remember? That night? That's what you told me."

I nod. "I don't trust anyone anymore."

"No one?"

She's right, I trust her, and it spills out. "I've been messing around. Behind Ellen's back."

Allie doesn't seem surprised. I didn't think I was *that* predictable.

"Is this before you split up, or after?"

"Mostly after."

"Mostly. Huh. But not with Anne."

"No. Not with Anne."

"What do you want to happen? Between you and Ellen?"

"I want us to get back together."

"And you said you ended this thing? Or was there more than one?"

"One. Yes. It's over."

"Then you just have to be patient. And put all of your skills to use in keeping this secret. Don't tell Ellen, especially. That won't work. Don't tell Sully. Don't tell *anyone*. Remember? Don't tell anyone."

I nod.

"Don't *ever* tell her."

"She already told me she doesn't want to know. Thanks, Allie."

"Thanks for the ice cream. Thanks for being my friend. For standing up for me with Sully."

But when I get back to my apartment, I think, *what if Pete's pulling the wool over Allie's eyes?* What if she doesn't know what he's up to? I wouldn't put it past him. He's gotten away with that sort of thing before, and he bragged about it to us. So what she said doesn't change much.

The self-help book and the picture are still on the floor where I threw them. I pick up the picture. I don't know if I like Alison more as a blonde or a brunette. I take out my phone and call Ellen.

After some small talk, I ask, "Do you remember that picture I was using as a bookmark?" If she says no, I can change the subject.

"What are you talking about? Why would I... oh. Yes."

"I can explain."

"You did. You don't have to explain anything."

"I think I should. I don't want you to misunderstand it."

"It was weeks ago. Why are you bringing it up now?"

"It's Anne and Alison. Goes back to when I was in college. I was carrying it because there was something I wanted to prove to Sully."

"Does this have something to do with past conquests? I remember you dated Alison. But the other one, too?"

"No, it's not that. Remember that night I got back from a game very late?" I want to add 'and you were upset' but I remember she was upset at the phone call from Olivia. "Did I tell you Sully dragged us to a strip club?"

"No," she says icily.

"That's one of Sully's things. It wasn't my idea."

"Sully doesn't seem like a decider. But then, neither are you. Why are you telling me all this now?"

"Because I want you to know. I was carrying that for Sully. To prove something to him."

"Was Anne the one who called a few weeks ago?"

"Yes. Did the picture bother you?"

"No. Yes, maybe it did. You're always looking at someone. Who isn't me."

"No, Ellen, that's not true." But that's only what I'd like to believe. I say something else that I wish is true. "I'm not like that anymore." Saying it doesn't make it real, though.

Ellen is skeptical, and she has every right to be. "How do I know that? I don't think it happens overnight."

"No, you're right. Like you keep telling me, I need more time. To prove myself to you. And to me."

"It can't be just words, Michael."

"How can I prove it?"

Ellen thinks. "I don't know," she says. "Start carrying a picture of *me* around as a bookmark."

"Seriously? I will."

"I have to go," she says.

"Please, Ellen."

"I have to go," she says again. "Pete's calling." And then she hangs up on me.

Pete's calling. I have to go. And what am I supposed to think?

Around 9:30 that night the phone rings. It's Olivia.

She calls again five minutes later, and then five minutes after that. I finally answer it.

"Where are you, Michael? You didn't say goodbye."

"Well, you didn't either," I say, but it's not funny, not with her breathing like that.

"I left a note for you."

"I saw."

"Are you coming over?"

"Can't." Meanwhile my brain is scrambling for a reason.

"Can't?"

"New roommate. We're hanging out tonight, getting to know each other."

"You're going to introduce me to him eventually."

I don't answer.

"You *can't* just write me out of your life," Olivia pleads. "Not after *yesterday*."

"Yesterday was nice. But I can't, Liv. I can't keep seeing you."

She hangs up.

Five minutes later she calls again.

"If you want to break up with me, be a man and do it to my face."

"I don't trust myself. Not around you."

"That's because we have something good."

"Maybe good now."

"What's that supposed to mean?"

"Don't you think this is all a little too fast?"

"You wouldn't say that if you've been waiting as long as I have."

"C'mon, you haven't been waiting that long. Not for me."

"Says *you*."

The silence between us becomes thick.

"Say it to my face," she says again. "If you can, I'll accept it. But I *won't* accept it over a phone. You didn't even leave a note. Say it to my face."

I'm shaking.

"I can't tonight."

"Tomorrow, then. Take some time to think about the mistake you're making."

"Fine. Tomorrow."

Maybe I can push this off day after day until I wear her down.

First Ellen, now Olivia. Both want something out of me I can't give. I don't know what it is.

Next day is Saturday. The new job starts in a couple of days. The phone rings early and I answer it.

"It's tomorrow. Where do you want to break up with me? Here?"

I know that would be a bad decision. "What about the park?" Somewhere open, public, someplace Liv can't perform her magic. Neutral ground.

Olivia thinks about it. Instead of flat-out disagreeing with me, she says, "I'll pack a picnic basket."

"Fine."

"What time?"

I pick my watch up off the floor next to my sleeping bag. "It's nine. How's noon?"

"Noon. Are you going to pick me up?"

I carefully consider that. As carefully as I can. Probably not enough. The trouble is picking someplace to meet in the park, that's not somewhere Ellen might go for a run. "Okay. I'll come by at noon."

Olivia sounds happy when she says goodbye and we end the call. She won't be happy at the park. I look out the window, which has a very limited view of the sky. There are a few clouds, but nothing threatening. I'm not getting a rain-out.

I shower and dress. The bathroom is very small and hasn't been updated in decades. The caulk between the tiles is crumbling. Water doesn't drain out of the sink very fast. I'm set to leave around 11:30, but I don't want to risk being early. I want Liv to be ready to go, not in some state of undress.

I call Ellen. I dial the house phone, not her cell number. If she's decided to run today, it probably already happened. The answering machine picks up. It's still got my voice on it. At the beep, I say, "Hi, El, it's me. I just want to tell you that I love you." I choke up and can't say anything more.

It feels like the first time I've ever told her that.

I get where Liv is coming from, wanting me to do this in the flesh. All I want is to be able to tell Ellen I love her. In person.

But first I must break up with Liv.

Not 'break up,' exactly. Maybe that's how she would put it. I came very close to needing a breakup. A heartbeat either way. But that little voice kicked my ass, it saved me from a position that would technically require a breakup. This is just... saying goodbye. It'll be hard enough.

The problem, as I see it, is how to say goodbye when you don't really know if you want to.

I get to Olivia's building five minutes late.

When I ring her apartment she buzzes the door open. I ring again. I want her to come outside, I don't want to go inside. She buzzes the door. She's not going to come outside. I go into her building. When I get to her door, I knock. Olivia opens it. She's wearing jeans and a pink Hello Kitty t-shirt, the most innocuous looking clothing she's ever worn around me. She looks good, of course, but it's a relief.

"I think I should stay here," at the door, I say.

"Don't be silly. I don't bite. Except that one time."

I take a step inside, let the door shut behind me. "How much more time do you need?"

"Five minutes. Oh. I picked up some finger paints. I thought we could have some fun, and forget this silliness. You can be my canvas, I can be yours."

"No. Thank you." I should've stayed outside.

There's no place to sit down, except on her bed, and that's out of the question. I stand by the door. Olivia makes lemonade in a thermos, and puts the thermos inside a picnic basket sitting on the coffee table. She shuts the lid, hefts the basket, and smiles at me.

"Let's go," she says.

As we walk to the park she hooks her arm around mine and squeezes my hand. I'm not sure whether it would be appropriate to pull away. Not inappropriate, more like impolite. Or impolitic. That's the word I'm looking for.

When we get to the park I steer us away from the Great Lawn and the ball fields and the running paths and find a spot on a grassy slope with nearby trees and boulders. I have to be careful. It's Saturday so a lot of people who know Ellen and me could be out here. Olivia takes a blanket out of the picnic basket and lays it down for us. I sit on an edge and she sits in the middle, touching me. She leans against me, puts her head on my shoulder. "This is so nice," she says. "Isn't it?"

"It's a nice day," I concede.

"I hope you like egg salad."

"That's fine. But maybe we should talk, first."

"I think we should *eat*, first."

Olivia hands me half a sandwich, egg salad on whole wheat bread, and a plastic cup with lemonade in it. It's not the easiest sandwich to eat without its insides falling out. Bits of shell crunch in my mouth. The lemonade is harsh. I realize it's only water with lemon juice.

She gets behind me, legs to either side of me, and starts to run her fingers through my hair, kissing my neck. It feels so good but I stop it. "No, Liv."

"Don't you like that?"

"Who wouldn't. But stop it, please."

"Only because you said 'please'." Then she wraps her arms around me, leans against my back, and soon she's kissing my neck again. Her lips are so soft...

I stand up. "This isn't going to work."

"Why not?" She's sitting legs akimbo at my feet. I take a step back.

"We have to stop seeing each other."

Her eyes flash, start to water. "Only *one* of us thinks he feels that way. If we voted, I bet *I'd* win. Part of you would have to vote for *me*, like it's trying to right now."

"You don't know what I'm thinking."

"But I do. I know what men want. I know because..." Olivia wipes tears off her cheeks with her palms. Then she puts both hands over her face and her body starts to shake. That's not fair.

I'm at a loss for words. She's damaged, that much is

certain. Maybe she's had a hard life. But it seems like, most of the time, it's not something she thinks about. She's gotten over it. That's what I tell myself. That's just me being unfair and unfeeling, I know. But it's what I have to think.

Around twenty yards away another couple is sitting, watching us. There I am, standing over Olivia, who's on the ground crying. I was planning to end this and walk away. What did I think was going to happen? If I walk away now, I'll look like a cad, that couple will vilify me. But it's more than just them. It's me, that's who will know I'm a cad.

I crouch and whisper, "Liv, please stop crying."

That doesn't work.

"Can I walk you home?"

Between sniffles and sobs, she nods her head.

"I just want to make sure you're okay."

She nods again and starts gathering things and loading them into the picnic basket. I hand her my empty plastic cup. "Thanks," she mumbles. She wants to hold my hand as we walk out of the park, and leans on me for the rest of the walk back to her place.

At some point, on the walk there, I decide that I'll do it in front of her apartment, say goodbye, so she'd be safe. But I'm worried about that. Maybe today was the wrong day. Maybe there's a different way to do this. Thing is, I'm not sure just cutting her off, not answering her calls, is going to do it. Not without me worrying forever that she might hurt herself.

Olivia is just not as tough as Ellen.

And I don't like the level of worry I'm feeling.

As Olivia unlocks and opens the door to her building, I realize it's too late to do this in public.

Once we're in her apartment, it becomes too late to do this now.

the pay-no-mind list

One night, I get together with Phil after work. We agree to meet at Atomic Dive Bar. A couple of wings, some beer, catching up with what's going on now that softball season is over.

"How's work?" Phil asks.

"It's only been a couple of weeks. I'm still settling in. But I'm happy."

"That's good to hear. What's it like after not working so long?"

"Not that bad." I tell Phil how the marketing people don't hover over me all the time. "Actually, it's a lot of fun. It's everything I always wanted."

The wings are the way we like them, atomic hot. I'm not hungry.

Phil is, though. Between wings he asks, "They have a softball team?"

"No. That's one of the few negatives about the new job."

"We've always got a spot in centerfield for you. What are you doing to keep busy? When you're not working. You don't look good."

I thrash about my memory to find something useful to say that doesn't involve Liv. It's been a couple of weeks since that break-up picnic. She acts as if that day never happened. "Mostly I read programming books. I'm learning a lot at the new job."

"Looks like you've been losing weight."

"I stopped going to the gym when I started working. Don't have much of an appetite anymore."

Phil grabs some extra napkins to try to get the grease off his hands. "That's not good."

"I know I'm not taking care of myself. But I just don't know what for. How's the family?"

"Did I tell you? Julie's pregnant again."

"A third? Are you sure you know what you're doing?"

Phil shrugs. "I should, by now. Have you talked to Ellen?"

"Not much. Sometimes, she calls. I've made a point of not calling her."

"Why?"

"I don't want to pressure her." Not until I can get Liv out of my life. "Do you see her in the office?"

Phil's working on the Super Bowl spot with Ellen. "The client is a tough one. You know him, right? Pete Sera?"

"Yeah, I know him. What's he doing?"

"One day he likes where we're going, the next day he wants to change it all up."

"I'm glad I didn't get involved. Does he... is he around a lot?"

"He likes to hold off-sites. Says it's to clear our heads, get us out of our usual routines. Feels like I've seen every hotel conference room in this city."

"Do you ever go somewhere else? Another city?"

"We did once, a few weeks into the project," Phil says. "That was a three-day thing outside Boston. Julie didn't like it, but this is such a big deal."

"What did he do, put you all up in a hotel somewhere? Was Ellen there?"

"It's her client."

"Lots of ways to get around, in a big hotel."

"Are you worried about Ellen and Pete? I don't see it. Ellen's pretty frustrated with him most of the time."

"Oh?"

"Like I said, the guy likes to change things up every other day. We're going over budget for sure, or just won't get it done in time."

"Ellen won't like that. I *know* she'll *hate* it."

"Do you still want to get back together with her?"

"I don't know how *she* feels, but yes."

Phil taps my bottle. "Then clear sailing and good luck to you, my friend."

Walking home, I come to a corner where I can go left, toward my apartment, or right, toward Olivia. I usually get together with Liv, but I'm not staying overnight. I'd rather start the day from the mattress that now sits on the floor in the center of my room. I still use the sleeping bag instead of bothering with sheets or a blanket.

There's a part of me that's missing. A part of me that Liv can't have. Only Ellen can have it. It's not something I can give to someone else. I hope Ellen is taking care of it.

Off-sites. That's just Pete's style.

It's starting to rain again. Liv's place is closer. I go right.

The thing is, I know Liv is home, and I know she'll want to see me. It's hard to pass that up on a wet night.

Hotels. All of those hallways, all of those doors, nobody knows what goes on behind them. A team dinner, maybe, in the hotel restaurant, and then everyone goes off to their own rooms. *Which one of them knocks on the others' door?*

I haven't thought of Pete in a while. I don't want to. He's

on my pay-no-mind list, along with Sully, along with Zander. The less I can think of them, the better.

Now thoughts of Pete and Ellen are flashing through my brain like wildfire. Wherever I turn, I see them together. It's like Zander and Anne. Again.

I slow my walk. This is my own fault. But I don't know what it is I said, what it is I did, that brought me here. Not that there's just one thing, but there has to be that one last thing that finally did it. I don't know what I could say or do to be back with Ellen. I know what I shouldn't do.

I know I should go back to my apartment and try to sleep on my mattress. Alone.

I resent having to be the one who's alone tonight.

Later, wrapped around Liv's warmth, my face in her hair, I think, *can I put Ellen on the list?* It feels necessary and impossible all at once. But I can't give up on her. I feel terrible even thinking about it. She still has that thing of mine that I'm hollow without. I can't give up on her like I gave up on Anne.

I did that as soon as I saw how Anne felt about Zander. Maybe there was still a little bit of hope left. But that ended well before her wedding day.

Liv always smells so nice.

I tried to stay away from Anne on her wedding day. I didn't think I'd handle it well. But I couldn't avoid her; Zander made me best man. Don't ask me why he did that. I've never been able to figure it out.

Just before the ceremony, it came into my head that I should just leave. I had the rings, and without the rings, they couldn't make it official.

Later, at the reception, Anne tried to pull me onto the parquet floor for a dance. I pulled away. Just like she remembered. A little after that, I left. I came back for Alison, but that wasn't fair to Allie; it doesn't matter if I did it to annoy Anne, or if I just didn't want to be alone. Allie always understood, or pretended she did.

That was the last time I saw Anne until seeing her at Zander's house before the camping trip. When she brought it up later I told her I forgot about it, but it was a big deal for me. Walking away on her wedding night was something I had to do.

Liv stirs against me. She nestles her face in my arm.

I slowly dislodge myself from her. I've done this before, on work nights like this.

She murmurs, "Don't go."

I whisper back. "I have to."

She pretends to sob. "Stay."

I kiss her perfect shoulder. "You know I have to go."

With that I carefully get off her bed. I look for my clothes, quietly put them on. She goes back to sleep, lets me go, not afraid of this being the last time.

Out on the street, in the sullen air before dawn, I think, *it could be that easy.*

I've walked away from things before. I'm good at it.

The first few days, Liv leaves plenty of messages on my phone.

I feel like I'm back in the Syndicate.

I'm breaking a girl's heart.

What I hate about the Syndicate, I see in myself. I'm going to cut this relationship off. I'm in command. We were good at this.

Zander would goad us into doing it if he didn't like who we were seeing. And he never liked who we were seeing. He was jealous of all of us, of anyone who would break his hold on us.

After a few days, the messages stop. But only for forty-eight hours.

Then she leaves me a long one, a weepy one, one that I listen to twice to make out all her words. There's no way I can bring myself to listen to it a third time. I delete it. I keep hearing it in my head. I can't delete that.

I'm afraid for her, but if I don't see this through, I'll never be able to do it.

There's a week of this, daily calls mixed with hourly ones. Finally I go through the trouble of getting a new phone and with it, a new number. Then something happens that changes things.

I call Phil to give him the new number and to get together again at Atomic.

We're standing at the bar, which is easier now in the off-season, just knocking back a few beers.

"See that girl?"

I look where Phil's pointing. "Who?"

"That one. With the curly hair."

It's Olivia. She's playing pool again. I want to run. Just like a UFO. Shows up when you aren't looking for her. Should I mention it to Phil? He called her that first, when it was just phone calls. I pretend not to know her.

"She used to work at KM," Phil says casually. "Maybe she still works there. I don't know."

"That one?"

"Yeah. She was on the corporate floor. With the execs. I think she was an administrative assistant, maybe a receptionist. You remember? She came to your farewell party. I only remember that because, well, look at her."

"Never saw her before."

"You interested? I could introduce."

I turn and put my back to her and hope she hasn't spotted me.

"No, Phil. Thanks for thinking about me. I'm okay.

How's Ellen?" I have to ask, because there's no reason Phil should be trying to introduce me to anyone.

"You two haven't spoken?"

"No. Not lately. I haven't given her the new number yet."

"She got herself pulled from that Super Bowl spot. I think she just asked. She's never done anything wrong by the agency that I heard about. Other than that, she's doing fine."

"The Super Bowl spot? That one was very important to her."

"Nobody wants to work with Pete Sera. There's been a ton of turnover on the team since the project started. If I could get myself off this project, I would in a heartbeat."

That's interesting.

"You still think nothing was going on? Between Ellen and Pete?"

"Are you still worried about that? Ellen's a pro. Nothing was going on. Anyway, I would've noticed something."

"Are you sure?"

"Well, *you* and Ellen *almost* went unnoticed. Trust me, there's nothing going on."

I rush Phil through his last beer. I want to get out of here before Olivia sees me.

But it's too late. Suddenly she's there, in front of us.

"Hi, Michael," she says.

Phil looks from me, to her, and back to me.

I don't know what to do.

"Don't pretend you don't know me."

"Maybe I should be going," Phil says.

"No. Phil, this is Olivia."

"Liv," she says.

"Hi, Liv," Phil says.

"You're making a big mistake, Michael."

"I'll wait for you outside," Phil says, and he heads for the door.

"It's over, Liv."

"You have no right telling me that. What I feel for you… it's not over."

"It's over for me."

"You can't *do* this," she says. I can see anger in her eyes, for the first time.

"I'm going to walk out that door, and I'm never coming back here. Stop looking for me."

"I *can't*," she says, and the anger is gone. All that's left is despair. But I'm not going to wait around for her to start crying again. I turn my back on her, and I walk out the door. She doesn't follow me.

"What was that?" Phil asks me outside on the sidewalk. "Is that why you and Ellen…"

"No. Ellen doesn't know about it. Please forget this happened, Phil. Don't mention it to anyone. It was a mistake. I really want to go back to Ellen."

"…Sure, Mike. I can do that. For you."

"Thanks, Phil."

Back in my room, I'm on my mattress staring up at the ceiling, admiring unusual stains and wondering how they got there.

Phil's a good guy. I can trust him.

Looks like I can never go back to Atomic Dive Bar again.

Not if I ever want to get back together with Ellen.

What if I've been wrong this whole time? What if there's nothing between Ellen and Pete?

That leaves me out on a limb. I can't claim she's messing around as an excuse for my behavior. Which I shouldn't have done, but I've grown up a little since then.

I'm just glad Olivia doesn't have my new number. Or know where I live. She scares me, now.

Olivia. Who worked—or still works—at Kraven Morrisey.

I sit up.

That's how she knew so much about me. *That's* how she had my phone number, my address.

But I *did* help push her car off the road. That couldn't have been arranged. That had to be a freak coincidence. Maybe the only one.

Did I ever see her when I was at KM? I don't remember being introduced. Farewell parties are always hectic, anybody-can-drop-by events. Any sort of party in a conference room tends to draw in random people. It's the free food.

I never went up to the executive floor. Avoided it like it was the inner circle of hell. That would explain why I don't remember her.

My skin is tingling with the excitement of this discovery. Or it's crawling from the thrill of finding out that yes, I have been stalked.

No one else belongs on my pay-no-mind list. They couldn't help themselves. The only one that truly belongs is Olivia.

syndicate rules

Over the next few weeks I give my new phone number to Alison, and check in on what she knows about Anne. I give it to my mom, and have a short conversation with her. I don't talk to my stepfather. I'm not ready for that yet. I don't tell my mom about Ellen; I don't want to put the situation into words, to make it real. And I don't know for sure what the situation is, anyway. We talk about the neighborhood. The DiNapoli's still live next door, and I hope to get some news of Anne from my mom, but there's nothing.

I don't call Ellen. I'm not going to beg anymore. I'll leave it to her to decide whether this thing ends and how it ends. I have no right to be part of that decision.

There's a giant hole in my life. Softball season is over, but this is something else. I'm not totally stupid. I know what the hole is.

It takes me a while to realize that by not calling Ellen, by not giving her my new number, I've made her decision for her.

And that's wrong, because I finally know at least one thing I want in my life.

Sunday afternoon I call to ask her out to dinner. She says

she'll meet me for drinks, and we get together at a little wine bar on the West Side.

Ellen is stunning. She's wearing her hair loose. She has to push it back from her face every so often, but I like that she's wearing her hair that way; she knows I like it like that. She's wearing that green dress she got in Cape May. It reminds me of better times. Maybe that's what she meant by wearing it. Ellen dresses deliberately. I forgot how tall she is, especially in heels. I don't see anything different, anything that could tell me whether she's moved on or not. All I can see, when I look at her, is how blue her eyes are. How they sparkle when she laughs. I want to make her laugh.

I pull Ellen's chair out so she can sit. "Thanks for meeting me, El. You look great."

"Thank you. Thanks for inviting me, Michael. After your phone number stopped working I thought that was it, I'd never hear from you again."

"I changed it."

"Why?"

"I thought I should disappear. For a while."

Ellen smells like she was at the beach. Like suntan lotion. It could be just that; it's comforting, familiar.

"It's been a long time. You lost weight."

"I was hoping you wouldn't notice," I say.

"Are you eating right? Are you *eating*?"

"No. I know. I'll try to eat more often. But I don't have much of an appetite."

"Call your doctor."

"I will," I say, and I won't.

I let her select wine. I've never been good at that sort of thing.

While we wait for the wine, I remember what Alison said: *never tell Ellen*. But there's something else she might want to hear.

"I called my folks. I gave them my new number."

"About time. I'm tired of covering for you."

"Covering how?"

"Your mom has called every week, as usual, since we've been... apart. I haven't told her why you're never home when she calls. I make excuses."

"Thanks."

"I figured you probably don't want them to find out about us from me."

"About us?"

"Breaking up."

As far as I know, the whole world knows Ellen has broken up with me. I'm the last one to find out.

"That's it? We broke up?"

"I think with the amount of time that's gone by, that's what it is."

"I don't want that."

"I don't either. This is not what I wanted to happen. I *hate* not having you around."

"Can't we just say we didn't break up?"

"I don't think so. It's like changing your phone number. You can't undo that."

"But you have my new number now."

"That's right. I have your new number."

"So *we* can start new."

"Where's our wine?" Ellen flags a waiter.

"Can I tell you what happened with my parents?"

"You can tell me anything, Em."

"My dad died when I was thirteen. It was sudden. Heart attack."

The waiter arrives with our wine. We wait for him to go.

"That must have been very hard for you," Ellen says.

"Yes. But what happened after was worse."

"Your mom remarried? And you didn't like your new stepfather."

"Not really. I mean, I liked him fine. When he was my uncle."

Ellen takes a moment to process this.

"Was your family very religious? Is that in the Bible?"

"No. It wasn't that. I guess he always had a thing for her."

"He married his brother's widow?"

"It didn't go over well with everyone else in my family."

"It's not normal. I can imagine. You not taking it well. Is that why you're estranged from your mother? Did you get along with your... uncle?... stepfather? What do you call him?"

"Sam. I was still young. It was too weird. I couldn't do anything about it. So I protested in teenage ways. I acted out. Almost didn't finish high school."

"You went to college."

"Yes, but I couldn't afford to go away to school. I lived at home."

"Is that why you don't have any college friends? I don't remember any."

"Yes. I don't have friends that I can count on. Maybe Phil."

"What about Sully? And the rest of your gang?"

"It wasn't a gang. And no, I can't count on any of them." I have to leave names out of it. I don't want to mention Pete. I don't know what I'd say. And I'm still playing by Syndicate rules. I can't talk bad about him to Ellen.

"Maybe that explains some of your disconnectedness. If that's a word."

"Maybe."

"What about the cousins you were with on Thanksgiving?"

"That stopped when the trips to the Zoo stopped. After my dad died. And when, well. When everybody stopped coming over."

"Did this cause a split in your family? Michael, this is turning into a very sad story."

"There was just... us. I had aunts and uncles, grandparents, cousins, but throughout the year, most noticeably on the holidays, we never went anywhere to visit, and never had visitors. We were the family shame."

"That must have been hard."

"Then there was the first year after I graduated, when I moved out. First Thanksgiving, I come home, there's no turkey."

This makes Ellen laugh, which makes me happy and lightens the mood a little bit. "You're never serious."

"No. But it was just, you know, a regular dinner. No turkey, no stuffing, no cranberry sauce."

"Did you make a scene about there being no turkey?"

"No, I didn't. Maybe a little bit. Then Christmas came around. Since I lived at home through college, this was my first time on my own. And Christmas, for me, had stopped being special. It hadn't been for a while."

"What happened on that first Christmas? Don't tell me you didn't go home."

"I just wanted to feel like a grown up. It seemed like it wouldn't be a big deal, not after the Thanksgiving that wasn't, and so many Christmases where it was just the three of us."

"You just didn't show up?"

"I made myself scarce. Didn't answer the phone. Until Christmas passed."

"I can't believe you. What did that prove?"

"That I was a bad son, I suppose. Or a bad nephew. It was always confusing." I stop as the waiter pours more wine. "They must've taken it hard. Now, it really was just the two of them. Next time my mom called, she said, 'missed you at Christmas,' and that was it. That's the only reaction they ever gave me. That, and there was never a family Thanksgiving or Christmas again."

"Oh, Michael. That's so sad. And this has gone on how long?"

"Years."

"You didn't have anything to hold on to. To ground you."

"All I really have is the softball team. And, for a while, you."

"Not in that order, I hope."

"I don't want to lose you the same way. By falling apart."

Ellen plays with the stem of her glass. "Don't worry about losing me. I'm not going anywhere. Worry about losing yourself."

Wine is not like beer or shots. You have to sip it. So we sit together quietly, each having interesting would-be conversations in our heads.

"Tell me about your job," Ellen says.

"There's this conference thing coming up, the company is sending me along with the rest of the team."

"Where?"

"San Francisco. We're going to learn more about Java. It's a new programming language."

"Sounds like a big deal."

"Conference tickets, airplane tickets, fly across the country, hotel, rental car. I was never treated like this by KM."

"You'll have fun."

It gets quiet again. It's my turn to come up with something to talk about. "Phil told me you're not doing the Super Bowl spot. It meant so much to you."

Ellen half-smiles. "You were right to stay out of it, Em. I should've listened to you."

"What happened?"

"It was just... out of control. I never had a project go that way before." Ellen is looking down at the table as she says this.

Not making eye contact. "I tried to warn people that it wasn't going to be a success. That the client... he was unmanageable. They wouldn't listen, and I didn't want to be part of it any more. I've never done that before."

I wait for her to say more, but she doesn't.

Then Ellen brings up something new. "Michael. I don't want to get married."

"To me?"

"To anyone. I don't want what comes with it."

"What comes with it?"

"You were going to propose to me because you thought you *had* to. That's not what I want."

"So is that it? For us?"

"No. That's not it. That's just what I've been thinking about. And what I decided I wanted. And didn't want. The ritual. I thought you should know. If that's not enough for you... I don't know. I guess it really is over."

"I don't know what to say."

"You don't have to say anything. It's not something you can fix." Ellen sighs. "That sounds like there's something broken. It isn't."

I would've married Ellen in a heartbeat. Or not. Whatever she wanted. And it wouldn't be because I had to, it would be because I wanted to, because I wanted to be with her, no matter what we called it. This is not like being let off the hook. It's like being dumped back into the ocean.

"What about kids?" I say.

"That's the same. I haven't changed my mind about that. It'll happen some day. When it's right."

We talk a little more, trying to make it normal. I walk her back to her apartment. When we get to the door of her building, what used to be our building, she stops, faces me, and says, "Well."

I don't know what I'm supposed to do.

"Can I call you some time?" She says the same thing.

"Any time," we both say.

We laugh, and there's a kiss on the cheek and a little hug, and then she goes inside.

Later that week, Alison calls.

"Anne's dead, Michael," she sobs.

Zander's dead, too. He shot Anne, and then killed himself. Alison saw it on the local news.

"You *lied* to me," she manages to say. "Don't deny it. She told me she was leaving him, just last week. She must have told him. She kept saying you're a phone call away."

"She had my number if she wanted to—oh. She didn't have my new number."

Allie says something like "What if she tried to call you? What if she needed help?" between tears.

"What *if* she called me for help? What could I have done?"

"Do you know how bad she wanted to leave Zander? I didn't tell you all of it because I was trying to keep her out of your head." She catches her breath, holds it for a few seconds. "Can you tell Sully?"

Damn. Sully. My life has been so peaceful without him. Almost normal. "Yeah. I can tell Sully. Are you okay? Are you with Pete?"

"Michael, please don't get mad."

"What am I going to be mad about?"

"Promise."

"I'm already mad. Tell me."

"I don't know where Pete is."

"What happened?"

"We're not together anymore."

That's it. Pete hurt Allie. I knew he would. I told him not to. But that's who he is. That's who he always was. I tried to convince myself otherwise, and I'm a fool for giving him a chance.

"What did he do?"

It doesn't matter what he did. He hurt Allie. That's all that matters. I don't need any more reason to despise him.

"He was seeing... someone else."

I hang up.

Anne's wake is Friday, in New Rochelle. I get there late, as the sun is setting. The front of the funeral home looks just like one of the handful of pubs and bars on this part of North Avenue. There's a large maple tree by the sidewalk and the branches shade the sign next to the driveway. Somehow, maybe deliberately, Zander's wake is here too. Why would his parents think that was a good idea? It seems more like a sick trick. Something Zander would do.

After the front door I turn left, toward Anne's... *room*. I don't know if there's a name for it. Chamber? This is all a bit alien to me. There's Sully, looking like an usher as he stands in the archway entrance. He took the news hard. He actually wept over the phone. If Zander was around he would have called it weak.

Now Sully's greeting everyone who approaches, shaking hands, offering hugs, pointing the way into the... the room. I wait as a group of mourners get past him, family maybe, and then approach.

"Thank you for coming—" he looks up from his offered hand and sees it's me. "Mike! You're here! I thought you were going to disappear again. This is tragic."

His eyes are red; it's obvious he's had to take some alone time. Or he's very stoned. Calling him to give him that news: that was hard. Seeing him now is a little comforting, to my surprise.

"Can you believe it? He shot her five times. In the back."

"Keep it down, Sully. Not so loud."

"She was trying to get out of there, Mike."

"I know. I've been following it in the newspaper. I can't believe he killed her. And himself."

"That doesn't sound like Zander."

I shrug. "He always called suicide the coward's way out."

"And he would never hurt Anne."

It is unbelievable. Not that he would never hurt her; I already knew about that. But that he would kill her. I don't know what else to say. But it's what the police are saying. As menacing as I thought he was, I never thought he would kill her. I put my hand on Sully's shoulder. "I have to go inside."

It's an open coffin thing. I barely remember the one for my father. Everyone is sitting in folding chairs, facing the open box. There's muted talk going on as family members and friends take the opportunity to catch up with each other. I've heard these things are good for the ones left behind. I'm waiting to feel good about anything. I kneel in front of the box.

That last time I saw her was weeks ago. I almost don't recognize her now. It's as if years of life, worry, and fear have gone away, and she looks like she did when I fell in love with her.

"Our timing will never be right, anymore," I tell her. Maybe that's a cruel thing to say, here.

Someone kneels next to me. It's Alison. She squeezes my hand and starts to cry, and that makes my eyes water, too.

"I'm afraid to see her dead," Allie whispers.

Anne's eyes are just closed, and she's about to wake. I have nothing to compare it to, but I imagine the coroner has done a good job. Then I look closer. Her eyes look glued shut. She looks less real than photographs I have, her yearbook picture, my memories. It's just a body; it's not Anne.

I put my arm around Alison's shoulder and she leans on me and I stay there until she stops shaking. Kneeling there with Allie, it's me that's dead, not Anne. I feel... grief... anger... it's hard to say. I'm looking at myself from behind again and waiting for something to happen inside me. I force myself to focus on Anne's hands. There are no rings on her fingers. I fold myself back inside me so I'm there.

I put my mouth close to Allie's ear. "Do you think Anne would approve of us kneeling here together?"

"Probably not."

Allie starts talking to Anne. "Everything's okay now," she says. "You don't have to run. You don't have to hurt."

I close my eyes and I see Anne smiling. It's a summer memory, she's just laughing and I catch her smiling at me, and she catches me catching her, a small thing, one time, long ago. A smile inside a smile. I need to keep it together, for Allie and for everyone else. For Anne.

I can't bear facing the dead. And now I can't avoid facing the living. I stand and turn around. Anne's parents are in the front row.

"Mike," Mr. D says as I bend down and hug Anne's mom. "She's beautiful, isn't she?"

"Always," I say. "Always. I'm so sorry."

"Oh, Mike," Mrs. D says. "The stories she told us in the past year... how he treated her... you would've taken so much better care of her."

"That's not what she wanted." What else can I say? I'm surprised Mrs. D would say that.

I could've kept her out of that box. I could've talked to her more about the hitting, helped her get out of there. I thought it was right, being able to resist Anne that day. I thought that's what mattered. I thought that was what was expected of me. Now I'm not so sure.

The me standing next to me wants me to admit I was a coward, that I was afraid of Zander, that I left her to him.

Allie takes a while talking with Anne's folks. There's a lot more crying. Looking around, I see my folks there, seated along the side of the room. I give them a small wave. I'll go over and talk, but not yet. Sully is still standing in the back, at the archway. I walk Allie to the back of the room.

Pete and Ellen are there, in the hallway, standing apart, ignoring each other. Maybe I should ask the funeral director to get another coffin ready.

Allie sees Pete and leans on me, clutching my arm with both hands and pulling me close. Her face is in my shoulder. "I can't," she whispers. "I can't be near him." Then she goes back inside the room.

Pete's telling a story. It's about how Zander kept trying to find out about Anne, in high school. "He probably bothered Mike the most," Pete says. "Mike finally had to set them up."

I remember Zander pestering me about her, how much power I felt I had over him, how I thought he would owe me his kindness forever. That was another betrayal. I should've never let him get close to Anne.

"It's wrong to be talking about Zander, here," I say. "Pete. Come with me."

"I'm sorry, Mike," he says, following me. "I know how much you cared about her."

Sully and Ellen watch us as we walk a little way down the hall and over to the far side of it, where we can have some privacy.

"Maybe we should go outside to talk," Pete says. "You look very upset."

"I like it fine here. If we go outside this will get loud and violent."

"Never thought Zander would do anything like this," he says, trying to distract me. He knows what this is.

"You wanna do me a favor?" I'm trying to keep my voice down so this stays between me and Pete.

"Is this about Alison?"

"I *told* you not to hurt her."

"She should've known I wasn't serious."

"Don't go near the people I care about. That's a very short list, and you know who they are."

"Mike, I know you're angry…"

"Remember when you wanted to talk about happiness? Go find it somewhere else. Find it *with* someone else. Find your own girl."

"This isn't appropriate right now."

"Don't give me that. I want you to leave. Now. Get out, or I'll take you outside and hurt you."

"Let me at least offer my condolences."

That makes me remember I'm here for Anne, not me. It's difficult but I calm myself and let him go. He goes inside the room. I stand at the back with Ellen and Sully.

"Thank you for coming, El."

"Oh, Michael. Alison called me. I'm so sorry."

"This is not your fault." That's all I can come up with? The best I can do? "You look great. You always did look good in black." That seems worse.

Ellen reaches out and squeezes my arm. "How are you doing?"

"Not well."

"Pete… he told me about Anne. What she meant to you. The girl next door."

I have no idea what Pete told Ellen about me and Anne, or why. What did *he* know? I never told him anything about how I felt. Certainly not about Anne.

"I don't think I can talk about Anne anymore. There's someone I'd like you to meet." I take her hand in mine. "It'll be quick." She doesn't let go. We walk back into the room, down the side aisle to where my folks are sitting. I stop in front of them.

"Hi Mom. Hi Sam. This is Ellen."

They both rise and give us hugs. Mom has talked with Ellen many times on the phone. It's almost like they know each other. "You're every bit as beautiful as you sound on the phone," Mom says to her.

"Mikey, it's been a while," Sam says.

"This must hurt," Mom says. "She was such a special girl."

"You know." I start to weep. "You know." My words get stuck in my mouth. I wipe my eyes. It's over quick. Not even enough time for anyone to whip out a tissue.

We sit together, turning chairs so we can talk to each other while respectfully still facing the box holding Anne.

"Sam, Ellen thought you were imaginary."

"I did not."

"Mikey can't wish us away," Sam says. "We're real." He reaches into his shirt pocket and takes something out. "Look what I found on your bookshelf. Just where you told your mother it should be." It's my polar bear cub.

"You found it!"

"You left a lot of your things behind," Mom says. "We tried to keep your room the way it was in case you came back. But you didn't."

"I thought I had a good reason. I can't remember it now."

"That's good. Why don't you two come over for dinner?" As if no time at all has passed since that Christmas.

"That's complicated."

"That would be wonderful," Ellen says, surprising me. We make arrangements for the week after I get back from the conference.

I stand up. "Please excuse me. There's something I have to do."

"Sure, Mikey. See you soon," Sam says. "Nice to finally

meet you, Ellen." We hug again. I hug Mom, Ellen hugs them both. We walk to the back of the room, where the remains of the Syndicate are standing.

"Sully says he wants to do something," Pete says for Sully. He hasn't left yet. "For the Syndicate."

"That's what we're doing now," I say. "This one last thing."

"C'mon, Mike," Sully says.

"Mike's right, Sully," Pete says. "The Syndicate is done."

Sully accepts it with a big frown. "At least we had that one last trip," he says.

"We did. But not all of us." I glare at Pete.

Pete's looking down at the carpet, like he's thinking about something. I'm thinking *now is not the time.*

Is he going to tell us why he missed that trip? I'm not ready for this.

Ellen lets go of my hand. Funny, I didn't notice she was holding it again.

"I'm killing the spot," Pete says.

"I never thought you would go through with it."

Pete tries to look at me, but ends up looking down again.

"I was *so* looking forward to it," Sully says. He's still Sully.

"It's Amazon," Pete says.

"You're giving up on this once in a lifetime thing, for another trip to South America?"

"Not that Amazon. They're going to do an IPO. And they're running a spot during the Super Bowl. They beat us to market. My company is doing a pivot. We're strategizing what to do next with the infrastructure we already built."

"Pivoting is your thing," I say. "And strategizing."

Sully's about to say something but I interrupt him. "Hey. You know what we have to do."

Pete nods. "I think I know what."

"No way," Sully says.

"Ellen, you don't have to come for this. But please don't go. We'll be right back."

"I'll sit with Alison. She and I could talk."

I lead Pete and Sully to the other side of the funeral home.

The other room is lonely. There are a few people there, family. The coffin is closed. We walk in and go to the front row, where Zander's parents are mourning. We were in and out of each other's houses so much that it's like we each had multiple sets of parents.

I bend down and offer my hand. "I'm so sorry, Mr. Lombardi. Mrs. Lombardi. It's me, Mike. Some of us came over to see you. Zander's friends." I'm not so sure about that last part, especially now.

Mr. Lombardi stands and turns to face me. "Thank you, Mike. Thank you." He's grateful to be standing instead of sitting there with his wife, staring at a fancy box.

I wonder what they're going through. How these poor people are suffering, I can't imagine. And mostly alone. It was an easy thing to do, to come over here. Zander was their creation, but not their fault. He was born out of an act of love. It just never stuck to him.

We don't stay very long. As we're leaving, Zander's dad pulls me to the side.

"We didn't know, Mike. The funeral director didn't tell us Anne was going to be here. I'm sorry about this."

I nod and shake his hand again. He doesn't want to let go.

"Do you think we could come over... offer our condolences? Anne was our daughter-in-law, after all. We loved her. We thought she would be so good for him."

"I think you should. I'll ask them if it's okay."

Anne's room is overflowing. She had—*has* so many friends, so many people loved her. *Love* her. I don't want to let her go.

I go inside and down to the front. When Mr. DiNapoli

realizes what I'm asking, he turns in his seat, and there's Zander's parents just outside. He waves them in. I step back and outside the room and rejoin the others.

"Thank you, Mike," Mr. Lombardi says again as we pass in the aisle. "You were always a good guy."

Outside the room, I ask, "Where's Pete?"

"He said he had to go," Sully says. "Left real quick. Didn't say goodbye or anything."

"That's good."

"Why's that?"

"I'm tired of his bullshit."

Sully laughs. "Pay-no-mind list?"

"I never want to see him again."

"Never?"

"As long as I'm alive. After, too."

"What were you two talking about?"

"Just that."

"Why?"

"He knows why," I say, "and I'm done talking about him."

"Wow," Sully says. "Serious."

one more time

After the wake I ask Ellen, "Can you give me a lift to the station?"

"Where do you live?"

"East side. Eighties," I say.

"I can drive you home."

The ride home is mostly quiet. It feels like there's nothing to talk about, nothing between us now. I don't know why I did this, why I got into her car. I don't think she wants to get back together with me.

"Did you know? About Pete's 'pivot'?"

"It's news to me," Ellen says. "It's like he just decided it, now. Like he decides everything. I don't know how the agency is going to take it. Most of us were ready for something like this. Pete not going through with it. He's been torture to work with. And you *knew* he would be."

"Don't blame me," I say.

"And you were right about Zander. I'm glad I never met him."

"It doesn't make me happy, being right about these things. Are you serious about dinner with my parents?"

"Yes. Maybe it'll help me understand you better."

I keep looking over at her. I can't see her eyes; it's dark. I'd really like to fall into them, get lost in them, again. I hope she takes me home instead of my place.

Ellen says, "I have to tell you something."

"You don't have to say anything, El."

"But I do. I'm going to tell you this one time, Em. And I don't want to answer any questions about it. I never want to hear about it again. I think you'll agree with me, that's what's best."

"What happened." Not exactly a question. More like a resignation.

"It's about Pete."

"What about Pete?"

"He started hitting on me. It was jokey, at first. But he kept saying things, and I realized he wasn't kidding. I told him I wasn't interested."

"Is that it?"

"No. I had to tell him more than once. He kept pushing for something to happen. Manipulating meeting times, controlling who was around. Trying to create situations. It was pretty obvious, what he was doing. I just didn't want you to find out from someone else."

"Let's do this, El. You never tell me the rest of what you're trying to say, and I'll forget you brought it up."

"Just like that?"

"That's right."

"But it's not that—"

"Whatever it is, it's not important. I don't want to ruin our chances of starting over."

We pull up to my apartment and double park. Every part of me is telling me to invite her inside except the tiny little voice, which tells me, *you can't show her you sleep on a mattress on the floor. You'd look pathetic.*

So I don't.

I lean over to give her a kiss, but just get hair and salty cheek. I use my thumb to wipe away a tear.

"I miss you," I say.

"Me too."

"I love you."

"Me too. I like what you said. About our chances."

I wake up late Monday morning. My alarm didn't go off.

I race to get dressed, finish packing my suitcase. I grab my brand-new company laptop and throw it into my Mega Group messenger bag.

Sully's giving me a ride to the airport. When I get down to the street the Striped Tomato is already there, double-parked.

I open the passenger door, move the seat out of the way, and throw my suitcase in the back. The messenger bag goes between my legs in the front seat.

"Hey, thanks for this. Again."

"No trouble for my best buddy," Sully says. He's not working today; he's not working at all. He got himself fired from Williamson. Chuck told Sully what he did, gloated about forcing me to bench him, and Sully reacted as expected. But it's made things right between us. That's good, because it's just the two of us now.

There's traffic. I keep checking my watch. You're supposed to get to the airport an hour ahead of boarding. I'm starting to cut it close.

"Can you go faster?" Sully is driving like he always does: just faster than all the other cars on the road. He pays the toll on the Triborough Bridge and takes us into Queens. We go right over the ballfields on Randall's Island. The way he's going, we'll pass Shea Stadium. Let's go, Mets. But not today. Make it a night game, I don't need the road to be full of cars right now. At least the traffic is not stop-and-go. It's just slow, but it's moving. They'll never be done with the roadwork here. It's as untangle-able as capellini.

"Catch a game next week?" Sully says.

"After I get back. Boy, I miss an afternoon in the sun. Beer, peanuts, the whole thing."

"It's on, then." Closer to JFK the construction gets worse and the cars back up. It's less than an hour to boarding now. But we should make it.

Everything goes down to one lane which frustrates both of us. "They couldn't do this work at night?" Sully complains.

We read the signs for my terminal, find it, and Sully gets off at the right exit. He pulls up to the curb. I shake his hand, open the door, and get my suitcase out. Let's see. Suitcase. Messenger bag. Wallet. Cell phone. Check.

"You sure you don't need a ride back?"

"Not a problem, Sull. I'll take the train. I can take my time coming home." Nothing to rush back to but my empty room. For the next few nights, though, it's going to be sheer luxury. Hotel beds. Real sheets and blankets. I'm looking forward to this trip.

I get my boarding pass. It's a long walk to the gate. From the way the numbering's going, my gate will be the last one. Figures.

As I near it I see a couple of guys from Mega Group. I wave and head over to them. They're in a bunch near the ticket desk.

Passengers are lining up at the gate, trying to be first on board. The line gets long. We're still off to the side. Someone pulls on my sleeve. "Michael. *Michael.*"

I turn around. It's Olivia.

Of all the jetways in all the airports in the world, she has to walk into this one.

"Excuse me, guys," I say, and take a few steps away from them. Olivia follows me.

"What are you doing here?"

She gives me a demure smile. "I could ask you the same question."

"Is this another 'coincidence'?"

"I had nothing to do with it."

"Stop following me around."

"I'm *not* following you. This is real. I swear."

Olivia's not using her museum voice again.

"Where are you going?" I ask.

"San Francisco. Some trade show or something."

"Really." It's just too hard to believe. "Who do you know that works for the airlines? Do you know someone at Mega Group?"

"Mega *What*?"

I grab her by the arm, twist it a little as I guide her a few more steps from the line.

"That hurts," Olivia protests.

"Tell me the truth. Don't lie to me. You've been stalking me since... a long time."

"That's a harsh word for it."

"It's what this is."

"No, Michael. I didn't set this up."

"Tell me about it."

"You're hurting me. Okay. I did."

I let go of her arm, look around. Everyone's too busy trying to jump the line to notice us.

"How did you set up the first thing? The empty tank of gas?"

"The empty tank? Oh. I didn't, I swear. That was real. I hadn't thought of you in—"

"You knew me before that."

"We never met, before that. But I noticed you, and I liked

you right away. And for a long time. And I thought, if a coincidence like that could happen, if someone from one world shows up in another, maybe life is trying to tell us something."

"That's supposed to make it better?" I signal to the guys that they should board, I'll join them soon. "When did you work at Kraven Morrisey?"

"Oh. You found out. Why didn't you recognize me?" She shoots back.

"That night? Everything happened so fast. And I don't remember—"

"You didn't remember *me*. We saw each other enough. Passing in the halls. And I was at your *party*. You don't remember?"

"No."

"Why didn't you see me? Why did you look through me?"

Of everything I've done, I've never been accused of *not* noticing a pretty girl.

"It was fun, though, wasn't it? You not knowing who I was. It was fate brought us together. And you keep trying to ruin it."

There's no one jumping the line anymore; it's gotten smaller.

I look back at Olivia. "What are you doing in San Francisco? How did you set this up?"

"I'm a spokesmodel for something called 'Orion Editor,' whatever *that* is."

"You have no idea."

"None."

"It's a code editor. A programming tool. Never mind."

"Whatever." Olivia shrugs. "That isn't why they hired me. All I have to do is keep you programmer fellas coming to our booth. I've done it before, at Comdex. Las Vegas. I'm a geek magnet." She touches the back of my hand briefly. "Don't you feel it?"

I can do this. Nothing has to happen. I look around for the team. They've boarded already.

Now she's holding my hand, with a big smile like sunshine. "You don't know how hard this was. You don't appreciate the effort I've been putting into this relationship."

I cringe just a little bit but Olivia catches it.

Someone announces over a speaker that it's last call for boarding. The clerk at the jetway door is looking at us. I wave. He takes it like "We'll be right there."

Olivia locks her eyes on mine. I can't look away. She sounds desperate now.

"We can make it like a honeymoon. Maybe we can stay out there. In California. Together. Make a new life for ourselves. Live in a shack on the beach."

For an instant I can see myself sitting in a tiki bar, and Olivia coming toward me wearing something tropical and revealing. I smell suntan lotion. But it's Ellen, at the wine bar.

"That's not going to happen," I say.

"Why not?" She's still holding my hand. I pull it back.

"You're not getting on the plane, are you," she says. Loud enough to turn heads, but there's no one in the waiting area anymore.

"What about the conference?" I ask. But I'm asking myself, and it doesn't matter. I've already made up my mind. I have to do this for Ellen.

"No. You won't. You're not *going* to the conference. You're afraid to go to the same *city* as me. You won't get on the same *plane*." Her eyes are wet, glistening, like sea glass.

"Get on that plane," I say. "You arranged this. I don't know how you did it. But you made a commitment to go work that show. Maybe for foolish reasons. Don't jeopardize your career. Don't burn bridges. But you have to let me go."

"I can't," she says.

I take a step back, breaking our stare. Then another.

There's no good way to say goodbye. And I've never been good at saying no to women.

I expect some kind of disciplinary action for missing the conference. Maybe I'm going to get canned. I want to hold on to this job.

I turn and slowly walk away, messenger bag over my shoulder, dragging my suitcase behind me. I can't look back. I try not to. I turn my head after about fifty feet. She's not following me. That's good. But she's still standing there.

The clerk says something and she reluctantly turns and walks toward the jetway. She looks back once, and then the gate closes.

I walk out of the airport. I feel light, weightless even. Like a brand new Clincher. I don't ever want to land.

9 798987 902523